THE
GIRL FROM AWAY
TRILOGY

THE
GIRL FROM AWAY
TRILOGY

The Girl From Away
The French Isles
Last Summer in Louisbourg

Claire Mowat

KEY PORTER BOOKS

National Library of Canada Cataloguing in Publication Data

Mowat, Claire
    The Girl from away trilogy / Claire Mowat.

Contents: Last summer in Louisbourg—The girl from away—The French Isles.

ISBN: 1-55263-489-2

I. Title. II. Title: The girl from away. III. Title: Last summer in Louisbourg. IV.
Title: The French Isles.

PS8576.O985A15 2002   jC813'.54   C2002-902942-2
PR9199.3.M679A15 2002

THE CANADA COUNCIL | LE CONSEIL DES ARTS
FOR THE ARTS | DU CANADA
SINCE 1957 | DEPUIS 1957

ONTARIO ARTS COUNCIL
CONSEIL DES ARTS DE L'ONTARIO

The publisher gratefully acknowledges the support of the Canada Council for
the Arts and the Ontario Arts Council for its publishing program.

We acknowledge the financial support of the Government of Canada through
the Book Publishing Industry Development Program (BPIDP) for our publishing
activities.

Key Porter Books Limited
70 The Esplanade
Toronto, Ontario
Canada M5E 1R2

www.keyporter.com

Design: Peter Maher
Electronic formatting: Jean Lightfoot Peters

Printed and bound in Canada

02 03 04 05 06 5 4 3 2 1

CONTENTS

The Girl
From Away

CHAPTER ONE

"Ladies and Gentlemen, welcome to Gander. Kindly remain seated until the aircraft has come to a full stop outside the terminal. For those passengers leaving us here, we hope you have enjoyed your flight."

The flight attendant repeated the message in French and then bobbed down the aisle, scooping up travel pillows and earphones. "Here we are Andrea," she said with a friendly smile. "Don't forget your tote bag and your nice leather jacket. And have a good holiday."

This was the first time thirteen-year-old Andrea Baxter had travelled by air on her own. The ticket agent had issued her a special ticket before she had boarded the plane in Toronto, with the names of her Aunt Pearl and Uncle Cyril at the bottom. In the departures lounge her mother had kissed her good-bye, and then had begun to cry when an attendant arrived to shepherd Andrea down the wide corridor leading to the plane.

Now, as the plane taxied toward the terminal at Gander airport in central Newfoundland, Andrea peered through the darkness and the light fall of snow. She could see a line-up of people inside the terminal, looking out the windows at the arriving passengers. Were Aunt Pearl and Uncle Cyril there? she wondered.

Her head bent against the wind, Andrea clutched her canvas tote bag, bulging with Christmas presents, and struggled across the tarmac. Her short, wavy hair had blown every which way by the time she reached the glass door leading into the bright building. The first person she saw was Aunt Pearl, bulky in her purple and green parka and sturdy boots.

"There you be, girl!" her aunt cried, running forward to hug Andrea. The attendant smiled and handed Aunt Pearl the envelope with *Mr. and Mrs. Cyril Baxter* written on it.

"Aren't you the smart one, flying all that way by yourself!" Aunt Pearl exclaimed, as they waited among the crowd by the baggage carousel. "Were you scared?"

"No, not a bit," Andrea said firmly. "It was lovely. We had dinner and everything." She wasn't going to admit to Aunt Pearl that, for the first few minutes of the flight, as she gazed back over the retreating lights of Toronto, tears had welled up in her eyes, making the lights go all blurry. Christmas away from home. Worse, Christmas away from her mother.

But this was no ordinary Christmas. Two days earlier her mother had married Brad. She and Brad were schoolteachers. They had decided to marry in

December when they both had holidays and could take their honeymoon in Florida. Brad loved Florida. Her mom had never cared for it. "It's crowded and those flat white beaches are boring," she had always said, before she met Brad.

"Aunt Pearl and Uncle Cyril would love to have you stay with them over the holidays," her mother explained, right after she dropped the bombshell about the Florida honeymoon—just for two, of course. "Honestly, darling. I talked to Pearl on the phone yesterday and she was delighted at the thought. Remember all the fun you used to have at her house?"

"But that was when I was just a little kid," Andrea protested.

"So? What's so different now? Your cousins have been growing up too. Jeff must be twelve, nearly thirteen now," her mom said reassuringly.

"But you and I always went there in the summer. It won't be much fun in the middle of winter."

"Oh, come on," her mom coaxed. "Who's the girl who loves storms? There'll be plenty of those in Anderson's Arm. More than here. You'll find all kinds of fun. Don't forget, the boys will be on holidays too."

It was true that Andrea loved winter storms. Even blizzards. Her mother and every other adult she knew grumbled about them because snow and ice made driving slippery and dangerous. But Andrea looked forward to wild days, even if she had to stay inside and watch the snow swirling horizontally past the windows of the seventh-floor apartment where she and her mom lived. Best of all, she liked to bundle up in her down-filled parka and tall boots and go out walking. She marvelled at the way the streets turned white and clean, and the way the falling snow muffled the noises of the city.

Andrea could remember being happy in Anderson's Arm on those summer holidays long ago, in the years after her dad had died. But her mom had always been there too. This time she would be far away, enjoying bright sunshine and white sand and palm trees. With Brad. Big, smiling, horrible Bradley Osborne, who seemed determined to take her father's place. "Well, he never will," Andrea told herself bitterly.

It seemed as if Brad had been hanging around their apartment forever. He had been there every Saturday and Sunday since last Christmas. Brad taught grade seven at a senior elementary school out in The Beaches. It wasn't the same school where her mother taught grade nine math. Her mom had met Brad during a professional development day. Too bad.

In some ways Brad was all right. He was always trying to be nice to Andrea, the way teachers act when you've done something clever like winning a prize for your science project. He took Andrea and her mom out to a lot of different places in his red sports car, even though there wasn't much room for Andrea in the tiny back seat. The visit to the Metro Zoo had been great. And last summer they had driven to Upper Canada Village, where people wore olden-days clothes and pretended to live in the past. That was fun, except when the village blacksmith mistook Brad for Andrea's father. How could he? With her petite figure and wavy brown hair, she didn't look anything like gangly, blond Brad.

Most weekends she and her mom and Brad went out to eat in a restaurant, usually an Italian one. Italian was Andrea's favourite kind of food. Her second favourite was Chinese.

The trouble was, whenever Brad was around, her mom didn't act the same. She got mad at Andrea for practically no reason at all, like the time she made a lot of noise sucking her milkshake through a straw. Her mother listened so carefully to Brad, as if everything he said was important or funny, even when it wasn't. Once Brad went home, she magically zapped back to normal again, wondering what Andrea wanted in her school lunch or fussing about whether she had a clean T-shirt to put on. But the next time Brad appeared at the door, grinning and sometimes carrying one of those silly bunches of flowers, Andrea again began to feel as if she didn't matter very much.

Now Brad would be moving in. He was going to be there every morning for breakfast. Would her mom suddenly think Andrea was eating her cereal too loudly? Brad's toothbrush and shaving stuff would be littering their tidy bathroom. At night she might even have to see him wearing his pyjamas.

Lately Andrea's mom had been talking about the three of them moving to a bigger apartment. Or maybe even buying a house. That only made Andrea angrier. She didn't want to move. She liked their apartment on Willow Drive in Willowdale. The address was amusing and besides, it was the only home Andrea could remember. It had a neat balcony where you could sit in the summer and look down into the leafy backyards of a whole row of houses. There were two bedrooms, one for her mom and one for her. She had her room fixed up just the way she wanted it, with dark red Venetian blinds, a fuzzy rug on the floor, posters on the pink walls, and Gloria, her favourite doll from when she was younger, sitting contentedly in the big wicker chair.

Andrea had two close friends, one living on the fifth floor and one on the ninth, who both went to the same school as she did. If she and her mom and Brad moved away, she probably wouldn't see them anymore. And who knows what kind of room she would have in their next home. If only Brad had stayed put in his own apartment in East York, and just visited once in a while! She could have lived with that.

Andrea often thought of her own father. He had died in an accident on a construction site five years after the family moved from Anderson's Arm, Newfoundland, to Toronto. Andrea was only seven then, but she still remembered her dad.

Her mother used to talk about him a lot, always glad to answer the questions Andrea asked, although lately she hadn't mentioned him as often. His first name was Albert. Her mother had often told Andrea how musical he had been, just like all the Baxters. Most of them could sing and play musical instruments without ever having had any lessons. Andrea's father had been able to play dozens of tunes on his mouth organ. He'd also had a strong voice, and enjoyed singing in the church choir.

When Andrea was ten, she had asked her mother if she could keep her dad's harmonica in the drawer of the little table beside her bed. It was still there. Sometimes she got it out and blew into it, intrigued by the humming notes. Someday she wanted to learn how to really play it.

Her mother had a photograph album with pictures of their wedding in Anderson's Arm, and all the relatives. As well, there was a photograph of Andrea's father in a silver frame that hung beside the mirror on her mother's dresser. He and Brad couldn't have looked less alike. Her father had dark eyes and bushy, dark brown hair that was almost curly. His nose was, frankly, a bit too long. Andrea was glad that she had inherited her mother's nose. Brad had a crooked nose. He was very tall and too thin, and his blond hair was thin too. He wore glasses and had awfully big feet. He had to buy his shoes in a special store.

When Andrea and her mom had travelled to Anderson's Arm during those summers before Andrea's mom got so busy taking summer courses at university, they had always stayed with Uncle Cyril and Aunt Pearl. Cyril was her father's brother. In a lot of ways he had been like a father to her. Andrea would never forget clam-digging and picnics with him and her cousins on the beach, and the fun they had swimming in the nearby pond. But Andrea never went along when they took the dory out to catch mackerel. She was afraid of being out in a boat on the ocean; she couldn't explain why.

In the evenings Uncle Cyril usually played his accordion. He even made up his own songs. He told funny stories that made people laugh. Spending Christmas with the Newfoundland Baxters wouldn't be so bad if only her mom could be there too, instead of...in Florida. With Brad.

Andrea had always loved Aunt Pearl too—the comfortable woman who smiled down at her now, eyes merry behind the pale blue frames of her glasses. She liked to say that Andrea was the little girl she had never had. "I prayed for a daughter," Andrea once heard Aunt Pearl confide to her mother, "but the good Lord saw fit to send me two sons instead."

"Where's Uncle Cyril?" Andrea asked glancing eagerly from one face to another in the crowd. "Didn't he come to Gander too?"

"Oh, no, my dear," said Aunt Pearl, looking less jovial. "Cyril's away at sea. Didn't your ma tell you? He's got a job on an oil tanker."

"Yes, but I thought he was supposed to be home for Christmas."

"And that's the truth. He's supposed to be. But there's been wonderful bad weather this past fortnight, and the ship is late getting to port. Could be a few days yet."

A few days! How many days? Andrea hadn't counted on this. Christmas was only days away...If Uncle Cyril wasn't home, Christmas just wouldn't be right.

"Don't look so sad, my girl," Aunt Pearl comforted her. "I miss him too. But we're some glad he got steady work. After the fish plant closed down . . . well, times have been hard for us on the coast. When Cyril got a chance to sail on the tanker, he took it straight off. Way it is, he's gone for a month and then he's home for a month. Could be worse."

"How are we going to get out to Anderson's Arm?" Andrea asked, suddenly remembering that Aunt Pearl didn't know how to drive.

"I caught a ride in with Mr. Noseworthy. He got the contract to collect the mail from the airport. There he is over there."

Andrea observed a glum man with his cap down around his eyebrows and his coat collar turned up over his ears. When her duffle bag came toward them on the carousel, he retrieved it and hurried toward the door.

"Better git goin'," said Mr. Noseworthy without a smile. "Dirty weather."

For the next half hour the three of them drove along the Trans-Canada Highway in silence, while snow danced in front of the truck windshield. Then they turned onto the gravel road leading out to the bay. Aunt Pearl began chatting about the boys and the weather, but Mr. Noseworthy still didn't say much. Even with the truck bouncing along over the gravel, Andrea felt so tired that she fell asleep, her head on Aunt Pearl's ample shoulder. When she awoke an hour later, they were pulling up in front of the green and white clapboard house belonging to Aunt Pearl and Uncle Cyril. The snow had stopped and the wind had died.

Anderson's Arm looked entirely different to Andrea this time. Everything, including the road, the rocks, and the three dozen wooden houses nestled along the shore, was covered in snow. A pathway of moonlight led out across the black Atlantic Ocean. Light shone from a few kitchen windows where people were still awake. Here and there coloured Christmas lights dotted the scene like confetti. "It looks like a Christmas card," Andrea told herself, as she and Aunt Pearl climbed the slope up to the porch stairs. The only sound was the tinkling of ice crystals forming along the shore of the bay.

Although it was after eleven o'clock, Andrea could see her two cousins peering out at her through the kitchen window by the chimney.

"Rascals!" Aunt Pearl admonished them, as she and Andrea entered the warm, welcoming kitchen. "You should be in bed."

The boys, dressed in their striped pyjamas, were grinning from ear to ear. Andrea hadn't seen them for three years. Of course they were more grown up now, just as she was. They both had freckles and dark hair like their dad and like Andrea's dad. Jeff, the twelve-year-old, was as tall as his mother. He had always been the shy one. Matthew, at ten, wasn't much shorter. His impish smile and mirthful eyes told the world that he was still the bolder one, the one more likely to make you laugh. Matthew was the first to speak.

"Couldn't sleep a wink, neither one of us. So we figured 'twould be best to wait up. We wanted to see Andrea as soon as she got here."

"Yes, I suppose you did, my dears. Not every day your mainland cousin comes here by her own self in an airplane," Aunt Pearl said indulgently.

"Hey, where'd you get that jacket, Andrea? That's neat," remarked Jeff, admiring her new, black leather jacket.

"Jumpin's! What a lot of zippers!" exclaimed Matthew, inspecting the zippered cuffs, zippered pockets, and the big zipper down the front. "Does everybody in Toronto wear stuff like that?"

"It's my Christmas present from my mom," replied Andrea proudly. "She bought it downtown at the Eaton Centre. She told me I could wear it before Christmas because she was going away."

"Some nice," Jeff remarked.

"Look what I see!" shouted Matthew excitedly, suddenly more interested in Andrea's tote bag full of brightly wrapped gifts than in her new jacket.

"You've got to wait till Christmas," Andrea teased, pulling the bag closer to her. "No peeking till then."

"Mom, can we have some lunch? Please, please," Jeff begged, hoping to prolong the excitement of Andrea's arrival.

"Tsk. It's late...Oh, all right," Aunt Pearl sighed as she filled the kettle for tea. "But only a mug-up, and we'd best be quick about it. There's half a pan of duff left from yesterday."

It didn't take Andrea and the boys long to finish the remains of the heavy pudding.

"Off you go to bed now," Aunt Pearl told them. "Up early tomorrow. There's plenty to be done."

Andrea had the small bedroom normally occupied by Matthew. Since the house was heated only by the large, black, oil-burning stove in the kitchen, there wasn't much heat upstairs. This room was much colder than her pink bedroom in the apartment back home. She hurried into bed and snuggled down under four patchwork quilts to try to get warm. Matthew had moved into the next room with his brother. The walls were thin, and she could hear them for a long time, giggling and whispering.

CHAPTER TWO

In the morning Aunt Pearl was full of plans for the day. "Well, girl, do you want to go off with the boys and cut down a Christmas tree, or do you want to stay and make a steamed pudding with me?"

"I want to do both!" Andrea replied.

"I venture you can," laughed Aunt Pearl. "There's enough baking to last all day. You git along with the boys first and find us a proper tree."

Though the north wind was fierce, the sun shone as brightly as if it were summer, and the snow was whiter than Andrea had ever seen snow before. The three of them squinted as they trudged along the snow-covered road beside the glittering ocean.

"I know where to get a good tree, sure," Jeff announced confidently.

"Dad always got the tree other years," said Matthew wistfully, as they passed a row of fishing boats hauled ashore for the winter.

"I'm pretty mad that he's not home by now," muttered Andrea.

There was only one road through Anderson's Arm. It curved parallel to the bay and ended at the last house. From there, Andrea and her cousins had to clamber around a huge rock and follow a path that led down into a valley where there were spruce trees as far as the eye could see. How would they ever decide which one to cut?

"This one here's first-rate!" Matthew called out.

"No, b'y. That's bent crooked at the top, look," objected Jeff.

"How about this?" Andrea pointed to a taller one.

"Naah. Got all the branches gone to leeward," said Jeff.

The three of them finally agreed on a bushy spruce tree growing in the middle of a circle of others. Jeff chopped it down with his hatchet. He and Andrea hoisted it onto their shoulders and carried it home triumphantly. Once they had their prize tree in the house, all fragrant and prickly, Jeff set to work building a base to hold it upright. Matthew fetched the stepladder and poked around in the attic until he found the carton of Christmas-tree decorations.

Andrea and her cousins spent the afternoon decorating the tree and helping to make the Christmas pudding.

"Tell us about your new dad," Aunt Pearl suggested, after she had set Andrea to work stirring up a scrumptious mixture of raisins, candied fruit, and maraschino cherries.

"Who, Brad? He's not my dad, but he's sort of okay, I guess."

"You call him...*Brad*, do you? Not *Uncle Brad* or something like that?"

"He's not my uncle, and he sure isn't my father. He's just...he's not like Uncle Cyril...Aunt Pearl, when will Uncle Cyril be coming home? Will he miss Christmas?"

"Don't fret. Ship's running late. Happens sometimes in winter. No, he won't miss Christmas altogether. There'll be fine times ahead, maid," she answered reassuringly.

Maid. That was Uncle Cyril's name for her. Andrea remembered her other visits here, when she was younger and had protested to Uncle Cyril that she wasn't a *maid*. A maid, she had explained indignantly, was someone who came to your home and made beds or did the ironing or cleared away the dishes after dinner. "Well, maid," Uncle Cyril had replied with a wink, "if you can't do that, then I sees hard times ahead for you and your man when you git married!" After that he made up a song about her. He played it on his accordion and sang it every time she came to visit:

Here's a little song about this fair maid:
She can't wash a dish and she can't make a bed.
How will she learn what she has to do
When she comes from away where the chores
* are few?*

At first Andrea didn't like that song at all, but her mother took her aside and explained, "That's how Uncle Cyril and Aunt Pearl talk. When they say *maid*, they mean young girl. You should be pleased. Most people don't have a song written for them."

After a while Andrea changed her mind. She wouldn't admit it, but she was secretly glad about that song. And it had a catchy tune all right.

Christmas morning dawned with a stiff easterly breeze and a threat of snow in the slate-coloured sky. Andrea's mood matched the weather. As she crawled out from under the colourful quilts, she couldn't help but think longingly of other Christmas mornings. For six years, it had been just herself and her mom, drinking cocoa while Andrea unwrapped the many small gifts her mother had tucked into her stocking. Andrea had always hung her stocking over the back of a big chair because they didn't have a fireplace in their apartment. Toronto Christmases wouldn't be the same anymore, now that her mom had married Brad. Andrea really missed her mom. And Uncle Cyril still wasn't home.

By the time Andrea emerged from her room, Matthew had turned on the tree lights. Aunt Pearl had put out some nuts for them to nibble. Once everybody started opening presents, Andrea's downcast mood lifted for a while. Her gift from

Aunt Pearl and Uncle Cyril was a beautiful hand-knit sweater in her favourite colour: a deep rose-pink. She loved every shade of pink; it flattered her fair skin and blue eyes. Jeff gave her a bottle of nail polish that almost matched the sweater. Aunt Pearl was delighted with the pearl earrings Andrea had chosen for her (true to her name, Aunt Pearl loved pearls). The boys were pleased with the gifts Andrea had brought them—a Toronto Maple Leafs hockey sweater for Matthew, and a book of pirate stories for Jeff.

With a few tears misting her glasses because Cyril wasn't there, Aunt Pearl finally unwrapped the package he had left for her. "Oh, my. Look at this. I always wanted one," she beamed, as she held up a small, black camera, complete with a roll of film.

The last gift to be opened was the one that Brad, Andrea's new stepfather, had given her just before she left for the airport. Andrea had been grouchy about it because it took up too much space in her already full tote bag. Now she felt ashamed as she opened the package and found a portable cassette player, complete with a headset and a tape of her favourite band. How had Brad known what she wanted? She'd never dreamed she could have this and the leather jacket too.

"Let's have a listen to it!" suggested the boys, almost in unison.

"Hey, let me try it," Jeff insisted.

"What would be the good of it?" Aunt Pearl asked, inspecting the tiny machine. "Why, we've got a radio in the kitchen. When we play it, everyone can hear the music."

"But Aunt Pearl, you don't understand," said Andrea. "I can play it outdoors or in my room and listen to anything I want, and it won't bother mom or Brad or anybody."

"Well, put it aside for now," Aunt Pearl said firmly. "I want us all to watch the Queen give her Christmas message on the television."

While they watched the Queen, the wind outside died down. Pale sunlight began to filter through the clouds. On the coast, whatever weather you got didn't last long. By eleven o'clock, when the four of them were walking down the road to church, the sun was shining and Anderson's Arm looked dazzling again with its blanket of snow.

The small white church with the tall steeple was packed with people. During the Christmas service the choir sang, "I Saw Three Ships Come Sailing in on Christmas Day in the Morning." When the Baxters left the church and walked back home, however, there were still no ships to be seen on the broad horizon.

A few minutes after they reached the house, the telephone rang. It was Andrea's mother.

"Hi, Darling! Merry Christmas! We miss you. How's everything going?" exclaimed a sunny but distant voice.

"Oh, Mom..." Andrea sputtered, suddenly feeling as if she might burst into tears. Jeff and Matthew were sitting on the kitchen daybed, hanging on every word she said. No one had ever phoned their house from Florida before. Their wide-eyed interest in the conversation forced Andrea to regain her composure in a hurry. Her mother sounded really happy as she told Andrea about the warm, sunny weather and the beach and the wonderful food. And Brad.

Andrea didn't want to let her loneliness take the edge off her mother's joy. "Everything is fine here, Mom. We're having fun, even though Uncle Cyril is still away at sea," she reported. "And tell Brad I love my present," she said resolutely.

Later, when she and Aunt Pearl and the boys gathered to eat their Christmas dinner, Andrea knew she must try not to let them sense her despondent mood. She realized it was even harder for them, having Cyril away on this festive day. If he had been home, everybody would be laughing at his jokes and listening to his music. As it was, with everyone trying to be cheerful for everyone else's sake, the mood turned out to be a reasonably happy one. Dinner was delicious—roast turkey with savoury stuffing and loads of vegetables: cabbage, carrots, parsnips, and potatoes. Even the mashed turnips, which Andrea usually hated, tasted good that day. There was lots of cranberry sauce, made from berries that Matthew and Jeff had picked in November. And there were three different kinds of Aunt Pearl's homemade pickles. The day was almost over when they finally delved into the luscious pudding that Andrea and the boys had helped to make.

That evening Andrea was surprised to see her aunt sewing something. Surely on Christmas Day Aunt Pearl could take a holiday from chores like that.

"Little something for Matt," she explained, "to cover his face." She was sewing what looked like a piece of curtain to an old woollen toque. What on earth was it?

"We're going mummering," announced Matthew, looking pleased at the prospect.

"You've heard tell 'bout mummers, surely?" asked Aunt Pearl. "Your mother must have told you. When we were all youngsters here together...oh, didn't we have some times then!" She chuckled.

Andrea dimly remembered her mom talking about it. Mummering was a dress-up occasion when people went visiting from house to house at Christmas time. They were in disguise and their hosts had to guess who they were.

"Hey, Andrea, I bet you never saw a mummer," said Jeff.

"Well...no," Andrea admitted.

"You mean they don't have mummers up on the mainland?" Matthew asked. "Some foolish place that must be."

"We have the Santa Claus Parade, the longest one in Canada, maybe in the whole world," Andrea retorted. "And another thing, the Christmas tree down by the city hall skating rink is ten times as big as yours. I bet you never saw anything like that."

"You'll see some surprises tomorrow night all the same," Jeff promised gleefully.

"That's weird, starting the fun *after* Christmas," Andrea remarked.

"Christmas just begun, sure," Jeff insisted.

"Seems we've always had the mummers. Goes back a long ways," Aunt Pearl explained. "They last the Twelve Days of Christmas. And then they stop the sixth of January, thank goodness. Sometimes I do git tired of mopping the floor."

CHAPTER THREE

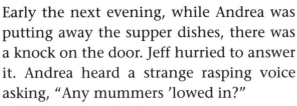

Early the next evening, while Andrea was putting away the supper dishes, there was a knock on the door. Jeff hurried to answer it. Andrea heard a strange rasping voice asking, "Any mummers 'lowed in?"

Three individuals wearing a comical assortment of other people's clothes were led into the kitchen. One was tall, one was middle-sized, and one was small; all had their faces covered. The two smaller mummers had filmy cloth covering their heads and shoulders, and the tall one was wearing an old Hallowe'en mask with the face of Pierre Trudeau on it. Andrea stared in fascination at the mysterious trio.

"You can sit down, mummers," offered Aunt Pearl.

The boys observed the masked visitors carefully. Matthew started prodding one of them around the ribs, jabbing at a pillow that was tied underneath a coat several sizes too large for him. Or her. You couldn't tell.

"Mummers, do you belong up the head of the Arm?" asked Jeff.

They shook their heads, and the veils swayed back and forth.

"Down the harbour?" asked Matthew.

Another shake.

"The Cove Road? Is that where your home is?" asked Aunt Pearl.

Suddenly they heard barking outside the door. Matthew jumped up and looked out. There, illuminated by the porch light, stood Jumbo—a large black dog, wagging his tail. He belonged to the Noseworthys.

"I know who you are! I know!" cried Matthew. "Show up, you Noseworthys!"

Once their identity had been guessed, the mummers had to reveal themselves. The three of them threw back their veils. They were, indeed, the Noseworthy children. Their father was the man who had driven Andrea and Aunt Pearl from the airport. Andrea had noticed them in church—Brian, a tall, unsmiling teenager with reddish hair; his younger brother, John; and their six-year-old sister, Molly. All the Noseworthys wore jackets and boots that were too large, making them look overweight and awkward.

"Darn," muttered Brian Noseworthy. "Should've barred Jumbo in his doghouse."

"How about a song for us?" demanded Aunt Pearl. It was the old tradition that mummers had an obligation to entertain their hosts. However, once they had removed their masks, these three suddenly became shy. At first they scarcely uttered a word. The boys looked at the floor and then sideways at each other, trying to hide their embarrassment. Brian finally cracked a smile, a slightly lopsided grin that encouraged Andrea to smile back at him. Only little Molly, who had curly hair and a missing front tooth, gazed unselfconsciously around at the Baxters, a big smile on her face.

"Has the cat got your tongue?" joked Aunt Pearl. Brian and John still didn't say a thing. Molly started giggling.

"Molly, my dear, is this the first time you've been out mummering?"

Molly nodded her head vigorously.

"Well, in that case, let's see if I can find you a little treat," said Aunt Pearl.

She cut several slices of her delicious, dark fruitcake and passed them around. "Remember, next time you come, I want to hear a story or a poem," she told the Noseworthys. Finally they replaced their face coverings and departed, first to take Jumbo home and then to call on other families.

More mummers came to call that evening. Aunt Pearl and the boys managed to guess the identities of most, but not all. One pair left as mysteriously as they had arrived, still masked and unknown. Andrea was intrigued. She was delighted when the boys suggested she go mummering with them the following night. They were still busy planning what they were going to wear when Aunt Pearl set out their "lunch" at nine-thirty—bread with bakeapple jam and tea.

"Mom gets this stuff at a special store in Toronto," said Andrea, spreading the amber-coloured jam on her bread. "I'm not all that crazy about it, but she is."

"Bakeapple jam? At a special store?" asked Aunt Pearl, surprised.

"Yeah. They don't sell it in the supermarket," Andrea explained, taking a sip of her tea.

"We don't get bakeapples at a store at all. We just go and pick 'em," explained Jeff.

"They're berries...like blueberries and foxberries and all those," added Jeff.

"Do they grow in your garden?" asked Andrea.

The boys started to laugh. They thought it was funny that anyone could imagine something wild like bakeapples growing in a garden, the same as potatoes or rhubarb. Aunt Pearl frowned at them for making fun of their cousin.

"They grow in the marsh," she told Andrea. "In every marsh. There for the taking. Last summer I put down twenty jars," she concluded. "So help yourself to some more!"

CHAPTER FOUR

"Aunt Pearl, what am I supposed to wear for mummering?" Andrea asked, as they were eating breakfast the next morning.

"No bother to find mummers' clothes," her aunt replied. "Jeff, you go to your closet. See if you can find a few things would fit Andrea. Something warm now. The wind today is colder than a merchant's heart."

"Oh, do I have to wear boys' clothes?" moaned Andrea, disappointed. "I was thinking I'd like to go dressed like . . . well, a bridesmaid or something."

"G'wan," teased Jeff. "It's only men that goes out mummering dressed like brides."

"That's mostly the way we do it," Aunt Pearl agreed. "Boys pretend to be girls. Girls pretend to be boys. Elsewise people could guess you right off. Wouldn't be so much fun then, would it?"

"Well, nobody will guess who I am," Andrea pointed out. "Nobody knows me."

"Don't be so sure," replied Aunt Pearl. "Anyone comes visiting Anderson's Arm is noticed."

That night, Andrea was so excited that she could hardly finish eating her supper. After trying on several sweaters and jackets, she had finally decided to wear a pair of Jeff's jeans turned inside out and a plaid shirt of Uncle Cyril's. The shirt was long enough to hide her leather jacket completely. She had borrowed a pair of rubber boots from Matthew. Though Andrea wouldn't have admitted it out loud, she knew she was lucky that her own boots, made of shiny black leather, were too small to fit Jeff or Matthew. She didn't relish the idea of lending her precious new boots.

The boys were both wearing long-sleeved, flannelette nightgowns belonging to their mother—a perfect disguise that adequately covered the many layers of warm clothes they wore underneath. All three mummers covered their faces with filmy squares cut from old, white, lace curtains that had once hung in Cyril and Pearl's bedroom. When they pulled their woollen caps down over their ears, the curtain material stayed in place. They could see where they were going, dimly, but no one could recognize them.

"Where d'you want to go first?" Jeff asked his brother, as the three of them made their way cautiously along the slippery road.

"How about the Noseworthys?" suggested Matthew.

Mrs. Noseworthy answered the door and hastily invited them in before the cold wind filled the kitchen.

"And mind you don't let old Jumbo in, neither,"

she added. The dog settled down again in his bed on the porch as the three mummers filed in and sat down. Brian and John were sitting at the kitchen table playing checkers. Molly was already in bed, and Mr. Noseworthy had gone to Gander to collect the mail. Ida Noseworthy was putting away the clean laundry. When she had finished, she sat down with her sons and they shrewdly looked over the mummers.

"Right, you mummers," she said. "I'd like a little song or dance. When I was your age, we had to entertain people before they'd give us a thing."

Jeff and Matthew got to their feet and haltingly began a clumsy step dance in the middle of the kitchen. Andrea remained perched on the corner of the daybed. She didn't know what kind of dance they were performing. She watched them with as much amusement as did Brian and John and their laughing mother who, fortunately, didn't seem to care that pools of melted snow were appearing on the kitchen linoleum.

"What's the trouble with this fellow? Can't he dance too?" asked Mrs. Noseworthy, pointing at Andrea, assuming she was a boy.

Jeff grabbed Andrea's hand, nearly pulling off her mitt, and yanked her into the middle of their crazy gyrations. All she could do was to start stomping and twisting, inventing a dance of her own, which wasn't easy when she was wearing borrowed rubber boots that were two sizes too big. But what did it matter if she did it wrong? After a few minutes of heavy-booted shuffling, they all sat down, hot and exhausted.

Right away Brian exclaimed, "I knows them, sure!"

"Who?" his younger brother asked.

"Baxters."

"Only two of 'em. Who's the other one, then?"

"Their cousin, the girl who came from away. You know, that pretty..." He suddenly covered his mouth with his hand, embarrassed that anyone should know he thought her pretty.

"Okay, show up, you Baxters! Show up! We knows it's you. Show up!" commanded John loudly.

Andrea and her cousins threw back the curtains that covered their faces.

"Just look at you, my dear," said Ida Noseworthy, admiring Andrea's disguise. She started taking cookies out of a round tin and placing them on a flowered plate. "I never thought to see you going around dressed like a mummer." She laughed. "But it suits you finest kind. And why not? You belong to Anderson's Arm. Born here, same as the rest us." She offered each of them a chocolate-chip cookie.

Andrea munched her cookie and said nothing. She didn't want to argue with Mrs. Noseworthy, a plump woman who seemed rather nice. But Andrea didn't think she belonged here at all. Her home was in Toronto, or at least it had seemed like home until Brad came and spoiled it.

"I knew 'twas Jeff's boots, see," said Brian Noseworthy, pointing to the boots Andrea was wearing. They looked like plain, black rubber boots identical to those worn by everyone in Anderson's Arm whenever the weather was cold and wet.

"How could you tell?" asked Andrea, puzzled.

"Easy. Patch."

"Patch?" She inspected the boots more carefully and noticed for the first time a small patch of orange-coloured rubber on the heel of one boot, covering what had been a leak.

"I minds the day Jeff put that patch onto it," Brian continued smugly. "Down in my dad's garage, in the spring of the year. He came by to get a drop of tire cement to make it stick."

"Hmmph," Jeff snorted. "I never figured you'd remember it forever and ever, amen."

"Time to git going," urged Matthew. Amid a chorus of good-byes, the three mummers trooped out into the frosty night.

"What say we call on Mr. Fudge?" suggested Matthew.

Mr. Fudge was the new United Church minister. He had recently arrived from St. John's, and everyone in Anderson's Arm knew he had yet to experience a Christmas season in which mummers invaded his home. Nobody went mummering in the city.

"No use going there," Jeff told them. "They're in St. John's visiting. I saw them drive away this morning. Hey, I've got a better idea. What say we go to the Keepings'?"

"Too darn far," protested Matthew.

Levi Keeping was Jeff's best friend at school, one of a big family where mummers were always welcome. The Keepings, however, lived at the other end of the community, a twenty-minute walk in good weather and even longer on ice-covered roads and paths.

"We can take the shortcut across the bog and then down along the shore and up over the hill. Be there in jig time," Jeff insisted.

"You tired, Matt?" Andrea asked solicitously. "Want to go home?"

"No way," said Matthew firmly.

Off they marched across the frozen bog, with reflected moonlight on the snow to show the way. The bog was nearly impassable in summer—several acres of wet land that felt as if you were walking on a field of soggy mattresses. Apart from the children who ventured there to pick bakeapples in August, most people avoided the bog until December. Then winter transformed it into a thoroughfare. The three Baxters threw back their veils to better see their way.

"I hope you guys know where we're going," Andrea said a bit apprehensively.

"Ha. I could find my way with my eyes shut," bragged Jeff.

"I been crossing this marsh all my life," added Matthew, as they trudged over the crisp snow.

"They really are sure of themselves," thought Andrea a bit enviously. "They belong."

"Are you going to stay here all your life?" she asked the boys. "In Anderson's Arm?"

Jeff thought for a moment. "I suppose. There's no better place than here."

"What do you want to be when you grow up?" asked Andrea.

"I dunno," replied Jeff.

"Ummm," said Matthew thoughtfully. "I'd like to go to sea on a big ship, like my dad."

"I know what I want to be," announced Andrea. She waited for them to ask her what, but neither did. There was only the crunching sound of their boots on the snow. Finally she stated, "I want to be an airline flight attendant. In the city, you can go to school and learn to be almost anything you want—like my mom. After Dad died, she went to university and..."

"Hey, what's that sound?" asked Jeff, interrupting her.

"What sound?" asked Andrea, stopping in her tracks.

"Shut up a sec. Listen!" he ordered.

The three of them stood still and listened. Then they all heard it, a long, melancholy sigh.

"Oh, my gosh," whispered Andrea fearfully. "Is that a bear?"

"Naah. Bears don't sound like that," said Jeff, trying to sound authoritative.

"When did you ever hear a bear anyways?" asked Matthew.

"Where's it to?"

"Has to be someplace handy to the beach."

"What if it's a wildcat or something and it runs after us?" asked Andrea nervously.

"Never heard of wildcats around here," said Jeff. "Okay, let's creep... really quiet... up to those rocks there. Nobody make a sound. Follow me."

At the far end of the bog was a mound of enormous rocks. Beyond that stretched Rocky Point Beach, where people went for walks in summertime and watched great waves roll in from some distant storm. Here the water was always too cold for swimming. Children, however, enjoyed themselves running along the shore and challenging one another to keep their feet dry as the breakers reached for their shoes.

Jeff climbed to the summit of the rocks first, and

gazed out over the great sweep of sand, pebbles and surf. "Holy jumpin's!"

"What do you see?" gasped Matthew, trying to catch up with his bigger brother. Andrea was right behind him, clambering onto the rocks. The three of them stared into the distance. For a few seconds, they were so astonished that no one uttered a word.

"It's a whale!" exclaimed Jeff at last.

At the far end of the beach, they could see the dark shape of a whale. Its gleaming body was partly in and partly out of the water. The gigantic mammal lay motionless in the surf as waves washed over it. Then suddenly it let out an explosive, whooshing sigh that could be heard the full length of the beach.

"My gosh, it's alive!" shrieked Andrea.

"And lookit! Out in the bay," Matthew yelled excitedly. "There's another one out there. And another. And another! There's a whole crowd of them." A pod of whales was swimming around in the dark water, breaking the surface from time to time.

"What are they trying to do?" asked Andrea, clutching at Jeff's sleeve. "Are they all going to swim ashore?"

"Jaysus, they'll be stuck for sure if they don't start swimming out to sea. When a whale gets stranded like that and the tide goes out, he can't move, and he can hardly breathe, and..."

"Hey, come on. I wants to see him up close,"

Matthew called, as he climbed down over the other side of the rockpile to reach the beach.

The three of them dashed along the moonlit shore, pounding through the wet sand in their heavy boots. The boys had to hoist the long night-gowns up around their waists so they could run. All three of the former mummers had stuffed their hats and veils into their pockets. Being mummers was now the last thing on their minds.

They were breathless by the time they got close enough to see the whale lying helplessly in the surf. Its bulky, rounded head was facing the beach, not the water.

"I sees his eye! His eye! He's lookin' right at me!" shouted Matthew, jumping up and down in excitement.

"Wow!" was all Andrea could say as she gaped in wonder at the hulking body only a stone's throw from where they stood. "It's awesome! The kids at school are never gonna believe this."

"Let's go up closer," hollered Matthew, as he danced on the shore. He was so thrilled by the spectacle that, as a big wave thundered in and filled one of his rubber boots with cold seawater, he barely noticed.

"Get back, Matt!" Andrea screamed. "If that whale rolled over, he could crush you like you were made of eggshells."

"He won't do that," shouted Matthew over the roar of the surf. "Whales don't harm people. They've got something like radar. They can..."

"Don't talk foolishness," Jeff yelled back. "That whale's in big trouble and won't be thinking straight. He knows he's about to die. So don't anybody get too close."

"But we can't let him die!" Andrea insisted. "Jeff, we've got to help him get free. What can we do?"

The boys just stared at the motionless whale. Finally Jeff spoke up. "There's nothing we can do. Look at the size of the creature. 'Twould take a tow truck to shift him an inch."

"But if we go for help as quick as we can...there might be something somebody could do," Andrea pleaded.

"No harm trying," said Jeff, though he sounded doubtful. The three of them ran to the other end of Rocky Point Beach, where they had to cross a field of beach grass and climb a small hill before reaching the main road.

"What kind of whale do you suppose he is?" Andrea panted, as they paused to catch their breath. "He's black all over, has a kind of round head, and he's long, nearly as long as...a streetcar. No, not that long. As long as a stretch limousine, I think."

"How long is a stretch limousine?" asked Jeff, mystified.

"How long is a streetcar?" asked Matthew.

"Oh, honestly!" cried Andrea, forgetting that her cousins had only seen those things on television and weren't sure of their size.

"We got a book at home, and it has pictures of all different kinds of whales. I can find out what it is," said Jeff confidently.

Just then they saw headlights approaching along the road a short distance away. "Hurry. Let's see if we can hitch a ride," called Matthew, starting to run again.

"My mom said I was never to hitch-hike," Andrea protested.

"Aw, come on. You want to help the whale or not?" Jeff cried in exasperation. "And anyway, Matt and I are here to protect you."

They recognized Mr. Noseworthy's truck, on its way back from Gander with the mail.

"Mr. Noseworthy! Mr. Noseworthy!" they yelled from the roadside, frantically waving their arms.

He slowed and then stopped and peered at them suspiciously out the side window. The boys were still clothed in long nightgowns. Even though Mr. Noseworthy had known them all their lives, he did not immediately recognize them. As soon as he did, however, he opened the truck door on the far side.

"Get in, then," he invited glumly. "Tired of going around mummers, eh? Too far to walk home?"

"No, no, you don't understand." They were all shouting at once as they climbed up and crowded into the front seat beside Mr. Noseworthy.

"A whale!"

"Stranded on the beach!"

"Long and black!"

"Can't move!"

"Seems like he can't breathe."

"He could die!"

"We gotta get help!"

"Beached whale, you say?" Mr. Noseworthy summarized, when he could get a word in. "Now that's a fine kettle of fish. Just what are you figurin' to do with him?"

"Don't know for sure. Maybe push him back out to sea," Jeff said earnestly, still a little breathless. Then he thought about how big a job that would be. "Well, not us. We got to get more people to help."

"It's possible that when the tide is high, a few hours from now, that whale might be able to swim away," Mr. Noseworthy mused as he changed gears. He steered the truck around the corner and rumbled up the Cove Road hill toward the Baxters' house. "A whale used to fetch a good price one time. You didn't think about that now, did you? Be worth more dead than alive. That's a lot of meat."

"Meat? You mean to eat?" asked Andrea, horrified.

"No, not fer us," he replied. "But, one time around here you could sell the meat to the mink farm for feed."

"What mink farm?" asked Jeff.

"You never heard tell of the mink farm? Gone now, of course. Before you was born. There used to be a fellow had a mink ranch down at Rattling River. Fur was a good price them days. I heard he made a nice bit of money."

"Ewww, that's disgusting," exclaimed Andrea, but her voice was lost amid the commotion as the truck stopped outside the Baxter house. Everyone scrambled out and hurried inside.

"Mom! You won't believe what we found..."

Quickly the boys related their amazing discovery.

"We're wondering what kind of whale it is," finished Andrea.

"A shame Cyril's not home just now. He'd know for sure," lamented Aunt Pearl.

"Oh, I really, really *wish* Uncle Cyril was here," said Andrea with a sigh.

"Pothead whale, I reckon," remarked Mr. Noseworthy. "'Twas the same thing a few years back down in Trinity Bay. They come ashore now and again. Nobody seems to know why."

"Where's that book Dad has, the one with all the different whales in it?" asked Matthew.

"Right here, slowpoke. I found it," said Jeff, who was already leafing through the pages, looking at the illustrations of all the world's whales.

"Let's see...we've got beluga whales, blue whales, fin whales, killer whales, minke whales...I don't see any pothead whales," Jeff said, as his brother leaned over the book with him to inspect the pictures.

"Got some other name in the book. Pilot whale. That's what they call it," snapped Mr. Noseworthy.

"Pilot whale. Sure, look. Here it is," announced Jeff triumphantly, holding up the book so they could all see the picture. "That's just like the one down on the beach. Flat nose and everything."

"Read us what it says," requested Aunt Pearl.

"'*Pilot whales. The origin of the name is not clear, but it may derive from the whales' habit of following schools of herring, thereby piloting fishing boats to good fishing grounds. Pilot whales are one of the smaller species, and are found in all seas of the world. They frequently beach themselves, often* en masse. *Marine biologists are still not certain why this happens.*'"

"What's 'en masse'?" asked Matthew.

"It's French. It means a whole bunch all together," replied Andrea smugly.

"So what they mean is the other whales we saw might come ashore too," Jeff concluded.

"What can we do, Aunt Pearl? That whale is

going to die unless we can somehow shove him out," said Andrea. "And what about the others?"

"There's nothing to be done tonight," said Aunt Pearl. "It's dark and it's late. We can't go round waking everyone. Besides, I wonder if anyone can help anyway."

"Maybe we should call the Mountie," suggested Mr. Noseworthy.

"Mountie couldn't do much, could he now? In the first place, he'd have to drive out here from the detachment at Seal Brook. Likely be midnight before he got here. And then what?" demanded Aunt Pearl.

"He's got a gun. I say 'twould be best to put that creature out of his misery," said Mr. Noseworthy gravely.

Aunt Pearl sighed and considered the matter for a moment, as Andrea and her cousins stood in anxious silence. "Well, someone could do away with the poor thing, I suppose. But then we'd have a dead whale on the shore. Stop and think about that, Isaac Noseworthy. The remains could still be there years from now. And the smell would knock you over before it finally rotted away."

"Got to be some use for him," Mr. Noseworthy insisted.

"Nothing I heard about," responded Aunt Pearl. "That mink ranch went out of business fifteen years ago. Even when it was a going concern, they never had a big enough freezer to hold all a whale's meat. Would only be wasteful if that poor beast died, and a proper nuisance."

"And horrible," added Andrea.

"The youngsters got the right idea. Best thing we can do is get that whale out of there alive," said Aunt Pearl.

"But how?" asked Jeff.

"Blessed if I know," replied Aunt Pearl. "But first thing in the morning we can all get to work on it."

CHAPTER FIVE

Not even the leaden eastern sky could dampen the excitement in the house next morning. The whole family was up and diving into breakfast by six-thirty. That was much earlier than the boys ate on school mornings. This day, however, nothing could have kept them in their beds.

The phone rang at quarter to seven. It was Isaac Noseworthy reporting that he had already driven down to the beach. The whale was still there and Mr. Noseworthy had been close enough to observe that the animal was still breathing. In the pre-dawn light, Mr. Noseworthy thought he had seen signs of other whales out in the deeper water.

"You know what? I bet the whales out in the bay are trying to talk to the one on the beach," announced Andrea.

"Talk?" laughed Jeff. "A whale can't talk."

"Oh, you know what I mean. Whales have underwater sounds they make, that other whales understand. I saw it on TV one time. I figure they must be worried about the one stranded on the beach. I think they care," Andrea said wistfully.

The boys stared at her, uncertain whether they shared her sentiment or not.

"I think I will give the Mountie a call before we

head for the beach," said Aunt Pearl, opening the telephone directory. "He'll be awake by now. Like as not we'll need to round up some people to help. And listen to me, all of you," commanded Aunt Pearl. "Everyone dress warmly. There's snow in that sky. Andrea, you borrow one of the boys' hats."

"I hate wearing hats," Andrea said.

"You'll be glad of a hat. You could be out there all day and no place to get warm," Aunt Pearl warned.

Grudgingly Andrea accepted a toque that had the words *Montreal Canadiens* knitted into it. She shoved it into her pocket.

"And you'd better borrow Jeff's old rubber boots again. And extra socks," Aunt Pearl added, glancing at Andrea's stylish leather boots. "If seawater gets into those, 'twould be the end of them in a hurry."

"Oh, all right," grumbled Andrea as she pulled on the patched boots. "Aunt Pearl, why don't you bring your new camera? You could get a picture of the whale."

"To tell the truth, I'm not altogether sure how to make it work," admitted Aunt Pearl.

"I can show you. Mom has one just like it," Andrea reassured her.

"I'll bring it then," Aunt Pearl agreed, and then turned to pick up the phone.

Aunt Pearl and Mrs. Ida Noseworthy rode in

the cab of Mr. Noseworthy's truck, while the Noseworthy and Baxter kids sat in the open back. They arrived at Rocky Point Beach just as snow began to fall. Andrea soon saw that they were far from alone with the unfortunate whale. News had travelled through Anderson's Arm faster than a northeast gale. The Keeping family was there, including all eight children. Even the three trouble-making Abbott boys had joined the crowd, looking less menacing than usual at this early hour. Men, women, and children were hurrying down to the cold beach to marvel at the sight of a whale with its body in the ocean and its massive head resting on the shore. Snow flurries obscured the seascape, making it impossible to see if other whales were still swimming in the deeper water of the bay.

"There's all kinds of them out there," Matthew assured everyone who spoke to him. "Last night, in the moonlight, it was clear as noon. I was the first to spot them."

"You were not. I saw the whale first," Jeff insisted, shoving his brother into the sand.

"Yeah, but I saw the offshore ones first," Matthew sulked, brushing sand from his jacket sleeve.

At 8:30 a tall Royal Canadian Mounted Police constable arrived. He looked cold, trudging doggedly across the beach from his car. The earflaps of his cap were down, and his dark blue nylon jacket was dotted with snowflakes.

"Sorry I'm late, folks. Took darn near an hour to drive here from Seal Brook. The visibility was practically zilch some places because of the snow squalls."

"Morning, Constable Wheeler," said Mr. Noseworthy, stepping forward to greet the Mountie. "We're just trying to figure what's best to do with this poor creature. I figured it would be best to shoot him and put him out of his misery, but..."

"Looks like a heckuva problem," agreed Constable Wheeler, peering at the unlucky whale through the snow. "To tell you the truth, this is the first time I ever saw a whale. I only got posted here last summer. I'm from Flin Flon, Manitoba. If it was a moose in trouble, I'd have a better idea what to do."

"We don't see that many whales ourselves, not on the beach like this," explained Mr. Keeping, a lobster fisherman. "Oftentimes we see them when we're out in boats, but they try to stay clear of us."

"I put in a call to a marine biology professor, a Dr. Elliott at Memorial University, before I left the detachment," reported the Mountie. "She's an expert at saving whales that get into difficulties. She told me she'd come herself as soon as possible."

"Take a nice while to get here, driving all the way from St. John's," observed Mr. Noseworthy.

"Well, she said she'd try to get a ride in a government helicopter. But by the look of that sky, I don't figure they'll be doing much flying," Constable Wheeler concluded.

"Might be too late," observed Jeff gloomily.

"The important thing, according to Dr. Elliott, is to keep the whale wet," said the Mountie. "If the skin gets too dry, that can cause dehydration. So, until we can figure some way to get him back in the ocean, we've got to organize a bucket brigade." He raised his voice. "I'd like you all to go home and round up every bucket you can. Put on waterproof clothes, if you have some, and rubber boots. Then get back here as fast as you can, okay?"

The Baxters, Noseworthys, Keepings, and others who had gathered on the beach hurried to put the Mountie's plan into action. Meanwhile new people kept arriving, eager to see the stranded whale. They stepped closer and closer, daring to touch the smooth, black skin, to marvel at the great head, to admire the broad tail, so much like the tail of an aircraft in its shape.

The high tide during the night had kept the whale partly afloat, but now the tide was receding, increasing the animal's peril. Without the buoyancy provided by the ocean water, the weight of the whale's great body began to press heavily on its lungs. Its breathing became laboured, and soon it was gasping for air like a person suffering from an asthma attack. Its breath, reported those close enough to catch a whiff of it, smelled like a hundred dead fish.

Immobilized, the frightened whale could only blink its tiny eyes as it gazed—seeing or perhaps unseeing—at the curious people watching it. From time to time it thrust its flippers back and forth across the damp sand. The effort was useless, however, and did nothing to budge its heavy body from its sandy prison.

"Does he know we mean to help?"

"A whale is a knowing creature."

"Looks poorly to me."

"His days are numbered, I'd say."

"Has to be a way to launch 'im off."

"They say he's got buddies out in the bay."

The challenge of trying to return the lonely whale to the sea soon united the community. Mr. Keeping and several others were wearing hip waders and rubberized jackets when they returned to the beach, ready for action.

"Won't do a pick of good if he dies here, will it now?" declared Mr. Keeping, addressing the crowd. "Best for everyone—ourselves and the whale too—to get 'im out of here alive."

It didn't take long to form the bucket brigade. Every able-bodied soul in Anderson's Arm wanted to help. The volunteers formed a long line across the beach from the surf to the stranded whale. Then they began passing along buckets of seawater from one pair of hands to the next. It was a wet job, and exhausting. Andrea soon realized she had never worked so hard in her life. Her arms ached. Despite the cold and snow, she was sweating, not freezing. She grabbed bucket after heavy, sloshing bucket from solemn Brian Noseworthy, who stood to her left. She swung each bucket over to Jeff, on her right. He, in turn, passed it to Matthew—and on and on, until it finally reached Mr. Keeping.

Moses Keeping had been chosen to stand beside the whale. He was the tallest man there, and had strong arms from years of hauling lobster traps into his boat. He took on the job of splashing bucket after bucket of cold water over the whale's back.

"Hey, watch it, clumsy!" scolded Andrea, as Jeff accidentally spilled some water inside her boots. They were the same old boots she had borrowed to go mummering, and were too big for her. Quite a lot of water splashed in.

"Ooops. Sorry. But it's only water," Jeff retorted. "I can think of worse things."

"Now my feet are all cold and clammy," Andrea complained. Swiftly she bent over to scoop up a handful of wet snow. She shoved it inside the collar of her cousin's jacket.

"Stop that!" yelled Jeff, flailing his arms at her.

"Quit carrying on, you two," ordered Brian Noseworthy, passing Andrea another full bucket. "We got a job to do here."

Constable Wheeler insisted that each person in the bucket brigade take a break every thirty minutes. Near noon, he took a breather himself and hiked back to the road where he had parked his car. Turning on his police radio, he called the police dispatcher to try to find out when Dr. Elliott might arrive. By then the falling snow had turned into swirling squalls that, every few minutes, obscured everything on land and sea.

Finally the Mountie received a message from Gander that the helicopter and Dr. Elliott were grounded there. Snow and high winds were making it dangerous to travel even by road. The police wanted to know what weather conditions were like at Anderson's Arm.

"Weather's no better here," replied Constable Wheeler, "but if we don't get this whale out on the high tide tonight, I'd say it's game over."

There was static on the police radio. "I'll put the doctor on. Hold on," came a distant voice. Soon a new voice could be heard. "Constable? This is Alison Elliott speaking. Here's what I suggest. Get hold of a boat, a sturdy one with a strong engine. And you'll need lots of rope. You've got to get a line around the whale's tail. Once the tide comes in and the whale is partly submerged, there's a fair chance that the boat can pull away until the whale is afloat. Do you understand?"

"Might be possible, ma'am," replied Constable Wheeler doubtfully.

"And you mentioned this morning that there were other whales near by. Is that correct?" asked Dr. Elliott.

"Yes, the kids who discovered the whale last night claim they saw more of them swimming out in the deep water. But there's so much snow this morning, we can't see if they're still there," said the Mountie.

"Most likely they are. Pilot whales live in extended families. If one gets stranded, the rest will stay nearby, and often end up on the shore too. It might be the leader who's on the beach," explained Dr. Elliott.

"Leader?" asked the Mountie. "How can you tell if he's the leader? One whale looks much like another to me."

"That's our problem. Whales do look the same to us. But the whales know who their leader is," said the faraway voice of the scientist.

"So that makes it even more important to get our beached visitor launched," said Constable Wheeler. "We sure don't need any more of them. Thanks. Over and out."

The Mountie plodded back across the wide beach. "We're going to need a boat, a sturdy one with a strong engine," he explained, as the whale watchers gathered around and the bucket brigade took a break. "Any of you folks got one?"

"Well, me son, I'd say most of us here got a boat of one kind or another," replied Mr. Keeping. "But fishing season's been over since November, and our boats all been hauled ashore. 'Tis a day's work to get one back into the water and fit to go to sea."

"There's one boat still in the water," offered Mr. Noseworthy reluctantly. "It's me old trap boat. Used to fish with her one time, but now Brian and I just take her down to the brook where we cut our firewood."

"Noseworthys' is just about the last house that's got a wood stove," Jeff explained to Andrea. "Rest of us all got oil nowadays."

"Isaac Noseworthy's kind of set in his ideas," whispered Aunt Pearl. "He likes the old ways."

"Thanks, Mr. Noseworthy," said the Mountie. "That's generous of you. Now, if you can show me where you keep your boat..."

Mr. Noseworthy and his son Brian headed for the truck. Aunt Pearl sent Andrea with them to borrow a dry pair of boots and socks at the Noseworthys' house. "Like as not you'll catch your death of cold, girl," she scolded, when she discovered how wet Andrea's feet were from all the water that had splashed in. "Wouldn't want you sick when we send you back to your mother and your new stepfather."

"Foolishness," muttered Mr. Noseworthy, as he turned the key to start the truck's engine.

"What's foolish?" asked Brian, who was sitting beside him.

"Still wonder if 'twouldn't have been the best thing all round to shoot that poor creature," grumbled Mr. Noseworthy, as the truck went slowly along the snow-covered road.

"No!" Andrea protested. "We have to try to save him. We absolutely have to. Suppose that whale was somebody we knew. One of us. Wouldn't we lie there hoping and praying to be rescued?"

"Hmmph. That might be. But he's sure sufferin' a long time for the sake of some wonderful idea that scientist up in St. John's has got."

Constable Wheeler followed the Noseworthy truck in his police car. Mr. Noseworthy parked the truck beside his house, and then got out and headed down the path toward the cove where he moored his boat. Andrea and Brian and the Mountie followed him. They, in turn, were followed by Jumbo, who had emerged from his doghouse wagging his tail, pleased to see some of his family returning home.

The *Rosebud* was nearly the same length as the whale. The vessel was old and scruffy and needed a coat of paint. There was a small cabin in the bow of the boat, but the rest was open. The bottom boards were littered with bits of bark and twigs from the load of logs that had been her most recent cargo. The boat was tied to a small, rickety wharf that Mr. Noseworthy called his "stage."

The wet snow was turning to spits of rain as Constable Wheeler scanned the *Rosebud*. He observed that there was no water in the hull, which told him there were no leaks. She looked seaworthy. So did the ancient engine, which her skipper was coaxing into action by turning a heavy wheel. At first it shuddered and coughed, but soon settled into a steady, reassuring CHUG...CHUG... CHUG...CHUG...CHUG...CHUG...CHUG... CHUG....

"Got some strong rope, Skipper?" called the Mountie.

"Finest kind. Right in me store there," shouted Mr. Noseworthy, gesturing toward a weathered grey shed beside the stage.

The Mountie stepped inside, gathered up several coils of rope, and hurled them into *Rosebud*'s forward hold.

"All aboard what's coming aboard!" bellowed Mr. Noseworthy over the thudding of the engine.

Brian climbed aboard quickly and Jumbo followed in after him.

"I thought you was planning to come too, Mr. Mountie," hollered Mr. Noseworthy, who suddenly seemed younger and more vigorous now that he was at the helm of his vessel.

"No thanks, Skipper. I got my work cut out for me on the shore."

"What about you then, girl?" Mr. Noseworthy called out to Andrea, who was standing uncertainly on the stage.

"I don't think I..." Andrea began.

"Come on. You been actin' like a fish out of water ever since you landed in Gander. You're the one with all the sympathy for that whale. Get on board with us. See what you can do to help."

Andrea stared at him, astounded. She hadn't thought of Mr. Noseworthy as a particularly perceptive person, but he was right. She did feel like a fish out of water in Anderson's Arm. She hadn't realized it had been so obvious to others, even to Mr. Noseworthy, of all people.

Constable Wheeler was becoming impatient. "What's it to be, Andrea? You can catch a ride back to the beach with me. Your aunt will be expecting you."

Andrea had always been leery of boats, especially grubby-looking ones like the *Rosebud*. She stood for a moment longer, wondering what to do. Then she turned to the Mountie. "No, thank you. I don't need a ride. I . . . I'll go in the boat with them. I want to help that poor whale find his way home," she said resolutely. Then she added, "All I really need is a dry pair of boots."

"I'll get you some, and socks too," responded Brian, leaping back onto the stage and running up toward the house.

"And fetch an oiled jacket for her as well," called Mr. Noseworthy. "No sayin' what the weather's going to do."

In a matter of minutes they were off. Mr. Noseworthy manoeuvred his boat out of the narrow cove and into the bay. Soon he was steering through choppy seas toward the point of land marking the beginning of Rocky Point Beach. Anderson's Arm looked quite different from the water.

For the first few minutes, Andrea was a little afraid, but she was relieved to find that the *Rosebud*, though unimpressive looking, moved solidly through the water. Being out on the water wasn't nearly as scary as she had expected. She was glad that she had taken Aunt Pearl's advice about dressing warmly and wearing a hat. She was grateful that Brian, who was turning out to be rather thoughtful, had found her a pair of dry rubber boots as well as a pair of thick, hand-knit socks. He had also found a fisherman's yellow jacket for her. Though it smelled oily and was too big, it did protect her new leather jacket and kept it dry.

As soon as they rounded the point, the boat headed into the wind and the waves, and every few seconds a shower of spray soaked them. When Andrea licked her lips, she could taste the salt.

Shivering, she huddled next to big, furry Jumbo, who was perfectly at home travelling in a boat, sitting quietly on the wooden seat between Andrea and Brian. His fur was wet with the snow and salt spray, which made him smell like an old mattress that had been left out in the rain. It didn't seem to matter though. He was a great source of shelter and warmth.

"Look! There's a whale," shouted Brian suddenly.

Without warning a huge head had broken the surface of the water, not far from the boat. Then an explosive blast of air and water vapour shot upward. A fin rolled by, and then the sleek, black mammal glided silently back into the depths.

"Thunderin' Jaysus!" exclaimed Mr. Noseworthy, adjusting the engine to its slowest speed.

"They're still out here!" cried Andrea.

"How many whales was it you and your cousins saw yesterday?" asked Mr. Noseworthy.

"I don't know exactly," she replied. "But I think

it must be the beached whale's family. They must be terribly worried about the one who lost his way."

"That might be, but we don't want to run into any of 'em," said Mr. Noseworthy, pondering the situation. "Brian, you keep a watch out to starboard. And you, maid," he directed Andrea, "keep an eye out to port."

Maid. There was that word again. Andrea shrugged. This was Newfoundland, and they used expressions that most people had never heard in Toronto. But she understood, now, what Mr. Noseworthy and her relatives meant. Newfoundlanders sometimes had another way of saying things. She felt rather pleased that they were treating her as one of their own. She huddled down in her position on the left side of the boat, concentrating on watching for more whales.

"We don't have to worry, Mr. Noseworthy," said Andrea. "My cousins told me that whales have radar. They know where we are, and they won't run into us."

"Seein' as our old boat got no radar, we won't be taking any chances," Mr. Noseworthy replied.

The three of them stared silently into the dark, rolling ocean. Even Jumbo was alert, his nose twitching as if at the scent of an unfamiliar animal. In a few minutes another whale made its graceful ascent from the cold depths. It sprayed a fountain of steamy vapour over them, and then noiselessly disappeared as they watched in fascination.

Luckily the snow was diminishing, so Andrea and the Noseworthys could now partially see the shoreline, the helpless whale, and all the people standing around. The boat made its way closer and closer to the beach, bobbing and rolling in the lively motion of the surf. Mr. Noseworthy flung his anchor over the side. "Close enough," he exclaimed. "I don't want the *Rosebud* beached like that whale there."

"Attention, Skipper, can you hear me?" came a metallic-sounding voice from the beach. It was the Mountie talking through a loudspeaker.

The crew of the *Rosebud* didn't have anything like a loudspeaker to use to call back. All they could do was shout in unison and wave their arms. "Yes! Yes! We hear you!" they cried. Even Jumbo barked.

"Right," replied the faraway voice of Constable Wheeler. "Next thing is to get one end of your rope to the shore. See if it will float."

Brian started uncoiling the heavy rope that lay in the forward hold.

"Hang on there, Brian, me son," Mr. Noseworthy called. "Way the wind is, 'twould likely carry it out to sea. I don't rightly know how we're going to get that rope ashore. The water's too deep for anyone to wade out from the beach and take it."

"Could somebody swim out for it?" suggested Andrea.

"Swim?" asked Brian incredulously. "A person would freeze to death in two minutes."

"All I meant was...if somebody had a scuba-diving suit, or something," explained Andrea, trying not to sound like an idiot.

"Or a fur coat like Jumbo," said Brian thoughtfully, patting the dog.

"Well sure, why not Jumbo? He could go," Andrea suggested.

The three of them stared at the dog, who wagged his tail, pleased at the sudden attention.

"My mom told me that when she grew up here, back in the old days, they had this dog, a big dog," explained Andrea. "And he would swim out in the ocean and retrieve things. I saw a photo of him. He looked something like Jumbo, but with a white chest and feet."

"Jumbo can swim with the best of them," agreed Mr. Noseworthy, fondling the dog's ear. "Yiss, Jumbo, old boy. I thinks we got a job for you."

News of the stranded whale had been broadcast over the radio, and the crowd ashore was now growing larger. A dozen people from nearby Round Harbour had arrived in the back of the truck that was used for snow ploughing. Several more had come on their snowmobiles from the small community at Rattling River. A television crew from St. John's was attempting to reach Anderson's Arm. Their journey, however, had been stopped at Gander.

"Probably just as well the road is closed," Constable Wheeler told himself. One thing he didn't need to contend with was a huge throng of sightseers. He had more important problems on his mind. Just how were they going to tie up the whale and tow it into the water?

"Who would like some tea?" asked Aunt Pearl, bustling along with a big thermos and some plastic cups. Mrs. Noseworthy was right behind her with a large bag full of molasses cookies. There had been no time for a meal at noon, so Aunt Pearl and Ida Noseworthy had gone home to fetch cookies and make tea.

Constable Wheeler helped himself to a large cookie, munched it, took a second one, and then aimed his loudspeaker at the *Rosebud*. "Attention, Skipper. We're ready to receive the line!"

Mr. Noseworthy had finished fastening a light rope to his dog's collar. "Jumbo, old man, here's your chance to be a hero," he announced. He strained to lift the heavy dog, hoisted him over the side of the boat, and lowered him into the icy water.

CHAPTER SIX

 There was a splash, and then a sodden Jumbo looked up at his master, indignant and surprised. He paddled around in a circle close to the boat, barking noisy demands to be hauled back aboard. Jumbo loved to swim but nobody had ever dumped him so rudely over the side of a boat into a wintry sea.

"Go Jumbo, go!" screamed Andrea, worried that the dog might freeze to death. But Jumbo only barked and whined and scratched at the side of the boat, his brown eyes pleading.

"No, boy, no! Go to shore!" Brian gestured, pointing to the beach.

But Jumbo wanted to be on board the *Rosebud* with his family. He looked forlorn and frustrated, as if he thought that suddenly nobody loved him.

On the beach, the villagers were straining their eyes as they watched the drama of the bewildered dog. One of the boys from Rattling River had a pair of binoculars, and a woman from Round Harbour had brought a small telescope. Jeff and Matthew and other bystanders took turns looking through these devices so they could see better.

"Constable Wheeler, why don't you call the dog through your loudspeaker?" suggested Aunt Pearl.

"What's his name?"

"Jumbo."

"JUM-BO! HERE, JUM-BO!" bellowed the Mountie through his loudspeaker. One after another, the other people joined in. "HERE, JUMBO! HERE, JUMBO!" they began chanting like a chorus.

Jumbo was growing cold and tired from swimming in circles. When he heard his name being called, he figured somebody wanted him, even if his family on the *Rosebud* didn't. The big dog turned and began to swim toward the voices on the shore. As the distance between dog and boat increased, the coil of rope started to unfurl. Jumbo paddled determinedly on, swept forward at intervals by the surging waves. The skipper and his crew watched in silence, too tense to utter a word. No one wanted to say what each was thinking: what if Jumbo didn't make it?

"Here comes the dog," called the Mountie urgently, as Jumbo approached. "Who'll volunteer to wade out for the rope?"

"Right. Let's go," said Moses Keeping to his neighbour, Alf Rose. Both men were wearing hip waders and rubberized jackets. They waded out into the cold seawater, waving their arms at the weary dog. "Over here, boy," they called.

Jumbo had no need of encouragement. By then he could see the beach ahead of him, and he was swimming furiously to reach it. Mr. Keeping had to grab him by the collar to stop him.

Quickly the two men wriggled the collar over the dog's head. Then they let him swim untethered toward the shore. Soon Jumbo was in shallow water, where he could wade. On the shore dozens of excited people crowded around the bedraggled dog. Unceremoniously Jumbo shook himself, splattering cold water all over his admirers.

"This dog deserves a medal!" exclaimed one woman.

"He must be perished with the cold," said Matthew, taking off his woollen scarf and trying to dry Jumbo's fur with it.

"Some smart!" exclaimed Aunt Pearl, patting Jumbo's soggy head as she gave him a molasses cookie.

"Moses! Alf! Can you get that line around the whale's tail?" shouted Constable Wheeler, standing at the water's edge.

"Yessir, we'll give it a try," they yelled back. Alf Rose quickly untied the rope from the collar the two men had taken from Jumbo's neck. They reeled the light rope in until the heavy tow rope Mr. Noseworthy had fastened to its other end finally reached them. Then they sloshed through the breakers over to the whale's tail.

"You get on the far side of 'im, Alf," called Mr.

Keeping. "We got to pass the line around his flukes."

"And what if he decides he don't like the idea?" enquired Mr. Rose. "Wild creatures don't like to be tied, you know."

"Not much he can do, is there now? Can't run away; he's got no legs. Can't bite us; he's got no teeth," replied Mr. Keeping.

Stooping on either side of whale's tail, the two men passed the loop of rope around the narrowest part, between the flukes and the body. Then, with frigid water slapping at the shoulders of his rubberized jacket, Mr. Keeping made it fast.

Suddenly the whale swung his broad tail up and then swiftly down with a great splash. The men leapt back, startled. At the same time the frightened mammal let out a mournful sigh.

"Me son, I told you he wouldn't like this," said Mr. Rose nervously.

"More likely in a hurry to get out of here," remarked Mr. Keeping as he double-checked his knot. Then he hollered to the constable, who was observing them from the beach. "She's fast!"

"START PULLING!" shouted Constable Wheeler to the crew of the *Rosebud* through his loudspeaker.

On board the boat, Mr. Noseworthy hauled up the anchor and then shoved the engine into gear. "Full ahead!" he roared. Andrea didn't know what to expect next. But she hung on tightly as the *Rosebud* headed for the open sea. White water from the labouring propeller churned under the stern. The tow rope lifted out of the water as the vessel tugged at the bulk of the partly submerged whale.

A series of towering waves tumbled in, and the whale began thrashing its tail. It rolled slightly to one side as another big breaker crashed on the beach. Then suddenly it was afloat, but barely. Before the weary, terrified whale had time to think of its next move, it was being towed—tail first— into deeper water.

"The whale is swimming! 'Tis off to sea! It's saved!" shouted the excited people on the beach, who had been eagerly watching the drama unfold.

"Not quite free yet," said Constable Wheeler, training his binoculars on the *Rosebud*, which was slowly proceeding out to sea. "They still have to get that line off the whale."

The *Rosebud*'s engine strained against the immense weight of the whale. It was attempting to swim now, arching its back and spouting weakly.

"He's in some rush to join his buddies out in the bay," Mr. Noseworthy speculated.

"Maybe it's a girl whale," said Andrea. "Everybody's been calling it *he* but it could have been *she* all along."

"Your guess is as good as mine," the skipper

responded. "Only another whale would know for sure." He turned to his son. "Brian, you bide back here and take the tiller. It's time to get that line off."

It was late afternoon by this time. The snow had stopped falling, but the sky was growing dark and the *Rosebud*'s crew could barely see the beach behind them. Brian sat at the stern, holding the boat on course with the engine going slowly, while his dad began hauling in the rope that was tied to the whale. The *Rosebud* and the whale drew closer and closer together, until they were almost parallel.

Mr. Noseworthy leaned over the side of the boat, peering down into the dark green water as the whale came alongside. It was barely moving now, exhausted after its long ordeal.

"You'll be leaving us, old fella, soon as you're clear of the rope. Just as well we didn't shoot you," said Mr. Noseworthy softly. He stood up and fastened a length of nylon rope to a cleat on the afterdeck. Then he tied the other end around his waist.

"Now listen here," he told Brian and Andrea. "In case I fall overboard, you youngsters haul me in again."

"Oh, Mr. Noseworthy. This is dangerous. I'm scared!" cried Andrea.

"Don't be fearful. Be careful," he replied. Then he grasped the gunwale with one hand and leaned out over the side. Thrusting his arm down into the ice-cold water, he groped for the end of the rope that held the whale captive. Suddenly a wave surged over his head and shoulders. Dripping with water and gasping for air, he heaved himself back onto the deck for an instant. After catching his breath, he tried again, this time leaning out even more precariously, reaching deeper into the water. Coughing and sputtering, Mr. Noseworthy hauled himself back a second time. This time he was clutching the end of the tow rope.

"Head for home, Brian," he commanded, half-choking with salt water.

"You did it, Dad!" exclaimed Brian with one of his rare grins.

"She's free! Our whale is free!" shouted Andrea.

The three of them watched the black body glide smoothly underneath the boat toward the open ocean and freedom.

"I've done a lot of jobs in me time," said Mr. Noseworthy, busily wringing the water out of his jacket, "but fishing around underwater after some whale's tail sure takes the cake." He looked around the boat at the shivering youngsters, and then gave Brian a course to steer for Rocky Point, barely visible in the fading daylight.

CHAPTER SEVEN

Early the next morning, the television crew finally arrived. There was no whale for them to photograph, however. All the whales had disappeared. The camera people scanned the horizon with binoculars, but there wasn't a trace of a spout or fin or tail.

Fortunately, Aunt Pearl had a whole roll of pictures of the beached whale in her camera. The producer was delighted to use them.

"Just imagine that!" she told Andrea joyfully. "My first camera and my first roll of film, and my pictures are going to be on television."

That evening the host of the six o'clock television news told the story in a dramatic voice. "The citizens of Anderson's Arm had to act on their own yesterday to save the life of a beached pilot whale." A film clip of Andrea, Jeff and Matthew appeared on the screen, and the announcer continued, "These young people were the first to sight the stranded whale."

"Jumpin's, it's us!" shouted Matthew in the Baxters' parlour, where the family was watching.

"Shut up and listen!" snapped Jeff, poking him in the ribs.

"Because a blizzard forced the closure of the Trans-Canada Highway," the announcer explained, "the concerned people of this small community received little outside help in their attempt to save the life of the whale. Constable Fred Wheeler of the Seal Brook detachment managed to reach Anderson's Arm, but bad weather grounded a helicopter carrying marine biologist Dr. Alison Elliott."

Even though Aunt Pearl's photos had been taken through falling snow and were a bit fuzzy, the black whale could still be seen lying in the sand. The dark shapes of people surrounded it.

"Using a local boat and the effort of many volunteers," said the announcer, "the people of Anderson's Arm were finally able to haul the whale out to deeper water, where it appears to have rejoined its companions. During the night this lucky whale and its pod evidently fled from the shallow bay and swam safely out to sea."

There was a panoramic shot of the now-empty Rocky Point Beach with not a whale or person to be seen on it. This was followed by a shot of Mr. Noseworthy patting Jumbo as the two of them posed beside the *Rosebud*.

"So all's well that ends well for whales in Anderson's Arm," the announcer concluded with a cheery smile. "And now over to you, Debbie, and the sports."

"Thanks, Ted. Last night in Atlanta..."

Aunt Pearl snapped the television off and

announced that supper was on the table and growing cold. "No time to waste. The mummers are still on the go. I want to have us fed and the kitchen tidied just in case anyone drops by."

"Mom, can we go out mummering again?" asked Matthew, stifling a yawn.

"Mummering indeed. Haven't you had enough excitement? Some other night, perhaps, but certainly not tonight. Now then, Andrea, you dig in."

"Oh, boy. Jiggs' dinner!" cried Jeff enthusiastically.

"Well, seeing as this has been a special day, I figured you boys...and Andrea...deserved a treat." Aunt Pearl smiled.

What Andrea was really longing for was a pizza with everything on it, even though she knew there was no pizza takeout place in Anderson's Arm. As soon as she got to Toronto, she told herself, that was the first thing she was going to eat. Only a few more days, and she would be home with her mom again. And Brad. She stared at the plate set before her. It was loaded with boiled vegetables—turnips, cabbage, and potatoes—and little bits of some kind of meat dotted here and there. It wasn't remotely what she wanted, but she was starving. It didn't take her long to finish her plateful.

"What kind of dinner did he call it?" Andrea asked Aunt Pearl, putting down her fork.

"Why, Jiggs' dinner, of course. Boiled dinner.

You mean to say your mom doesn't cook this for you up in Toronto?"

"No."

"Well, she ate lots of it herself when she was a girl. Every Sunday, sure."

Jeff and Matthew had also finished theirs, and were already back at the stove for a second helping when suddenly there was a loud BANG BANG BANG on the storm door.

"Goodness," clucked Aunt Pearl. "Who's coming to call when we haven't even cleared the table yet? Matthew, you go and see who it is."

Matthew opened the door to face a solitary mummer—a large figure wearing a heavy jacket and work pants, with a towel tied clumsily over his head.

"Come in, Mummer," called Aunt Pearl. "We haven't finished our supper, but you can bide for a minute." She inspected him carefully. "Sit down, and we'll try and guess where you belong."

"Is it somewhere along the Arm?" asked Jeff.

The mummer made a gruff snorting noise, but didn't answer the question.

The boys stared at the towel-covered face. Jeff exchanged a glance with his mother. Then Matthew got a sudden fit of the giggles, but stifled it when Jeff jabbed him in the ribs with his elbow.

"Well, Mummer. Seems you don't have much to

say for yourself," observed Aunt Pearl. "How's about you sing or dance for us?"

"Yeah. Yeah!" yelled the boys.

"I got an idea. Jeff, you go upstairs and fetch your father's accordion," Aunt Pearl suggested.

Jeff bounded up the stairs, returning in a flash with the shiny instrument. Andrea was surprised. Imagine lending Uncle Cyril's accordion to this stranger! He might not know how to play it. He could even break it.

The mummer hoisted the accordion strap over his shoulders and started fingering the keys, still with his gloves on.

"What song you want?" he whispered hoarsely.

"Oh, just whatever comes to mind," Aunt Pearl said with a smile.

He started to play. He played as if he had been doing it all his life. What was he playing? Andrea thought the melody sounded familiar. Suddenly it dawned on her. It was "Here's a Little Song About This Fair Maid." But how did the mummer know that tune?

All at once it struck her. "It's Uncle Cyril!" she shrieked.

"It's me all right. Got here as quick as I could!" he cried, yanking the towel from his head.

"Dad! Dad!" the boys squealed, leaping toward him. "We knew it was you! We knew right away."

"Our little joke," Aunt Pearl explained, patting Andrea's arm. "Cyril called earlier to say he'd be home this evening. So we decided, what with it being the time for mummers and all, to surprise you and the boys."

"Oh, Uncle Cyril!" Andrea gasped, not sure whether she was laughing or crying. "I'm so glad you finally got here. You missed Christmas and I was so..."

"Christmas hardly begun, sure!" Uncle Cyril exclaimed, snatching her up and whirling her around the kitchen as if they were at a dance. "Just you wait, maid, fine times still to come."

That night Andrea snuggled down under all her quilts as a rising wind rattled the panes of glass in the window. She felt so happy. At last Uncle Cyril had come home. She had helped save a whale's life. She had overcome her fear of boats. And the fun of Christmas in this surprising, wonderful place wasn't over even yet.

Such a short while ago she had been reluctant to come here. Now she was in no hurry to leave. In a funny way, maybe she did belong here.

CHAPTER EIGHT

"Andrea! Andrea! Here we are!"

Her mom was waving from the midst of a crowd of people in the arrivals lounge of Toronto's Pearson airport.

"Mom!" sobbed Andrea, running to hug her mother. For a moment she couldn't say another word because she thought she might really start to cry.

"And here's Brad," said her mother, beaming up at her new husband.

"Hi there, kiddo," smiled Brad. "How was your trip?"

"Oh, it was great! I've got so much to tell you," said Andrea.

"We have a lot to tell you too," replied her mother happily, as they headed for the parking garage and Brad's red car. The newlyweds both had suntans, and were wearing matching, bright-yellow shirts under their winter coats. Their flight had arrived earlier that afternoon from Daytona Beach.

"Oh, Sweetie," said her mom, throwing her arm around Andrea's shoulders. "You know, I was so worried about you after your flight took off for Newfoundland. Being there in the winter isn't the same as summer, with picnics and everything. I got thinking maybe you'd find it boring."

"Mom, I wasn't bored. I was..."

"Brad and I decided," her mother interrupted, "that next Christmas we'll all three go to Florida. You'll love it. Can you imagine going swimming on Christmas Day? It was something else."

"Mom, I've got an even better idea," countered Andrea.

"What's that?"

"Next Christmas, let's all go to Anderson's Arm."

"Ah, come on," laughed Brad. "You mean to say we'd have more fun in Anderson's Arm than in Daytona Beach? What a kid!" He chuckled as he reached forward to grab her duffle bag so he could carry it out to the car.

"You know something, Brad? You just might," Andrea replied solemnly.

"That's my girl," smiled her mom. "I guess you've found your roots are in The Rock."

Tears sprang to Andrea's eyes. It was true. During those last few days in Anderson's Arm, she had really begun to feel at home, the way she imagined the whale felt back in the ocean. Not that there weren't things she missed about Toronto. Like takeout pizza.

By the time they reached the car, Andrea had decided. She would try to meet Brad halfway, no matter how difficult it was. She knew her attitude toward him diminished her mother's happiness. She had been too selfish.

"You know one reason for us all to visit Newfoundland?" she asked, sliding into the back seat.

"What's that, Sweetie?" asked her mother.

Andrea swallowed hard. "Well, Uncle Cyril and Aunt Pearl haven't met my new stepdad yet. Maybe they should."

THE
FRENCH
ISLES

CHAPTER ONE

"Where on earth is Sierra Leone?" asked Andrea.

She had been in her bedroom sitting at her desk trying to finish her homework, although she had actually been thinking about her toe-nails. She didn't like the cinnamon-coloured nail polish she had painted them last week and was wondering if a deep pink shade might look better. That was when her mother had interrupted her with this bombshell.

"It's nowhere I've ever been, my dear, that's for sure. It's in Africa. The west coast of Africa—a place I never thought I'd live to see," replied her mom dreamily.

"But why would you want to go there for six months?" asked Andrea, bewildered.

"Sweetie, we have to stay that long in order to get the job done. Try and understand that there's a need for teachers, for people with certain skills who can make a difference in that place. It's an opportunity for us to see another part of the world. You see, Brad has always wanted to do this kind of thing, to go to—"

"Oh, I might have known it would be Brad's idea! He's just full of great ideas, isn't he?" Andrea shouted angrily and stomped out of the room, slamming the door behind her.

Brad was her stepfather. He and her mom were both teachers. They had been married for only a few months and already he wanted to change things. When he moved in, he brought his CD player and tons of opera music, along with all his books and bookshelves and two really ugly paintings. Now the living-room was so crowded there was hardly room to sit down. He kept saying he wanted the three of them to move out of their apartment in the Toronto suburb of Willowdale and buy a house in the country somewhere. He used to have a really neat sports car and then all of a sudden he sold it and bought a stupid van. And now the latest—he wanted to go to Africa and teach school in some weird place. Andrea wished her mother had never married him. She wished she had never even heard of Bradley Osborne.

"Now, is that a nice way to behave?" her mother scolded, following Andrea through the living-room to the little balcony that was Andrea's favourite place to go when she was mad.

"I guess not," Andrea finally replied after a gloomy silence.

"You know how Brad is," her mom said in a soothing voice. "He wants to see the world and he believes we have to help people who haven't been as lucky as we are. And he's right. Think how fortunate we are. We have everything we need, and even money left over for eating out on Friday nights."

Andrea had to admit that once in a while Brad was okay, especially the times they ate out at Alberto's restaurant, where you could get the best pizza in Canada, and the best spumoni ice-cream in the world, and even a second helping if you wanted one.

"Yeah, I know, Mom. I know all that," Andrea muttered. "It's just that... Africa? What about me? Am I supposed to come, or what?"

"That's what we have to talk about. We'd love it if you came with us. You'd be more than welcome. But there are a few... well, a few challenges. This particular place where we're going has no secondary school. We'll be teaching people who have never had a chance to get an education. There's been political unrest and there are a lot of refugees. There's a housing shortage so we could be living in a tent for a while. But if you do come with us, you could complete your school year by correspondence from Canada. And, of course, you'd have Brad and me there to help you, in the evenings."

"By candlelight, I suppose," said Andrea sarcastically.

"Probably lamplight or something like that."

"Ugh."

"Don't you be saucy, young lady! When I was your age, back in Newfoundland, we had lots of winter storms that knocked out the electricity. Plenty of times we did *our* homework by lamplight and we got along just fine," said her mother firmly.

"Well, it didn't happen last Christmas when I was there," Andrea countered.

"They've got better technology nowadays," her mother explained. "And that brings me to the other possibility. You did enjoy being there in Anderson's Arm last Christmas when Brad and I were away on our honeymoon, didn't you? You told me you did."

"Yup," nodded Andrea. At first, she had been reluctant to go to the Newfoundland outport her parents had come from but, as things turned out, it had really been a lot of fun.

"You know, you could spend those months in Anderson's Arm. I've been talking to your Aunt Pearl and Uncle Cyril on the phone. They said they'd love to have you stay with them. Your cousins think you're the greatest. I'm just asking you to think it over for a few days," concluded her mother in a tone of voice that Andrea knew meant serious business. Then she gave Andrea a hug.

"Okay, I will, Mom," Andrea promised, a little reluctantly.

"That's my girl. I know this is tough. Don't forget, you're the most important person in the world for me. It's just that there are so many people out there. Brad and I want to help wherever we can."

What kind of place was Sierra Leone? Andrea wondered. Her mother had brought home a couple of library books about west Africa. Frankly, thought Andrea, the pictures didn't make the place seem very appealing. The houses looked beige and dusty. Some of the people didn't wear shoes. Her mom said they ate a lot of rice and peanuts and sweet potatoes. Andrea didn't like sweet potatoes at all.

A couple of days later, she got a letter from her aunt Pearl Baxter. It was full of news about Uncle Cyril, who was going to buy a boat, and about her cousins, and lots of other people she had met in Anderson's Arm the previous Christmas. There were even some photographs Aunt Pearl had taken with the camera Uncle Cyril had given her then. Andrea felt sort of homesick for all of them. They had been so nice to her.

In the end, it wasn't so difficult to make up her mind. When it came to a choice between Sierra Leone, Africa, or Anderson's Arm, Newfoundland, Anderson's Arm was the hands-down winner. She would certainly miss her mother but all the other Baxters were family, too. Six whole months! She looked at her clothes closet and began thinking about what she should take with her.

"Andrea's mother was always the brazen one, wasn't she, Cyril?" remarked Pearl. Andrea was sitting between Aunt Pearl and Uncle Cyril in the front seat of her uncle's new truck. He called it his "new" truck but it must have been at least five years old. He had bought it a month earlier from a car dealer in Gander, the town where they had just collected Andrea at the airport.

"Yes, girl. Your mother was some smart and that's the truth. Soon as she married Albert, seemed like the pair of them couldn't wait to git going down the road," added Cyril as he steered his rattling truck along the Trans-Canada Highway.

Albert Baxter, Andrea's real father, had been dead a long time now—over seven years—but Andrea remembered him with love. Cyril, his brother, was her favourite uncle. He was a man who loved to make people laugh, and he looked and acted quite a bit like her dad.

"But neither of *us* wanted to leave," explained Aunt Pearl. "We could never be content if we lived away, Cyril and me. The Arm is where we belong."

"People are like trees," declared Uncle Cyril thoughtfully. "Some can be dug up, roots and all, and moved to another place and they flourish finest kind. But others now, you dig them up and try to plant them somewhere else, and they just wilt and die."

"I'd say Andrea takes after her mother," smiled Aunt Pearl. "Content wherever she be—Toronto or Anderson's Arm."

"I guess so," agreed Andrea. But when she thought about it for a while, she wasn't too sure. What would it *really* be like spending such a long time with her relatives in a small outport?

Cyril Baxter turned off the highway along the coast road. Gradually a blanket of grey fog crept towards them. Uncle Cyril turned on the lights and reduced his speed. It became cooler. Andrea reached for her black leather jacket and wriggled into it. It was her very favourite jacket, a Christmas present from her mom last year.

She started thinking about her mother, soon to be far away in some place that was terribly hot. It dawned on her that her mother must be brave. At first, Andrea had just been angry—angry at Brad because it had been his idea to go to Africa, angry that her mom didn't simply tell him to forget it and refuse to go. But the more she thought about them, about the difficulties of teaching school in such a place, the more she began to realize that it wouldn't be easy for them either. Staying with her aunt and uncle and cousins was no big deal in comparison. It was easier than trying to live in a tent in Africa.

"I hope you likes t'eat scallops," remarked Uncle Cyril, interrupting her reverie.

"They're okay. I tried them a couple of times. Back home, Mom and Brad and I used to eat out every Friday night. Mom was always tired after teaching all week so we'd go to different restaurants, sometimes Italian, sometimes Chinese, sometimes seafood. That's where I tried scallops. The restaurant was called The Twin Mermaids. It had a sign out in the front with two mermaids swimming, sort of like synchronized swimming. It was neat," Andrea reminisced.

"Hah! I don't say you'll be eating in them places now, not in Anderson's Arm," laughed Cyril, "but soon as fishin' season begins, you'll get all the scallops you can eat, free of charge."

"We're some lucky," explained Aunt Pearl, "that Cyril got a licence to fish for scallops. These times there's no codfish to speak of but it seems there are scallops to be found out in the bay."

"Got me own boat now, maid," added Cyril proudly.

Maid. Would they ever stop calling her a maid? Andrea wondered. She knew what they meant, though. Maid was their word for a young girl. It didn't mean she was a maid who cleaned houses or hotels the way it did in Toronto. Of course, she was no stranger to housework. She had always helped her mother because, ever since she could remember, her mom had been teaching school and didn't have time to do everything herself. Andrea had learned early in life that she had to help tidy up the mess in the kitchen, make her bed, and get the laundry into the washer and then the dryer, and remember not to mix the white clothes with the coloured ones.

The road got bumpier the closer they got to Anderson's Arm. And the fog got thicker. Andrea was still day-dreaming about her mother. She started remembering Friday nights, and all the fun they had deciding where they wanted to go to eat. For a few seconds she even thought about Brad in a kindly way. Then she was afraid she was going to cry. She didn't say a word for a long time. Her mood had grown as grey as the fog.

"Spring of the year we always gets the mauzy days," sighed Aunt Pearl, peering through her glasses at the wet, hazy world that lay ahead of them.

Spring? Was this supposed to be spring? Andrea wondered. It was the middle of June. It had been summer when she left Toronto that morning on her flight for Newfoundland. And what did "mauzy" mean, anyway? It had to mean wet or foggy or misty. They had so many strange words to describe things here, even the weather.

As Uncle Cyril's truck chugged resolutely up the hill and turned a corner, Andrea was able to make out the dim profile of the Baxters' trim wooden house through the mist. The truck ground to a halt in front of it. Uncle Cyril turned off the engine and they climbed out just as a fog-horn wailed mournfully in the distance. For one dark moment, Andrea wasn't sure if she had made the right decision after all.

CHAPTER TWO

"There's not much to do around here, is there?" lamented Andrea to her cousin Jeff. "Plenty to do," answered Jeff matter-of-factly. "We got to get this deck painted before tomorrow. Forecast calls for rain." Jeff was serious about the job. He had just turned thirteen and was more than a year younger than Andrea. He had straight dark hair and freckles on his nose. Andrea had light brown hair which was naturally wavy and got curlier when it was wet. She was now slightly taller than he was. In the past six months, she had grown faster than he had.

Andrea, Jeff, and her other cousin Matthew, who was only ten, had almost finished painting the new porch that Uncle Cyril had recently built on the back of the house. The boys called it a deck, even though Andrea kept insisting it was a porch.

When it was time to stop for supper, they took their paint brushes down to the "store," which was really a shed, where Cyril kept his fishing gear. They swished the paint remaining in each brush on the old door of the shed. Then they left the brushes to soak in a can half full of turpentine. People had been cleaning their paint brushes on the old door for years, leaving a rainbow of colours. Now it looked like one of the abstract paintings that Brad had hung in their living-room. Andrea was going to mention this similarity to the boys but decided not to in case they laughed at her.

"When we're finished painting—like tonight, after supper—what're we going to do then?" she asked, returning to her earlier complaint.

"I'm going over to Levi's house tonight. I promised to help him mend lobster traps," said Jeff.

"I think I'll watch TV," added Matthew. "'Northwood High' is on."

"Oh. I guess I'll wash my hair then," said Andrea without enthusiasm.

Back at the house, Aunt Pearl had put their supper on the table. There was cold meat, potato salad, and pickles, with ginger cake for dessert, and lots of tea. Andrea hadn't been too fond of tea until she visited Anderson's Arm last Christmas but now she decided she liked it.

"I wish there was something to do or some place to go," she remarked to no one in particular.

"Could be I got just the ticket for you, maid," declared her uncle.

"Oh, what's that?" Andrea asked.

"I'm looking for a crew to fetch my new boat."

"You mean to go fishing?" asked Andrea, horrified. She didn't care for fishing at all.

"Can I go, Dad? Can I?" pleaded Jeff.

"Me too? Me too?" Matthew begged.

"No, not to go fishing. Not yet. First, I got to collect me new boat from the feller what sold it to me. Jeff, you're big enough now so you can come along to spell me off at the wheel. Matt, you got to bide home and keep things shipshape here. There's room for one more and we need somebody who can cook," announced Cyril.

Andrea looked over at Aunt Pearl. "Aren't you going to go?"

"Don't say as I will. I never was one for going about in boats," replied Pearl. "Looks to me like Cyril has you in mind for the job."

"You said you wanted to go somewhere, didn't you?" Jeff reminded her. "And you knows how to cook, don't you?"

"Of course I can cook—well, sort of. But I'm not altogether crazy about boats myself," she added uncertainly. "How far away is this place anyway?"

"A nice ways," said Cyril, stroking his chin. "Wilfred's Harbour is on the southwest coast. No road down there."

"No road? How do you get there?" asked Andrea, surprised.

"On the water," laughed Cyril. "What else would a boat float on?"

"I know that." Andrea felt a bit silly. "I know you'll be sailing your boat back on the ocean. What

I meant was how do we get to Wilfred's Harbour in the first place? Is there an airport?"

"Airport?" snorted Cyril. "Only way to get to Wilfred's Harbour is aboard the coast boat. We drive down to Bay d'Espoir and then we get aboard the steamer, as we used to call her. That's how it was around here when I was a youngster. No road to Anderson's Arm them times."

"This, um, coast boat. Is it big?" enquired Andrea.

"Big enough. Bunks to sleep in. Hot meals, too. But not near so big as those old steamers was. You mind, Pearl? There was the *Bonavista* and the *Burgeo* and the *Baccalieu*," Cyril reminisced, reciting the names of ships that had sailed into Anderson's Arm a long time ago.

"I was wondering," Andrea began thoughtfully, "those boats—are they like the Love Boat? You know, on television? With a captain in a white uniform and dancing in the evening and all that stuff?"

"Dancing?" laughed Aunt Pearl. "I never heard tell of anyone dancing on the coast boat unless it was dancing with joy to get where they was going. Wonderful stormy in the winter, I can tell you."

"You can be sure they has a captain," Cyril laughed. "Finest kind of skippers, too. They knows the ocean better than any fish."

"Wish I could go," grumbled Matthew.

"Bide your time, my son. When you're bigger, we'll fish together. That's a promise," Cyril consoled him. "Don't take on now. We won't be gone more'n a few days. What about it, maid?" he asked Andrea.

"Well, if you're not too fussy, I suppose I could be the cook," Andrea agreed haltingly.

"Can you make a sandwich? Open a can of soup? Boil the kettle for a mug-up?" asked her uncle, outlining the job requirements.

"Oh, sure, I can do that. Whenever Mom had to work late I used to get supper ready."

"There you go then!" exclaimed her aunt. "'Twould be something to write and tell your mother about."

"True," nodded Andrea. "There's not much else happening here to write about."

Mr. Noseworthy, who lived in the next house along the road, owned a van in which he collected the mail and hauled things from one place to another, and sometimes he used it as a taxi. He agreed to drive Cyril, Jeff, and Andrea to a town called St. Alban's, which was located on the shore of a huge bay in the south of Newfoundland. It was a long drive through a landscape of small trees, enormous rocks, and large ponds. Once they saw a big brown moose wandering near the road. They stopped the van for a minute to look while the moose walked lazily away and disappeared into the forest. Andrea thought this was very exciting. She had seen one before at the Metro Toronto Zoo but it was altogether different to see such a big animal in a place where it was free to roam wherever it wanted to go.

It took most of the day to reach St. Alban's and then they had to wait several hours on the wide government wharf for the coast boat to arrive. It sailed in just before dusk, a modern-looking, diesel-powered vessel, about the length of a Toronto Island ferry but streamlined like the cruise ship on television. Cyril watched it intently as it eased up to the wharf.

"That skipper knows what he's about," he said with admiration, "but all the same, I'd sooner ship aboard one of the old steamers."

Once they got on board, Andrea was assigned to a tidy little cabin right next door to an identical one where Uncle Cyril and Jeff slept in the upper and lower bunks. However, the ship did not resemble the Love Boat that Andrea had been secretly hoping to see. A lot of people were travelling with babies and small children. Some of the passengers were very old. They weren't wearing evening clothes, just the usual jeans, shirts, and sneakers they wore at home. There were no waiters in white jackets. The captain wore a dark sweater with some unspectacular insignia on it. Supper was served in a small cafeteria. There wasn't any orchestra and there was no place to dance even if there had been music. Everybody went to bed early.

The next morning they reached Wilfred's Harbour. The harbour was large but the community itself was tiny. A semicircle of brightly painted houses was clustered on the rocky slopes at the foot of a high cliff. The ship was soon moored beside the wharf, and within minutes the three of them made their way down the gangway, carrying their luggage and sleeping bags and the box of oranges and homemade bread that Aunt Pearl had insisted they take with them. Several mail bags and some cartons were unloaded, and within twenty minutes the ship was heading out to sea again.

After this rapid departure, Wilfred's Harbour was incredibly quiet. It took Andrea a few minutes to figure out why this was so. There were no cars or trucks anywhere; there wasn't even a street, just a broad pathway meandering around the houses. Apart from the chatter of some excited children who had come down to the wharf to watch the ship arrive and depart, the only persistent sound was the screeching of seagulls.

Mr. Spencer, whose boat Uncle Cyril was about to buy, was waiting on the wharf. The two men went off to arrange the transfer of ownership, leaving Andrea and Jeff sitting on their duffle bags to wait for them. The sun was shining and, for a change, it was warm enough to shed their jackets. Andrea felt relieved to be on dry land again.

"I wouldn't want to live in this place," she remarked, taking in her surroundings.

"Don't look too bad to me," Jeff observed.

"Well, it is pretty but there's no road and no cars. How do people get where they want to go?"

"They walk, sure. Or they travel in a boat," replied Jeff.

"Yeah, but what if they want to go to some bigger place—you know, like Toronto?"

"They get aboard the coast boat, just like we did. Then when they get upalong, they can take a bus or a train or a plane," he explained patiently. "But I don't say as many of 'em would want to go to Toronto. What would they do when they got there?"

"Oh, honestly!" sputtered Andrea. How could Jeff not think about all the things there were to do in Toronto? She was always telling him about the Royal Ontario Museum, where her whole class went to look at Chinese tombs and things, and the North York Sports Complex, where she went swimming in an Olympic-size pool, and the Eaton Centre, where you could buy absolutely anything you wanted if you just had enough money. And there were all those restaurants besides. Jeff listened to her politely but he didn't seem the least bit impressed.

For a long time Andrea and Jeff hardly exchanged a word. It was fulfilling just to sit there and soak up the warm sunshine and to eat some of the oranges. At last Uncle Cyril and Mr. Spencer returned. By this time they were chatting like old friends.

"My dear man, I'm sad to see her go but I got no choice. Fished all me life but I never seen the likes of this," Mr. Spencer was saying solemnly.

"Fish is some scarce," agreed Uncle Cyril.

"Foreign trawlers. I say that's the reason, sir," explained Mr. Spencer earnestly.

"Too many boats after too few cod fish and that's the truth," added Cyril.

"The way it is on this coast, we got them St. Pierre fishermen crossing the line besides. Who knows what they're up to in the dark of the night?" asked Mr. Spencer, suspicion in his voice.

"'Tis hard to say," Cyril nodded.

"Seeing as I'm getting me pension now, I decided to retire," said Mr. Spencer. He stood on the wharf and looked down at his former boat and gave her a friendly salute as if he were saying goodbye to an old friend.

The boat was called *Blanche and Marilyn* and had the name painted in large white letters on the stern and on the bow. It now officially belonged to Cyril.

He looked down proudly at the vessel. "Well, girl, what do you think of her?" he asked Andrea.

Andrea was disappointed. The boat wasn't very big. There was a deck over the forward section, a cabin in the middle, and the stern was wide open like a big row-boat. Built of wood, it was painted dark green on top, with the hull a muddy grey colour. The *Blanche and Marilyn* looked sturdy, but not very comfortable.

Uncle Cyril didn't wait for Andrea's reply. He climbed aboard and looked up at Jeff and Andrea from the deck. "All aboard, crew!" he commanded.

Jeff jumped down onto the deck right away, as enthusiastic as his father and just as intrigued by everything around him. Andrea lingered on the wharf, wishing the coast boat hadn't sailed away. It had been a lot nicer than this scruffy-looking fishing boat.

"Hey, c'm'ere, Andrea!" called Jeff. "Come and see your new quarters."

Andrea cautiously climbed down the ladder that had been built into the side of the wharf. From the bottom rung, she had to leap onto the deck of the boat, and she landed with a thud. She followed Jeff through the wheelhouse and down into the cabin, which was in the bow and looked about the size of a large doll's house. It was dark and smelled funny. She peered inside with a sense of dread.

"Is this the kitchen?" she asked, observing a row of battered saucepans hanging on hooks.

"The galley, sure," replied Jeff.

In the dim light from a single porthole, she could see a two-burner propane stove and a tiny little sink with a hand pump beside it. Above the sink was a cupboard holding plastic mugs and plates. In the middle of this cramped triangular room was a wooden table fastened to the floor. There were built-in benches on either side. It didn't look the least bit comfortable.

"Where does anybody sleep?" asked Andrea in alarm. The boat didn't seem to have any beds.

"Me and Dad sleeps on the settees," Jeff explained, pointing to the two benches. "You get the forepeak."

"The what?"

"The forepeak. Look here." He pointed towards a narrow, dark space right up in the bow. It wasn't high enough to stand up in but there was a bunk of sorts with room for one thin person. It was, Andrea noticed with relief, at least separated from the rest of the cabin by a plywood partition.

"You'll get used to it," said Jeff with the air of someone who understood everything there was to know about going to sea.

"Who do you suppose Blanche and Marilyn are?" Andrea wondered aloud.

"Most likely be Mr. Spencer's daughters. Or perhaps his wife and daughter. Some of his family, anyhow."

"How long do you think it will take to get to Anderson's Arm in...this?" Andrea asked warily.

"Jig time. Won't be more than two or three days, if we gets good weather," replied Jeff.

"That doesn't sound like jig time to me," stated Andrea flatly. She was beginning to wish she had stayed home with Aunt Pearl and Matthew.

"Um...Jeff...there's something I was wondering..."

"What?"

"Where does a person...go?"

"Go? Go where?"

"You know, stupid...go to the bathroom. Where's the bathroom?"

"No bathroom on board. This is a fishing boat. We just do it overboard." Jeff shrugged and then tried to suppress a laugh.

"Overboard!" gasped Andrea, horrified at the prospect.

"Aw don't fret. We'll find you a bucket someplace," Jeff reassured her. He started poking around in a locker full of odds and ends under the steps. He soon found a battered steel pail and handed it to Andrea.

"Thanks a whole lot," she said without gratitude.

"We'll make a sailor out of you yet," he grinned.

Just then Uncle Cyril appeared in the cabin doorway, clutching several bags of groceries in his arms. He handed them to Andrea. "All right, cook, here's your first duty. Get those cans and jars stowed so they won't roll around if we gets a breeze. Best be quick, too. We got favourable weather today so we're getting underway right now."

With that, he returned to the wheelhouse and started the engine. Mr. Spencer untied the lines and tossed them aboard. He watched wistfully as the trim little vessel backed away from the wharf. With Cyril at the wheel, the boat headed for the narrow gap in the rocks that marked the exit from the peaceful, sheltered harbour. Andrea looked back to see Mr. Spencer and several children waving goodbye. Gradually, the tiny community of Wilfred's Harbour disappeared from view. Ahead lay the open ocean.

CHAPTER THREE

Fog. They had seen nothing but thick, wet fog since leaving Wilfred's Harbour. When this journey began, Andrea had figured she would have all kinds of things to write her mother about, but what was there to say? For nearly two days they had been feeling their way along at a snail's pace. Fog and more fog. It was getting pretty boring but at least the sea was calm.

It was just as boring eating so many peanut butter sandwiches—until Uncle Cyril decided to try out his scallop-fishing gear. This was a bulky, complicated piece of equipment made of metal and nylon mesh. It hung over the stern of the boat and, when lowered into the sea by a powerful winch, it was towed slowly along the bottom of the ocean. When it was hauled back up, it could contain several bucketfuls of scallops. As it happened, the place where Cyril had tested his gear was not a particularly good fishing ground but they did catch enough for a meal for the three of them.

Cyril cut the scallops out of their shells and fried them in a pan over the little stove. After that they sat on deck in the fog and stuffed themselves. It wasn't the least bit like the last time Andrea had ordered scallops at The Twin Mermaids in Toronto.

Then, there had been candles on the tables, check-ered table-cloths, and fishing nets hanging from the ceiling holding an assortment of sea shells. Nevertheless, sitting here with the ocean all around them, the fresh scallops tasted better than anything Andrea had ever eaten in a restaurant.

Jeff picked up one of the empty shells and, curl-ing his index finger around the edge, propelled it into the ocean sideways so that it skipped along the surface half a dozen times before it sank.

"Hey, don't do that," Andrea protested.

"Why not?"

"Because the shells are pretty. I want to keep them and put them around my room when I get back to Anderson's Arm."

Jeff and his father laughed. "There'll be plenty more where those came from," said Cyril, "but if you want them you can have them."

After dinner, Jeff took his turn steering the boat. They were proceeding very slowly because of the poor visibility. Every now and then, Cyril shut off the engine and they listened for the sound of fog-horns on the shore or bell-buoys on the ocean. If they heard anything, Cyril consulted a small book called the *Aid to Navigation*. It listed every fog-horn, bell-buoy, and lighthouse on the coasts of Newfoundland. Each horn had its own distinct sequence of sounds. It might be two short blasts and then one long one, or maybe four short ones in a row. This enabled mariners to know where they were in relation to the coast, even when they couldn't see it—like today.

Unfortunately Cyril had no navigational charts for that part of the coast. He explained to Andrea that a chart is a map of the ocean. There were several on board but they all described the shoreline to the *west* of Wilfred's Harbour. The *Blanche and Marilyn* was now heading east.

For the past several hours, they had heard only the gentle lapping of a quiet ocean, but they had seen something that thrilled Andrea. Through the mist she had suddenly seen a large, dark face with plaintive brown eyes looking right at her.

"Look!" she gasped, tugging Jeff's sleeve and pointing out at the hazy surface of the water.

Quickly the face disappeared below the water as silently as it had appeared.

"Only a seal, sure," Jeff observed nonchalantly.

"A seal! A real seal!" squealed Andrea.

"What's so special? There's t'ousands of 'em."

"I never saw one before. Well, yes, I did see one once in the aquarium at Niagara Falls. But I never saw one...just swimming around like that."

"You'll see plenty more," said Uncle Cyril. "Sons of guns eat more fish than I do these days."

"Dad, where do you think we're to?" asked Jeff a bit anxiously.

"I reckon we got to be somewhere south of the Burin Peninsula by now," said Cyril, stroking his chin.

"What if we're lost?" asked Andrea plaintively. She had never doubted Uncle Cyril's ability before. He had been going to sea all his life in one sort of ship or another. But all this fog—it made her wonder how safe they were.

"What if we run out of food?" she worried.

"Don't you fret, girl. We can always drag for scallops. Or we can head for shore and put into some outport and buy some grub," Cyril added reassuringly.

"But how will we find any places in the fog?"

"Fog don't last for ever. The wind will shift and blow it away," proclaimed Jeff, who was obviously enjoying being in charge of steering the boat.

Cyril had stopped the engine again and they were drifting silently.

"Listen," he said urgently. "Do you hear something?"

All three of them strained to listen. In a few seconds they heard it—a low-pitched, thudding sound.

"That's a vessel's engine, a pretty big one, too, and not far off," Cyril estimated. "Hope to heaven she's got her radar working and can see us."

They sat in alert silence, the baritone rumbling growing louder as some unseen ship drew nearer.

Then they heard a change in pace—a slower vroom . . . vroom . . . vroom—indicating that the oncoming ship was slowing down.

Suddenly, out of the fog emerged the outline of another vessel very much larger than theirs. It was only a dozen metres away.

"Well, here's a bit of luck," smiled Cyril. "Now we can ask these fellows where we're to."

The vessels drifted closer to one another.

"Ahoy there, skipper," hollered Cyril. "Can you give us our position, please?"

A man wearing a uniform was holding a loud hailer as he stepped out on the wing of the bridge of the other vessel. His ship didn't have a name, only a number painted in very large figures on its side.

"Il est défendu de pêcher ici! Restez-là! Vous devez nous suivre! C'est un patrouilleur de la pêcherie."

"Thunderin' Jaysus!" exclaimed Cyril. "What in creation is this all about?"

"I think he's talkin' French, Dad," whispered Jeff, suddenly less sure of himself.

"I know it's French," said Andrea nervously.

"Can you understand him?" Jeff asked, surprised.

"What's he sayin'?" her uncle demanded urgently.

"He says it's a patrol boat and we're not allowed to fish here and that we have to follow him. Somewhere."

"What in the name of all that's holy for?" cried Cyril angrily. "We're not fishing!"

"*Avez-vous compris?*" called the uniformed man. "*Il faut que vous nous suiviez*, Blanche et Marilyn*!*" he repeated, pronouncing the name of the boat "Blonshay-Maree-leen."

"He says we have to—" Andrea began.

"You tell him we're *not* fishing. Tell him we're not sure of our position. This fella's making a mistake!"

"Well, I'll try," said Andrea, clearing her throat. "*Nous ne sommes pas pêcheurs,*" she yelled. "*Nous sommes perdus. Pouvez-vous me dire…*" She had to stop for a minute to try to think what to say. She didn't know how to ask for a navigational position in French. Her class had never studied that in French immersion.

"Ask him where we're to," repeated her uncle.

"*Où sommes-nous, s'il vous plait?*" she shouted.

"*Ce sont les lieux de pêche réservés pour les pêcheurs de pétoncle de St. Pierre et Miquelon. Il est interdit aux Canadiens de pêcher ici!*"

"*Mais nous ne pêchons pas! Nous sommes en route à* Anderson's Arm," shouted Andrea in frustration.

The two vessels had now drifted so close together that the loud hailer was no longer needed. The first man was joined on deck by two other uniformed men. They ignored Andrea's explanations as they scanned the *Blanche and Marilyn*, pointing at the scallop-fishing gear at the stern of the boat.

"Mademoiselle," said the man who appeared to be in charge, *"Ce n'est pas vrai. Voilà la preuve."* He was pointing to the small pile of scallop shells Andrea had saved to take home and decorate her room.

Andrea gasped. Were those few shells evidence of some terrible crime they had committed?

Her uncle spoke up again. "Now look here, we never fished them around here, me son. We fished them hours ago, back near Red Island in Newfoundland. A feed for our dinner is what it was. I just bought this boat and I'm ferrying her home where I got me licence to fish scallops."

It was no use. Apparently none of the uniformed men understood English. Andrea pleaded with them in French but they simply would not believe her. The scallop shells were right there on the deck in broad daylight. If only Andrea had let Jeff hurl them all into the ocean.

"Vous êtes en état d'arrestation, mon capitaine," said the captain of the other ship. *"Ne résistez pas!"*

"We're under arrest," sobbed Andrea.

"A fine kettle of fish this is," growled her uncle. "I guess we got no choice. We got to do what he says, for the time being, but don't you youngsters fret. We never broke any rules and we'll be clear of this lot in no time at all."

"Well, at least we're not lost any more," remarked Jeff, trying to put a bright face on the situation.

"Where are we? Where are they making us go?" asked Andrea, through her tears.

"St. Pierre. Can't be far," explained her uncle. "I knew it was close by but in this fog...well, I never stopped to think about their new regulations and all. Been lots of trouble about the fishing boundaries between them and Newfoundland this past while."

"I always wanted to see St. Pierre," said Jeff, "but not like this."

"What's so special about it?" Andrea asked.

"It's French. Foreign port," explained Cyril.

"You mean French, like Quebec?"

"No, no, girl. St. Pierre is altogether different. It's a small group of islands hard by the coast of Newfoundland but they belong to France. Not exactly belong—more like they're a part of France, like a territory is in Canada. For hundreds of years, St. Pierre has been their fishing base on this side of the ocean. Nowadays, with fish so scarce, it seems the two governments have got the ocean hereabouts all carved up like it was a patch of potato gardens. No one is allowed to fish in the other fella's space."

"But how can they tell where the lines are?" asked Andrea. "The ocean all looks the same."

118

"It's all marked on the charts. What you do is get your position on the loran—that's a navigation machine. No problem to know where you're to. Trouble is, I don't have one but I'll buy one soon as I make a bit of money from scallops."

"I wonder if it's going to be like Paris?" Andrea wondered hopefully. She had read a lot of stories that took place in Paris.

"Don't say as it will. Likely be more like St. John's," speculated her uncle.

"I was thinking how it might be more like Gander. I know they got an airport there. An international airport," Jeff put in.

They were all wrong. It wasn't the least bit like any of those places. They followed the police boat for nearly an hour and finally emerged from the fog inside a broad harbour. In front of them stood a tidy town that was unlike anything they had ever seen. Andrea stared in fascination. Part of France, she thought. Now she really would have something to write her mother about.

Chapter Four

"Jail?" spluttered Cyril. "You got it all wrong, sir! I never fished so much as one scallop in your territory. I was only—"

"*Capitaine Baxter, on vous accuse d'avoir violé les traités de pêche entre la France et le Canada. Malheureusement, je n'ai pas le choix. Il faut que vous restiez ici jusqu'au moment où on entendra votre cause,*" pronounced the stern-looking police officer from behind his wide desk. He wore the same kind of uniform the men in the patrol boat had worn.

"What's he sayin' now?" Cyril asked Andrea, who looked back at him with tears in her eyes.

"There's some treaty. He says...you broke the law. And you have to go to jail," she gulped, hardly able to tell him, "until your case can be heard in court!"

"Jumpins, Dad! That might take months!" blurted Jeff, who was close to tears as well.

"Now look here," Cyril demanded of the officer. "Surely I got the right to call the Canadian Fisheries people over in St. John's. Someone there will get me out of this mess."

Andrea translated, and the police officer sighed and crossed his arms across his broad chest. "*Eh bien!...*" he muttered, a flicker of a smile crossing his face. Somewhat grudgingly, he shoved his telephone across the desk so that Cyril could reach it.

Cyril was able to reach a telephone operator in Newfoundland who connected him to the Department of Fisheries. The distant phone rang and rang. Finally, a recorded announcement asked callers to leave their number and told them that their call would be returned. It didn't say when. "Why in the name of Old Harry don't they answer the phone in person?" grumbled Cyril with growing impatience.

"Maybe they're closed today," suggested Jeff.

"What day is this?" asked Cyril.

"I'm pretty sure it's Saturday," Andrea replied.

While they had been travelling, they had lost track of the time. On board a ship, one day seemed very much like another.

"I'm some vexed," said Cyril wearily. "That means we got to wait till Monday."

"You know something?" Andrea said quietly, not wanting to add to her uncle's troubles. "Monday's a holiday. It's Canada Day—July the first."

"Lord love us! They won't be at work Monday neither," sighed Cyril. He turned to the officer who was waiting patiently and in a slow, polite voice said, "Now then, sir, you can put me in your jail if that's what you got a mind to do but what about these youngsters here?" He pointed at Jeff and

Andrea. "You can't go putting them in prison. They got nothing to do with this. They're innocent, you hear me? Innocent!"

"Ah, oui, les jeunes," nodded the officer, who now seemed to have grasped what Cyril was saying to him. After all, the word "innocent" was the same in both languages, even if it was pronounced differently. He looked at Jeff and Andrea with friendly concern and asked, *"Vos enfants, capitaine?"*

Andrea explained her family relationship to the police officer. *"Jeff est son fils. C'est mon oncle, le frère de mon père. Mon père est mort."*

"I just remembered something," interrupted Cyril. "We got some family over here. On Pearl's side. Her mother's sister—Henrietta was her name— she came over here many long years ago to take a job in a hotel. Married a local fellow and raised a big family before she finally passed on. Now then, if I can just remember the name of the man she married...let me see...I believe his last name was Rowe or Roo or some such name as that."

"Qu'est-ce qui se passe?" enquired the policeman, wondering what they were talking about.

"Il est possible que nous ayons des cousins ici," explained Andrea. *"Leur nom de famille est Roo ou quelque chose comme ça."*

"Roux? La famille Roux, peut-être?" suggested the officer helpfully.

"Peut-être," nodded Andrea. *"Henriette c'était la tante de ma tante."*

The officer reached for a St. Pierre telephone directory and leafed through it until he came to a page on which there were three listings for the last name of Roux. He explained to Andrea that he would start calling and enquire about anyone who was descended from a former Newfoundlander named Henriette.

"Uncle Cyril, what's going to happen to us?" whispered Andrea, while the police officer talked rapidly to one person after another on his telephone.

"Don't you fret. This has all been a mistake and we'll be out of here before you knows it. Let's just hope, seein' as how we got some cousins here, there might be someone you and Jeff could stay with. Only a day or two. Won't be long," he said reassuringly.

"But what if there aren't any relatives? What if they all moved away or died or something?" asked Jeff anxiously.

"Don't seem too likely," concluded Cyril. "What I heard was Henrietta had a dozen youngsters."

"Bonnes nouvelles!" exclaimed the policeman with a smile, putting down the receiver. He told Andrea that he had located a woman who was a daughter of Henriette Roux and had explained the situation to her. Madame Cécile Foliot was a widow

who rented rooms to tourists. She was coming to the police station right away.

Madame Foliot soon arrived, driving a sea-green Renault. She was a large woman whose dark hair was streaked with grey. She wore black slacks and a black blouse, gold earrings, and grey shoes. Her finger-nails were painted bright fuchsia.

"Ah, les pauvrets," she cried sympathetically the moment she caught sight of Andrea and Jeff. They were both so nervous by then they could barely manage to smile. *"Quel dommage!"* she murmured.

"Dites au revoir à votre père maintenant," ordered the policeman.

"C'est mon oncle," Andrea corrected him. "Goodbye, Uncle Cyril. I hope it's going to be okay where you're going," she added solemnly, trying to keep her voice from faltering.

"S'long, Dad," said Jeff bravely. "I hope you won't be there very long."

"I'll be all right, never you fear. Now then, you be sure to help this good woman all you can. She's your long-lost cousin. Jeff, you phone your mother soon as you can but don't go getting her all riled. Just tell her we're in St. Pierre. Tell her we'll be home soon," said Cyril firmly as the police officer ushered him down a corridor and through a door that slammed ominously shut behind them.

The three of them watched him go, then they

walked out to Madame Foliot's car. Andrea and Jeff sat in silence as she drove them through the maze of narrow streets. The cars and trucks didn't look the same as they did at home. Most of them were French. The surrounding landscape looked a lot like it did in Anderson's Arm, with big, rocky hills, but the houses were quite different. Most of them were two stories high and some had three floors. They had been built very close together and quite near the street. Nobody had a front lawn. There weren't very many trees and none was any taller than a house.

There seemed to be dozens of small shops and most of them were located on street corners. Andrea wondered what was sold in them. She had so many questions. Just how long would they have to stay with Madame Foliot? What if Uncle Cyril was in serious trouble? What were they going to tell Aunt Pearl? What would her mother say, far away in Africa? She hoped her mother wouldn't hear about it until long after it was all over. With any luck, that would be soon.

"Faites comme chez vous!" chirped Madame Foliot cheerfully as she led Andrea and Jeff up a flight of stairs and showed each of them to their rooms. It was a big house with a lot of bedrooms. There was a sign outside that read "Auberge Cécile."

Andrea had gathered up all her belongings from the *Blanche and Marilyn* and stuffed them in her duffle bag. She now dropped it on the floor and sat down on the edge of the bed. She caught sight of her reflection in the bedroom mirror and realized she looked a real mess. No wonder Madame had called them poor little things. After all the travelling, and then living on her uncle's boat, her clothes were getting dirty. Her hair needed washing. Something dark and greasy—engine oil, maybe— had spilled on one of her white sneakers. She hoped that Madame Foliot had a washing machine. She had noticed that there was a big, old-fashioned tub in the bathroom down the hall. She would ask Madame if she could take a bath this evening. After a while her thoughts drifted back to Uncle Cyril. What must it be like where he was, and how was he going to manage since he didn't speak French?

She walked over to the window, brushed the curtain aside, and just stared out at nothing in particular for a long time. There was a small garden below her, enclosed by a fence. Someone had planted rows of something—vegetables maybe— but so far only small green plants were showing. An orange cat was sitting on the fence. It was beginning to rain. A tear ran down Andrea's cheek. "What am I doing here?" she asked herself. "What are we going to do?"

"A table! Dépêchez-vous, mes enfants," called Madame from the bottom of the stairs.

Andrea snapped out of her dark mood and went to look for Jeff.

"There's food," she told him. "Let's go."

Jeff looked just as depressed as she had been. He had been lying on his bed staring at the ceiling but he got up and followed Andrea downstairs.

There was a big, oval-shaped table in the dining-room. A teen-aged boy with curly, dark brown hair was already sitting down. He wore a black sweatshirt with paint splattered on one sleeve. He was, they learned, Madame Foliot's son, and his name was Philippe.

"*Mon bébé*" was the way she introduced him, which Andrea thought was really kind of silly because he was no baby. It turned out that he was seventeen and the youngest of a family of five, the rest of whom had married and moved away.

"*Bonjour,*" said Andrea politely.

Jeff didn't say anything and just sat with a for-lorn expression on his face.

"*Ton frère ne parle pas français?*" asked Philippe, after they had begun to eat.

"*C'est mon cousin. Je n'ai pas de frère. Il parle un petit peu,*" she said, looking at Jeff hopefully. She knew he studied French at school but was too shy to say anything.

Jeff was picking at his food. It didn't taste like the food he was used to at home. They had been served some kind of stew which Madame described as "ragoût." Jeff wasn't sure he liked it. Luckily, there was a basket full of bread on the table and he ate as much of that as he could without appearing too greedy. There was rhubarb pie for dessert and that was really, really good. When Jeff was offered a second helping, he smiled for the first time since he had arrived in St. Pierre et Miquelon.

When dinner was over, Andrea knew they couldn't postpone phoning Aunt Pearl any longer. Jeff didn't want to place the call in case he encountered a French-speaking operator, so Andrea volunteered to do it. She still wasn't sure what to say.

"Hello, Aunt Pearl. It's me," Andrea began carefully.

"I'm some glad to hear your voice, my dear. Not hearing from you for a nice while, I was a little worried," replied Pearl. "Where are you to?"

"Umm, you remember your aunt?"

"Aunt? Which aunt?"

"Your Aunt Henrietta. You know, the one who went to St. Pierre and got married? Way back when?"

"Yes, I remember all right," answered Pearl, sounding puzzled. "What's that got to do with anything? Poor soul is dead and gone now."

"Umm, well, we're here visiting with her daughter."

There was a brief silence as Aunt Pearl tried to absorb this astonishing information. "You mean to tell me you're in St. Pierre? And you're visiting Henrietta's daughter?" she asked in amazement. "I never knew Cyril was planning to go there."

"Well, we didn't really plan to, but..."

"And which daughter would that be?"

"Her name is Cécile. Cécile Foliot."

"Yes, I recall there was a Cécile. And a Marie. And Annette...and Yvonne and...well, there was quite a crowd of them. How on earth did you find her?"

"We had some help."

"We lost track of Henrietta's family over the years, seeing as they lived so far away. I'm surprised Cyril even remembered Henrietta's name. Can I have a word with him now?" asked Pearl.

"Ah...well...he's not here right now," she faltered. "But Jeff is. I'll put him on."

"Hi, Mom."

"How you getting on, Jeffie, my son?"

"Okay, I guess. I wish I was home."

"Hurry on home then."

"We can't. Not until Dad gets out of jail."

"Jail!" exploded Pearl.

"It's all a big mistake," Jeff began. "You see, we got lost in the fog. And then this police boat arrived. They said we were fishing in their territory. And we weren't fishing at all. They made us come here. And they put Dad in jail. So me and Andrea are staying here with these cousins."

"Angels and saints!" exclaimed Pearl, in a state of shock. "Jeffie, could you let me have a word with Cécile?"

"No, I don't think so, Mom. She only talks French," he explained.

"And I only talk English," sighed Pearl.

"Aunt Pearl, it's me again," said Andrea, grabbing the phone from Jeff. "I can speak to her. She seems really nice. She's got this big house, and the food is pretty good, and we're all right, so don't worry about us. You see, the trouble was that when Uncle Cyril tried to phone the Canadian Fisheries people no one was there because this is a long weekend. That's why he's in jail. He's innocent but he couldn't get anyone to help him."

"We'll just see about that!" said Pearl with determination. "I'll get hold of one of those bloody paper pushers if it's the last thing I do!"

"I sure hope so," said Andrea plaintively. "Will you call us back? The number is 508 41.55.55."

"You'll be hearing from me. And soon!" cried Pearl as she wrote down the number and then hung up the phone.

CHAPTER FIVE

Andrea awoke on Sunday morning and heard the distant clanging of a church bell. It took her a few seconds to realize where she was and to remember the alarming events of the previous day. The rain had stopped falling and sunshine was filtering into the bedroom beneath the green window blind. She got up, raised the blind, and looked out. The sky was clear blue and the distant ocean was as dark as ink. The tidy town of St. Pierre looked quite different today, with all the brightly painted houses resembling a multi-coloured quilt. Andrea noticed a blue, white, and red flag flying from the top of a building.

"I'm in France," she thought. "This is St. Pierre but it's also France." For the first time, she felt a little bit of excitement about being here.

Andrea and Jeff arrived downstairs for breakfast just as Madame Foliot was leaving for church. Philippe was already at the table so they joined him. Breakfast consisted of bread and butter and jam. There was nothing else except coffee, which neither Andrea nor Jeff liked. Apparently the Foliot family didn't eat cornflakes, or Sugar Pops, or anything like that. There were no muffins and no eggs, either. Just long, skinny, warm loaves of bread.

"Some good," said Jeff with his mouth full. "This bread's not store-bought. It's homemade, like Mom makes sometimes." He reached for more.

"Holy Moley. Philippe's mother must have got up awfully early to bake it," Andrea remarked, feeling a bit guilty that she hadn't been on hand to help this woman who was being so kind to them.

"Elle l'a acheté à la boulangerie," Philippe interjected, then he pronounced, slowly and carefully in English, "at...the...bakery."

Andrea looked across at him in surprise. "We didn't know you could speak English, Philippe," she said.

"A little," he grinned. "I study it at school."

"And I study French! I'm in French immersion. Or, at least, I was. I'm really from Toronto but right now my mom's away so I'm staying in Anderson's Arm. That's in Newfoundland."

"I have been to Newfoundland," said Philippe.

"Whereabouts?" asked Jeff.

"Burin and Grand Bank and St. Lawrence. I play soccer. Sometimes we go there. Sometimes they go here," he explained.

"Come here," Andrea corrected him politely.

"Bet that's good fun," added Jeff.

"Fun? Yes," agreed Philippe. "Do you like fun? Today perhaps? It is Sunday and I do not work."

"Umm, what kind of fun?" asked Andrea cautiously. "We don't have to play soccer, do we?"

Philippe laughed. Andrea could see his strong white teeth. One of them had a gold cap on it. He was actually quite cute looking. "Not soccer. Today we can make fun to see St. Pierre. It is something new for you, no?"

"Well, yes, it is," Andrea replied. "I suppose we could see some more of it. We're not doing anything special."

"Nothing special at all," added Jeff.

"Laissez-moi vous piloter," offered Philippe.

Andrea washed the few breakfast dishes and then the three of them set off down the road while Philippe explained that he had a summer job as a painter. He and several other students were painting the rooms in the high school. When that was finished, they were going to paint the rooms in the elementary school.

"Jeez, b'y, you got stuck with school the whole year long," Jeff said sympathetically.

"This is different. For this I receive money," Philippe explained proudly, as he led Jeff and Andrea past the school so they could look in the window and admire the fresh coat of cream-coloured paint.

All roads in St. Pierre seemed to lead to the harbour. Soon they were walking across the public square beyond which were several wharves crowded with ships. Most of them were fishing vessels—big, rusty, deep-sea draggers that looked as if they had survived a lot of bad weather. Some were French but several were flying flags Andrea and Jeff did not recognize and they had strange names painted on their sterns.

"Espagnol," said Philippe, pointing to a large dragger. The home port painted on the stern was Bilbao, a city in Spain. "They arrive here for fuel and supplies. Sometimes because of big...ah... big...*orages*," Philippe tried to explain, groping for the right word.

"Storms," said Andrea helpfully.

"Oui. When big storms arrive on Le Grand Banks, many ships come here," Philippe concluded.

"They must be catching t'ousands of fish," remarked Jeff, who was impressed with the size of the draggers.

"More like millions or trillions," countered Andrea.

"True enough, t'ousands," agreed Jeff.

"Oh, Lord," thought Andrea as she remembered that "thousands" in Newfoundland didn't mean precisely that. It meant an enormous quantity of whatever they were describing. It was tricky enough trying to help Philippe along with his English, but every once in a while Jeff would use a word she had to translate, too.

"And they shouldn't be taking so many of 'em.

Dad says the trouble is too many foreign fishing boats are out there and that's why the cod stocks are going down, and he says—"

"Oh, look! There's the *Blanche and Marilyn*!" Andrea sang out, rapidly trying to change the subject. Jeff didn't seem to realize that in *this* place, he and Andrea were the foreigners. This was no time to start criticizing anybody.

"That's Dad's boat! Right there," cried Jeff, pointing it out to Philippe, who stared at their unoccupied boat, which looked rather sad and lonely tied to one of the docks. "And we'll be going home in her soon."

Following another road that led up a hill to the edge of town, they came to a large cemetery. Rows of crosses ended at a cliff above the sea. The graves were very close to one another. Andrea and Jeff were surprised to see that the coffins were above the surface of the ground, boxed in concrete.

"This graveyard is weird," Andrea observed. "Everywhere else they bury dead people *under* the ground."

"Rocks," Philippe tried to explain. "Too much rocks." He pointed at the surroundings, which were mainly solid rock with only a thin layer of moss or grass.

"Too *many* rocks," Andrea couldn't help saying, thinking to herself that Philippe still had a way to go with his English.

Philippe shrugged. "Come. *Mon grand-père et ma grand-mère.*" He led the way through the maze of graves. At the far end of the cemetery stood a pair of crosses side by side at the head of two cement tombs. One bore the inscription "Louis Philippe Roux 1908-1981." The other read "Henriette Ethel Roux 1910-1990."

"That must be my mom's aunt," noted Jeff solemnly, "but look at that. They spelled her name wrong. It should be Henrietta with an 'a'."

"That's the French way, stupid," proclaimed Andrea righteously. "She probably changed the way she spelled it once she decided she was going to stay here."

"She never changed the way she spelled her middle name," observed Jeff.

Andrea thought for a moment. "I don't think there is a French way to spell Ethel."

"Anyhow, this place gives me the creeps. It's probably full of ghosts." Jeff shivered as a cold breeze from the ocean swirled around them.

"I kind of like it here," said Andrea dreamily. "I like places with ghosts."

"I don't. I want to get going," said Jeff impatiently.

"*Alors*, we go to the café now for a...*petit coup*," directed Philippe.

"Right!" beamed Andrea.

"For a what?" Jeff asked Andrea warily. "What kinda stuff do we get at the café?"

"Un petit coup!" teased Andrea. "Hah! I won't tell you. It's a surprise."

As they entered Aux Marins, a little cafe in the centre of town, Jeff was apprehensive. He didn't like strange food or drinks. In fact, he didn't like restaurants at all, except for the burger place in Gander where his family sometimes ate when they went to town to shop.

Philippe ordered a Coke. Andrea decided she would have one, too. Jeff ordered a Pepsi, relieved to find a familiar beverage in this odd place.

The café was rather dark inside and looked more like a bar, which it also was. It was the sort of place that would certainly have been off-limits for a girl of Andrea's age back home. Over by the window, a young couple sat staring dreamily into each other's eyes as they sipped red wine. At the counter, a man wearing rubber boots and sea-going clothes was quaffing something amber-coloured from a very small glass as he chatted with another man who was drinking beer.

There were tables and chairs on the sidewalk just outside the front door so Andrea suggested that they sit at one of them. She sipped her Coke slowly and looked around. The café overlooked the harbour and the *Place du Général de Gaulle*, which was the centre of town. Philippe told them that it was named in honour of the leader of the Free French in World War II. In the middle of the *Place* were bright flower beds and, surrounding them, benches where older people were sitting and chatting. Off to one side several men, dressed in their Sunday best, were playing some kind of game—rolling big metal balls against one another.

Even though the shops were closed, this was a busy place. The three of them sat and watched as the passenger ferry made its daily departure for Newfoundland. A fat man walked by, pulled by a Labrador dog on a leash. A young mother pushing a dark blue baby carriage trotted past them. Three boys on bicycles pedalled by in a great hurry to get somewhere. All the while, a parade of Renaults and Peugeots zoomed along the road that encircled *Place du Général de Gaulle.* Andrea remembered the only place you could go for refreshments in Anderson's Arm was a chip truck parked near the wharf. In contrast, this was so...well, so French. She decided then and there that she liked it.

While they were having their drinks, they heard the sound of an airplane. The airport, across the harbour, was visible from where they sat. They watched as a twin-engined plane circled the town before descending.

Philippe glanced at his wrist-watch. "Air St.

Pierre, from Halifax. Many people come to St. Pierre now. From Canada. From United States. From everywhere. Tourists—they like St. Pierre in summer."

"Well, I can see it is sort of special," agreed Andrea. "It's too bad we have to leave right away—just as soon as my uncle gets out of jail."

"Could we go and visit him?" asked Jeff. He had downed his Pepsi and now was anxious to leave.

"Alas, not possible," replied Philippe, shaking his head. "Those *gendarmes*...they are...how do you say...?"

"Strict?" suggested Andrea.

"*Oui*. They are not *St. Pierrais*. They are sent from France. Sometimes they are not happy to come here."

"That's no big surprise," muttered Jeff, who didn't share Andrea's growing interest in this place. He was beginning to feel he had been exiled here himself.

"They say it is...*rustique*. Also it is cold...too cold," Philippe continued.

Andrea didn't say anything. She didn't want to hurt Philippe's feelings but it really *was* pretty cold for the end of June. She was glad she had brought along her black leather jacket and a turtle-neck shirt.

"*Ah, mon Dieu. J'ai oublié quelque chose!*" exclaimed Philippe, abruptly jumping up and yanking his wallet out of his pocket to pay for their drinks.

"Qu'est-ce que c'est?" asked Andrea, wondering what it was he had forgotten.

"Cet avion... I forget. Two people arrive on this airplane to stay at Auberge Cécile. Tourists. No, not tourists—scientists. I have promise to be at home to help my mother to understand. They do not speak French."

"You're the translator?" Andrea smiled quizzically.

"Yes," admitted Philippe, who began to laugh so that you could see his perfect teeth and the one with the gold cap. "Not good maybe, but I try," he apologized.

"I'll help you, if you like," Andrea volunteered shyly.

"Bonne. Okay," smiled Philippe, and they hurried out of the café. *"A qui arrivera le premier!"* he challenged.

And the three of them ran all the way back to Auberge Cécile.

CHAPTER SIX

A man and a woman were hauling luggage out of a Citroen taxi as Andrea, Jeff, and Philippe arrived, somewhat breathlessly, at the front door of Auberge Cécile.

Madame Foliot was standing in the doorway to greet her two new guests. *"Bonjour!"* she cried vigorously. *"Nous sommes enchantés de vous avoir chez nous!"*

"Hello there," replied the man. "I'm Tom Horwood and this is Karen Corkum, my wife. What a lovely day."

"Philippe, apporte les bagages tout de suite, s'il te plaît," requested Madame, pointing at the growing mountain of duffle bags, brief-cases, and mysterious-looking crates and boxes that kept emerging from the back of the small taxi. *"Vous avez la chambre numéro cinq, en haut. Faites comme chez vous,"* she welcomed.

"Did you catch that?" whispered Dr. Horwood to his wife.

She shook her head.

"Maybe I can help you," Andrea offered. "Your room is number five. If you follow me, I'll show you where everything is."

"Well, now, here's a young lady who really knows how to speak English," said Dr. Horwood,

141

much relieved. "And what would your name be?"

"My name is Andrea. Of course I speak English. You see, I'm really from—"

"Now that is something I do admire," interrupted Karen Corkum enthusiastically, "a kid who's at home in both languages."

"So, Andrea," said her husband, "if you're not too busy, maybe you'd be kind enough to stick around for a bit, until we get organized here. We're heading off to do some studies on Miquelon for the summer and we have to make a lot of arrangements... buy supplies, hire a boat, make phone calls, that kind of thing."

"Sure, no problem," smiled Andrea.

At noon, Madame placed a bowl as big as a bird bath full of steaming soup in the middle of the dining-room table. She asked Andrea to ladle it out to the other guests.

During the meal, the new arrivals mentioned that they had been married for less than a year and were both marine biologists. Tom Horwood was engaged in research at the marine laboratory in St. Andrew's, New Brunswick. Karen Corkum was a lecturer at Dalhousie University in Halifax. In the course of the school year, they could be together only on weekends, which was one of their prime reasons for working on a combined project this summer. They were going to do a field study of the Grey seal.

Andrea did her best to explain all this to Cécile Foliot and to Philippe, who both listened with keen interest.

Jeff was listening, too, and after a while he asked, "What kind of guns have you got?"

"Guns?" repeated Dr. Corkum.

"Right, guns. See, I was just wondering, well, how are you going to kill those seals?"

"Kill them? Ewww! That's disgusting," Andrea protested.

"No, no, no!" answered Dr. Horwood emphatically. "We didn't come here to kill anything. We're here to study living seals. We want to learn more about where they go, what they eat, how they look after their young—not how they die."

Jeff considered what they had said and then declared, "My dad says there are too many seals. They eat all the fish and that's the reason...well, part of the reason fishermen can't catch enough fish to make a living these days."

The two biologists exchanged glances, then Dr. Horwood cleared his throat. "Ahem. Well, there are differences of opinion on the question of whether seals are bad for the commercial fishery. That's one of the main reasons we're here—to help find some answers to that question. We intend to carry out an intensive study of the Grey seal in the great lagoon up on Miquelon. We plan to—"

The telephone rang.

Philippe got up to answer it. His mother and Andrea began to clear the table. *"C'est pour toi,"* he called to Andrea.

It was Aunt Pearl.

Andrea listened silently for what seemed to the others like a long time, then she exclaimed, "No kidding!" After another moment she said, "Wow!" Another silence lapsed before she cried, "That's brilliant!"

"What's happening? Lemme talk to Mom! Lemme talk!" Jeff pestered.

Andrea ended the phone conversation with a firm "Okay, okay. We'll get there! Goodbye," and then hung up. "Jeff, she says to give you a hug from her, but she had to hang up because she was waiting for an important call. Wait till I tell you! It looks like all hell's breaking loose."

"Goodness, what's going on?" enquired Dr. Horwood.

"Qu'est-ce qui se passe?" asked Cécile.

"That was my Aunt Pearl," Andrea began.

"Ah! Ma cousine!" said Madame Foliot brightly.

"I'll try and explain. It seems Aunt Pearl has been talking to, well, just about everybody. The minister of Fisheries, the premier of Newfoundland, some guy from...oh, I forget...foreign something."

"Foreign Affairs?" suggested Karen Corkum.

"I think so. Anyway, the day after tomorrow a bunch of them are coming here. And Aunt Pearl is coming, too...on the plane from St. John's! She wants us to be there to meet her at the airport."

"Mom's never flown in an airplane before!" exclaimed Jeff.

"Well, she will soon. And the government people all agree it's been a real fiasco, and Uncle Cyril never should have been put in jail, and they're going to get him out of there fast. And, oh, I nearly forgot—Aunt Pearl needs somewhere to stay." Andrea turned to Madame Foliot. *"Ma tante a besoin d'une chambre. Est-ce qu'elle peut rester ici?"*

"Bien sûr!" said Cécile, smiling, *"Ce n'est pas la place qui man que, c'est ma cousine!"* she exclaimed, raising her hands in a dramatic gesture, pleased at the chance of meeting a distant relative she had never expected to see.

"Do I read this correctly?" asked Tom Horwood, who was trying to catch the drift of the conversation. "These women are cousins but they've never met?"

"Right. Their mothers were sisters. In Newfoundland. A long, long time ago."

"And, uh, somebody's in jail?" enquired Dr. Corkum tactfully.

"Yeah, my dad," replied Jeff, "but he's not

supposed to be there at all. It's been a big mistake. Just wait. He'll be outta there quick as a wink."

Monday was Canada Day—in Canada—but in St. Pierre it was just an ordinary day when life went along as usual. Philippe went back to work painting the school. Jeff volunteered to go with him and help. He was getting fidgety just hanging around.

Andrea, on the other hand, was very busy. The scientists kept her occupied all day. First they had to go to the bank. Next they rented a post-box. Then they looked for a boat to hire to take them to the island of Miquelon. That wasn't a problem since there were all kinds of small fishing vessels not being used because of the fish shortage. After that they bought a boat-load of food since they were going to be camping for several weeks far from any store.

When they finally got all their supplies organized, Karen Corkum (she had asked Andrea to call her Karen) suggested that the two of them go shopping for perfume. St. Pierre, she explained, was famous as a source of French perfume at bargain prices.

"Mmmm. Mmmm! Try this," she suggested as she sprayed some Chanel No. 19 on her wrist. They were sitting side by side on a pair of stools at the counter in a small shop called Topaze. Twenty or thirty bottles of perfume stood in front of them. They all smelled wonderful. With the day's work behind them, their biggest concern now was trying to decide which of the many scents they liked the best.

"What's your favourite?" Karen asked Andrea.

"Miss Dior, I think. But..."

"But what?"

"I don't have any money. I can't afford to buy it," Andrea acknowledged sadly.

"Well, you do have *some* money," Karen smiled. She was quite pretty in a thin sort of way, Andrea thought. "You've got the money you earned today helping us."

"Oh!" said Andrea, brightening, not having realized she was going to be paid.

"So go ahead and choose some perfume. And why not buy some for your mother in Newfoundland, too?"

"My mom's not in Newfoundland; she's in Africa. I won't be seeing her... well, not for a long time," Andrea explained, suddenly feeling a pang of sadness. It really would be a long time.

"In Africa?" asked a puzzled Karen. "I thought someone said you lived in Anderson's Arm, Newfoundland."

"Yes, I do, but only till January. I really live in Toronto. My mom got this job teaching school in

Africa, so I had to come here—well, not here, but to Newfoundland to stay with my aunt and uncle. Then my uncle went to collect his new fishing boat and, oh—it's a long story," Andrea sighed. At the moment, her life wasn't simple at all.

"My goodness," commented Karen sympathetically.

"It's not so bad. I kind of like travelling around. And St. Pierre is really okay. I wouldn't mind staying here for a bit longer...if only my uncle wasn't in jail."

CHAPTER SEVEN

On Tuesday morning, the fog returned. When Andrea awoke, she could hear a foghorn bleating hoarsely from a distant rock far out in the bay. She ran up the window blind but couldn't see further than the back yard, where the orange cat was once again sitting on the fence.

"What if the plane can't land?" asked Jeff anxiously, as they were eating their bread and jam at breakfast. "It's thick as soup out there."

"They've got radar and all that stuff. They'll get in," said Andrea reassuringly.

"I bet Mom is scared to death right now."

Near noon the fog lifted a little, and by two o'clock there was just enough visibility for the flight from St. John's to land on the single runway of St. Pierre's small airport.

The first passengers to leave the plane were two men dressed in dark business suits. Both of them were carrying brief-cases. Right behind them came Aunt Pearl, wearing a beige raincoat over her best summer dress, which usually she wore only to church. She looked anxiously around for a familiar face.

"Mom! Mom!" Jeff called.

"Here we are!" shouted Andrea.

The three of them collided at the door that led

from the customs and immigration counter into the main terminal. Pearl hugged them both and then burst into tears.

"Oh, my dears," she said between sobs, "I been some worried about you and Cyril."

"Don't worry," comforted Andrea. "People here have been very kind to us. I'm sure everything will turn out right."

"I'm some glad to see you, I can tell you that," Pearl said, pulling herself together. She took off her glasses and fished in her handbag for a handkerchief. "Now then, these two gentlemen—this one is Mr. Snow and this one's Mr. O'Leary—they're from the government, and they're going to get Cyril out of that prison."

Soon the five of them were crowded into a taxi headed for the Prefecture, the government administrative building, where they were met in the entrance hall by the same *gendarme* who had put Uncle Cyril in jail the previous Saturday.

"Bonjour, mes enfants!" he greeted Andrea and Jeff cheerfully. *"Vous êtes-vous bien amusés ici à St. Pierre?"*

"Oui merci," answered Andrea politely.

"What did he say?" whispered Aunt Pearl.

"He was asking if we had been enjoying ourselves here," Andrea translated.

"Tell him I wants to go home to Newfoundland."

"Shh, Jeff. He did the best he could for us," Andrea scolded.

"I guess so, but I still wants outta here."

Mr. Snow and Mr. O'Leary were ushered into an office occupied by an important-looking man who had grey hair and was wearing a dark grey suit. Then the office door was shut, leaving Aunt Pearl, Andrea, and Jeff to wait anxiously out in the hall. They sat down on a wooden bench. No one wanted to say what they were all thinking: what if these men couldn't get Uncle Cyril out of jail after all? They were in a foreign country now; the rules were different. Finally, Andrea broke the apprehensive silence.

"How did you like flying, Aunt Pearl?" she asked, with a grin.

"To tell the truth, it wasn't too bad at all. Gets you where you're going in a hurry. And they gave me a glass of ginger ale besides."

"Mom, where's Matt?" asked Jeff, who hadn't had time to think about his younger brother in the midst of all the excitement.

"Matt is staying over with the Noseworthys," she replied, just as the office door opened.

"Madame Bax-tair," said the man with the grey hair and the grey suit, *"j'espère que vous pourrez pardonner cet incident fâcheux. Votre mari sera ici aussitôt que possible."*

Pearl Baxter stared at him uncomprehendingly.

"It's okay, Aunt Pearl," whispered Andrea. "He says Uncle Cyril will be here right away."

It was true. In a few minutes, another door opened and through it strode Cyril Baxter, smiling from ear to ear. Pearl and the kids darted forward and hugged him. The *gendarme* smiled. Mr. Snow and Mr. O'Leary smiled. The man in the grey suit, who was the chief administrator of the French territory of St. Pierre and Miquelon, smiled too.

Everyone shook hands. It had all been a dreadful mistake. There was no real evidence that Cyril had been fishing in forbidden waters. He had been telling the police the truth. He should never have been arrested. After apologizing, the chief administrator insisted on paying the cost of Aunt Pearl's airplane ticket.

"I got to admit," confided Cyril once the family was inside a taxi heading for Auberge Cécile, "it wasn't altogether bad. The bed was some hard but the place was clean and they gave me all the home-made bread I could eat for me breakfast. What do you think of that?"

"I think it came from the bakery," said Andrea knowingly.

"Only torment was the other fella in there. He was some drunk. He moaned and hollered the whole of the first night and I never got a wink of sleep. But in the morning they sent him home, and after that I was on me own and the place was as quiet as a church bell on Monday. By and by, they got me a radio so's I could hear a station over in Newfoundland, and last night some fella came by with a bunch of French picture magazines to look at."

That evening, Madame Foliot gave a party. Not only were they celebrating Cyril's release from jail but also the occasion when Cécile and Pearl, who shared the same grandmother, had finally met one another. These two cousins had something of a communication problem, of course, and Andrea had to work overtime translating for them while Cécile turned over the dusty pages of an old photograph album.

"*Voilà ma mère, ma grand-mère, et ma tante il y a longtemps,*" said Cécile Foliot, pointing to a photograph of a smiling woman standing between two young girls wearing old-fashioned clothes. The black-and-white photograph was small and slightly out of focus.

"Look at that now!" repeated Aunt Pearl. "That's my mother standing beside my grandmother and my aunt, all those years ago. Look at this, Jeffie, my son. There's your great-grandmother when she was a young woman and your grandmother when she was a girl."

Jeff glanced at the faded photograph but wasn't particularly interested. He was engrossed in listening to the conversation his father was having with the two scientists. They planned to leave the next day to spend the rest of the summer on the lonely shores of the Grand Barachois, a shallow bay on the island of Miquelon.

"Hard to credit," remarked Cyril, "that you got a machine that records the noises those old horse-head seals makes underneath the water. Can't help but wonder what good that would be to anyone—except maybe another seal."

"We hope to determine, among other things, the distance the young Grey seal ventures from its parents as it grows in size and strength," explained Dr. Horwood earnestly.

"And what if they don't say anything? What if they figure you're getting too nosy and they don't make a sound?"

"Well, then," chuckled Dr. Horwood, "we'll have to look for some other means of communication. Whatever we discover, it's never wasted time. There's so much still to learn about the life of the Grey seal."

"*A table!*" called Cécile from the dining-room. That evening the table had been set for a celebration. There was a lace table-cloth; two tall, white candles on either side of a vase full of wildflowers;

and coloured paper streamers hanging from the light fixture in the ceiling. Andrea was surprised that Uncle Cyril's release from jail meant so much to Madame Foliot.

However, she was not nearly as surprised as Dr. Tom Horwood was when, with a flourish, Cécile Foliot handed him a colourful greeting card and a bottle of wine with a fancy ribbon around it.

"Bonne fête!" Cécile cried. *"Bonne fête!"*

"What *is* all this?" laughed Dr. Horwood.

"Madame is wishing you a happy birthday," Andrea told him.

"What? Oh, I'm afraid there's been a mistake. My birthday is in November. November the ninth, in fact," said Dr. Horwood, feeling a little embarrassed. Where in the world had Madame Foliot got the idea that this was his birthday?

"Pardonne, Madame, le professeur dit que son anniversaire est au mois de novembre," Andrea began.

"Ah, mais non, mais non," insisted Cécile, and then she retrieved a calendar from the kitchen. *"Regarde. La fête de St. Thomas. Aujourd'hui. Le trois juillet,"* she persisted, pointing to the tiny square for July the third which did indeed have *"St. Thomas"* printed in it.

"Today is the feast of St. Thomas," Andrea explained.

"It is?" said an astonished Dr. Horwood. "If you

say so then. Where I grew up, in Digby, Nova Scotia, we didn't celebrate this sort of thing."

"Eh bien! Bonne fête!" chirped Madame Cécile, handing Tom the corkscrew with which he was to open the bottle.

Philippe, who always became shy when he had to say anything in English, nevertheless volunteered to explain. "Here in St. Pierre each person have a special, ah...*fête.*"

"Celebration," said Andrea.

"A celebration on the day of our saint. My special day is in May."

What a brilliant idea, Andrea thought, wondering if there ever was a St. Andrea.

Cyril turned to Tom Horwood. "Look here, me son, I don't say as I understand entirely, but if they wants to give you a fine time, I'm for it." He held out his wine glass so that it clinked against the one Tom was holding. "We can count our blessings today. We got good reason to celebrate. We'll be heading for Anderson's Arm tomorrow. I'm mighty glad of that. And I'm some grateful that cousin Cécile here has been so kind to Jeffie and Andrea and to all of us."

"Well, then, a toast to Madame Cécile Foliot," said Dr. Tom Horwood, raising his glass. "I now have an excuse for another annual party I didn't even know about before."

"I'm sorry to hear that you're leaving, Andrea," said Karen Corkum. "You've helped us so much. We were hoping you could be our liaison person here in town."

"You were?" said Andrea, happily surprised.

"Yes. You see, we need someone to arrange for supplies and messages and things. We can call on our portable radio-telephone from our camp at Miquelon. The trouble is, with our French being so limited, well, we would have problems trying to communicate," explained Karen.

"Gee, I'd really like to do that for you," sighed Andrea, "only I guess I can't."

"And of course we would pay you a small salary—but if you're leaving, then I suppose we'll have to find someone else," she said, sounding disappointed.

The party went on for a long time, and at the end of it there was even a birthday cake for Tom. Everyone had a lot of fun on this unexpected and joyful occasion. But Andrea began to feel wistful. She had been offered a summer job and, what was more, it sounded like an interesting job in a place she was reluctant to leave. It was late when she finally got to bed, and she had trouble going to sleep. She wanted that job and she wanted to stay here. Could she make it happen?

CHAPTER EIGHT

 Next morning fog was shrouding St. Pierre more thickly than ever, and it was accompanied by a cold drizzle of rain. When Andrea awoke and heard the fog-horn, she felt very gloomy. It wasn't merely the weather. She knew she should be happy because her uncle was out of jail and they were all free to leave. The problem was that she liked being here. Now it occurred to her that Cécile Foliot might let her remain at Auberge Cécile if she helped with the work, but would Aunt Pearl and Uncle Cyril permit such a thing? She *had* to find some way to stay.

The weather forced everyone to change their plans that day. Having got lost once, Cyril decided it would be wise to wait for better visibility before setting sail for Newfoundland. Dr. Horwood and Dr. Corkum also decided to postpone their journey as they preferred to begin their expedition on a day that was not quite so damp. Philippe's work day was cancelled because they were now painting the exterior doors and window sills, and it was too wet to paint outdoors. With their plans on hold, the visitors lingered over breakfast—all except Andrea. With her new plans in mind, she decided this was the time to be super-helpful. She volunteered to run down to the bakery for another loaf of bread when it appeared that more was needed. Then she washed and dried the breakfast dishes and put them away in the cupboard. When she saw Cécile dropping laundry into the washing machine, Andrea offered to keep an eye on it and, when it was done, to load it into the dryer and then to fold it up. This left Cécile free to go to the *épicier* and buy her groceries.

"*Ah ma p'tite Andrée,*" sighed Cécile as she was buttoning her raincoat, "*C'est dommage que tu doives partir. Tu me manqueras.*"

"*Et moi aussi, Madame.*"

"*Tu aimes St. Pierre, n'est-ce pas?*"

"*Oui, beaucoup.*"

"*Vraiment, tu es arrivée juste à temps,*" she smiled.

Andrea smiled back. It was encouraging that Cécile felt she had arrived "in the nick of time." It could mean Cécile needed her. Maybe she wanted Andrea to stay.

After the noon meal, Andrea realized this was her chance. She had to take the plunge and ask her aunt and uncle if they would let her stay on in St. Pierre.

"Well, I don't know what your mother would say, I'm sure," said Aunt Pearl, looking concerned. "Cyril and me's supposed to be looking out for you."

"I know, but Cécile is your cousin, so it's still in the family. Anyway, I can look after myself. And I have a chance to earn some money working for Dr. Horwood and Dr. Corkum, and that will help once school starts and I have to buy books and things."

"I know. I know that, my dear, but you're awful young to be away in this foreign place by your own self," argued Aunt Pearl.

Uncle Cyril had been very quiet and he looked thoughtful. He finally broke in. "I do believe Cécile is a good person and very kind. 'Tis a shame we can't have a proper talk with her about all this."

"I've already talked to her," pleaded Andrea, stretching things a little. "I know she likes me and that I'm welcome here, and she does need help. She's got a lot of tourists coming from now till the end of August. There's all the laundry and the cooking and everything. Philippe can't help her much because he's gone all day at work."

"Surely she's going to need that room you're in to rent out and make some money," Aunt Pearl reasoned.

"Yes, but you know what? There's a cute little bedroom on the third floor......in the attic. I could sleep up there," Andrea explained.

"You're some determined, maid," clucked Uncle Cyril. "I got to admire you for that."

"That's right! I really *will* be a maid!" laughed Andrea. "Cleaning and washing and cooking to pay for my room and board."

"Well, I suppose it might be all right," said Aunt Pearl cautiously. "I'm going home with Cyril and Jeff on the boat so you could use my return plane ticket when it's time to come back."

"Oh, Aunt Pearl, that's wonderful! Thanks a million," she cried, giving her aunt a big hug. "I'm going to miss you, all of you. It's just that this is an opportunity I don't want to miss. It's only for the summer. I'll be back in time to start school."

"Now, hold on, hold on. There's two things. First, we got to sit down and try and talk with Cécile when she gets back from the shops, and second, you got to write a letter to your mother right away," insisted Uncle Cyril.

"I will. I will," agreed Andrea.

When Cécile returned, she said she would be very pleased to have Andrea stay with her for the rest of the summer. She had been thinking of hiring someone anyway. Andrea would be ideal.

Dear Mom,
    You'll never guess where I am. I'm in
St. Pierre and Miquelon. It's just near
Newfoundland (maybe you know that) but it's
really part of France. Is it ever neat! We met this
family named Foliot. They're Aunt Pearl's cousins
from years ago. Madame Cécile Foliot is really
nice and she asked me to stay here for the rest of

the summer and help with the work. She takes in
tourists. And I've also got this other summer job
part time working for some scientists who are
doing research here.

    Cécile has a son named Philippe and he's
very...

Andrea had just begun a new page but now she
ripped it up and threw it in the waste-paper basket.
It might be better not to mention Philippe. Her
mom might get the wrong idea. She began the second page again:

    The research has to do with seals. It's a man
and a woman (they're married). They pay me to
help them because they're going off on another
island near here and I can look after things for
them here in town.

Andrea paused and thought about what to say
next. Better not say anything about Uncle Cyril getting arrested. That would make her mother worry.
She continued the letter.

    It's cold here even though it's July. There's a
lot of fog. I hope it's nice and sunny where you
are, Mom. I hope everything is okay. How is Brad?

In case you're wondering how we got here, it was in Uncle Cyril's new fishing boat. It's sort of a long story. Aunt Pearl says she'll write and tell you.

I miss you a whole lot, Mom. Write soon.

Love and kisses,

Andrea

Andrea took the letter to the post office, where she bought a strange-looking stamp with a picture of an old-fashioned airplane on it. Her letter had a long way to go to reach her mother in Sierra Leone.

The next day the weather changed. The fog disappeared and was replaced by a breezy, overcast day with huge puffy clouds that sailed across the sky as far as the horizon.

"Following breeze for home. Finest kind, me son," Cyril said to Jeff. Since dawn the two of them had been down at the wharf making sure everything was shipshape aboard the *Blanche and Marilyn*. Jeff could barely contain his excitement and happiness to be finally heading for home.

Aunt Pearl had lingered at the *auberge* to pack their belongings and to fuss over Andrea.

"I don't know, my dear. I just don't know. What if I hear from your mother and she says you got to return to our place?"

"Then I'll come right back, okay? I promise. I've got a plane ticket. Don't worry, Aunt Pearl. Mom won't object. I mean, if she can go to Africa, why would she mind if I stayed in St. Pierre for a while? I'm not that far from Anderson's Arm—not like she is."

"I suppose," sighed Pearl. "I'd best be sending along the rest of your summer clothes then. You'll surely need them if you're to be here till the end of August."

At that point, Cécile came in with an armload of clean towels. *"Ah, Perle,"* she said with sincerity, *"ne vous inquiétez pas. Andrée sera heureuse ici. Elle m'aidera. Elle sera bientôt de retour."*

Aunt Pearl smiled, even though she hadn't understood a word.

"She says don't worry about a thing," explained Andrea.

Dr. Corkum and Dr. Horwood were also up early that morning. Andrea helped them load their equipment into a truck. They and their gear were destined for the same big wharf where the *Blanche and Marilyn* was. The scientists had hired a fishing boat to ferry them to Miquelon, a voyage of several hours. So it was a morning of farewells as Andrea waited on the wharf and waved goodbye, first to her aunt and uncle and her cousin, and then, twenty minutes later, to Karen and Tom.

When she returned to Auberge Cécile, the house was very quiet. Cécile had gone to the hairdresser. Philippe was back at work painting the school. There was no one around except the orange cat, who started meowing to be let out. For a few minutes Andrea felt terribly alone. She wondered if she had made the right decision. However, there wasn't much time to think about it. Tomorrow a family of four was due to arrive from Ottawa, and it was Andrea's job to make up their beds and be sure their rooms were dusted. After that, she had to move her clothes up to the cosy little room on the third floor, her new home for the summer.

From the small window up there, she had a bird's-eye view of the entire town. On this day she could easily see the coast of Newfoundland twenty kilometres away. Down on the street below, a man and a woman walked by pushing a stroller with a little boy in it. A small brown dog trotted along in the opposite direction, carefully watched by the orange cat.

What was going to happen during the days and weeks ahead? Would it all be wonderful and exciting, or would it turn out to be boring and awful? Andrea studied the airplane ticket to St. John's before carefully tucking it into the zippered pocket of her duffle bag. She went back to the window and stared dreamily at the street below until she saw

Cécile's sea-green Renault heading back up the hill. That snapped her out of her day-dreams and she hurried downstairs. It was time to set the dinner table again.

CHAPTER NINE

"Such incredible luxury!" declared Dr. Karen Corkum as she stepped out of the upstairs bathroom at Auberge Cécile, wrapped up in a huge white towel. She was patting her hair dry with another towel. "You can't imagine what a treat it is to soak in a big bathtub full of hot water after four weeks of keeping clean with only one pail of water every day, heated over the campfire."

"Sounds awful," commented Andrea. She had been changing all the bedsheets and pillowcases in preparation for a new bunch of guests who would be arriving that afternoon.

"It's not really. You'd be surprised how well we manage—how well anyone can manage—if they use their ingenuity and figure out how to live on a simpler scale. It can be quite a lot of fun."

Karen had had to return to the town of St. Pierre because she had lost a filling from one of her teeth. Andrea had arranged a dentist appointment for her. Karen's tooth had been repaired and now she had a day left over before she had to return to the camp-site and her work.

"I've always loved camping," Karen chatted as she ate her breakfast, "but I must admit this is a wel-come holiday for me to be here. And, oh, how I love this bread! This is the same kind you send us every week, isn't it?"

"Sure is," Andrea confirmed. "Direct from Boulangerie Rémy."

"I'm going to miss it when we leave," Karen remarked. "Goodness, summer is half over and we still have so much work to do. Odd thing, when we started our research early in July, we thought we were observing a stable population."

"What's that?"

"A fixed number of seals. An extended family whose members live together. But lately...well, we don't know. A couple of them have disappeared, gone away somewhere."

"There was something I was wondering, Karen," Andrea ventured.

"What's that?"

"Doesn't it get kind of lonely up there? Just you and Tom and those seals?"

"Not as much as you'd think. For one thing, we are quite busy with our work. And then, from time to time, we do see the occasional person. The other day there were a couple of back-packers, from Denmark. They stopped to chat with us. And before that there were the two men who check the navigational markers. We saw them in their boat so we invited them to join us for coffee. And, of course, some nights there are...those lights. They reassure us that we're not entirely alone in the world."

"Lights? What kind of lights?"

"Out on the ocean. A boat of some sort."

"Who?"

"Haven't a clue."

"Aren't you afraid?"

"No. They're way offshore somewhere. Sometimes Tom and I amuse ourselves speculating about what they're doing."

"Maybe they're smugglers," suggested Andrea.

"We wondered about that but I doubt it somehow. They never come ashore. They don't appear to rendezvous with anyone else. Anyway, it's not our concern."

"Spooky."

"It is, in a way."

"Oooh. I would love to see something like that. I love mysteries."

"Really?" Karen laughed. "I guess I did too when I was your age. Well, I suppose I had better get going. Seeing as I'm here in the midst of things, I might as well use my time to do a little sight-seeing and maybe some shopping. Perhaps I'll go back to that perfume shop. Wasn't it fun? Do you want to come with me, Andrea?"

"Damn it. I mean, darn. I can't. I have to get the laundry done before Cécile gets back from the store.

Then I have to peel the potatoes and after that I have to set the table, and all that stuff," Andrea grumbled.

"Of course. Well, another time then," said Karen warmly.

Shortly after Karen left, Cécile returned with the groceries and she also brought the mail. At last there was a letter for Andrea from her mother.

Sierra Leone, July 20
Dearest Andrea,

I was so happy to get your letter. It's too bad it took so long to get here but I guess the mail is slow where you are and even slower where we are.

I hope you're okay, sweetheart. I was surprised to learn you are in St. Pierre instead of Anderson's Arm, but I also got a letter from Aunt Pearl who assured me you are in good hands. I never knew she had a cousin out there. Just remember to say thank you to her for being so kind. But in St. Pierre it would be *"merci,"* right?

Brad and I are truly enjoying our work here. We are training teachers who will continue this work after we leave. We are renting a nice little house and we do have electricity but only for two hours a day. That is enough because it is very warm so we don't need any heat except for cooking.

The only thing I don't like is the snakes. Most

of them are poisonous. We have to be careful where we walk at night.

Along with teaching literacy skills, Brad is organizing carpentry classes for the boys and I am starting sewing for the girls.

Remember that I miss you very much. Brad sends his love to you. Write soon.

All my love,

Mom

Andrea folded the letter up and put it back inside the blue air-mail envelope, intrigued by the stamp with a bright red bird on it. She tried to picture her mother in that far-away place. She didn't like snakes either. Maybe, she day-dreamed for a fleeting moment, Brad might get bitten by one of those poisonous snakes and then her mom would have to come home, and the two of them would move back to Toronto, and it would be just like it used to be. Then she thought about the same snake biting her mother. That was horrible. She didn't want to think about that. She put the letter in the pocket of her jeans and went back out to the dining-room to clear away the breakfast dishes.

August had been the busiest month for tourists in St. Pierre. Most of the time all the rooms at Auberge Cécile were occupied. Cécile and Andrea rarely had any time to themselves. However, Cécile was such a cheerful person that working with her didn't feel like hard work. Throughout those busy weeks in the middle of summer, she and Andrea had become very good friends. Andrea wouldn't have missed this experience for the world. She enjoyed meeting the guests and often helped with the translating. Most of the guests had been a lot of fun and some of them even left a tip for her when they checked out. As well as her work at the *auberge*, Andrea loved traipsing all over town to get things done for Karen and Tom.

Everything had been perfect, except for one thing. All along she had been hoping to get to know Philippe a little better. A lot better, actually. He was friendly enough, in his way, but the trouble was that he was always so busy. He worked long hours every day and then almost every evening he was out playing soccer. When he finished playing soccer, he and his buddies usually ended up at a discothèque called *Le Joinville*. By the time he got home, it was late and Andrea had already gone to bed. She was dying to know what went on at *Le Joinville*. She had dropped a few hints to Philippe that she was interested in seeing what it was like. Unfortunately, Cécile had overheard her, and she told Andrea in no uncertain terms that no one was allowed inside until he or she was sixteen years old. It was the only time Cécile had been really stern with her. She said the police would come and throw people out of the disco if they were too young. Andrea got scared then. She didn't want any more encounters with the police. But she was still curious to know what went on inside this popular night spot.

One morning in late August, Andrea was surprised, and pleased, to see that Philippe was still at home, dawdling over a second cup of coffee at the breakfast table.

"Aren't you going to work this morning?" Andrea asked him. He was usually out of the house before eight o'clock.

"*Ni aujourd'hui, ni demain,*" replied Philippe.

"*Pourquoi?*"

"*Mon travail est fini. Toutes les écoles sont peintes maintenant,*" he shrugged.

So he was out of a job, Andrea thought, realizing that he would probably be staying around the house now and she might see him more often. Her work was dwindling as well. They were expecting a couple of tourists from the United States this week but no one else after that. As Cécile had remarked at breakfast, once the nights grew chilly and the northerly winds strengthened, the tourist season was almost finished for another year.

That morning Philippe was engrossed in a French motorcycle magazine called *Moto Verte*. He told Andrea that he hoped his summer earnings would be enough to buy a Peugeot 103. She peered over his shoulder at a photograph of the trim red motorbike. Yes, she thought to herself, it would be neat if he got one. She could even picture herself riding on it, too.

The phone rang.

"Damn it. Darn it," muttered Andrea under her breath. She didn't want anything to interrupt the delightful day-dream she was spinning of zooming around town on a motorbike with Philippe, the two of them, close together.

The phone kept ringing. Andrea picked it up.

"*Allô.*"

"Hello, Andrea. Over," called Karen Corkum. Her voice sounded faint and static-ridden over the radio connection from their camp on Miquelon island. She and Tom had now spent nearly eight weeks studying the habits of the Grey seal.

"Hi, Karen, what can I get for you? Over." Andrea reached for a pencil and notepad.

"We won't be here much longer so we don't need a lot this week. Could you get us some more of that wonderful bread—four loaves—and a few of those delicious French pastries? And a couple more tins of that pâté we like. And some Brie cheese and a dozen eggs. And do you think you could locate an underwater camera filter, one that fits a Zeiss 400? You might have to try a few places but we really need it. Over."

"Mmm-hmm. Okay," replied Andrea, jotting things down.

"And Andrea, Tom and I were wondering if you would like to come up here for a few days? Do you think Cécile could spare you? Is the inn busy now? Over."

"No, we're not busy here at all. Over."

"Great. When you get all the stuff together for the boat tomorrow, pack up your sleeping bag and come on out, too. This is actually a very interesting place and I have the feeling you'll like it. We'll be closing out our camp on Monday or Tuesday so you can return to St. Pierre with us then. How does that sound? Over."

"Fantastic! I'll be there," cried Andrea. "Over and out!"

"Guess what," she said excitedly, after hanging up the phone. "Karen and Tom have invited me to go up there for a visit—to Grand Barachois. Gosh, I wonder what it's like?"

"Grand Barachois? A lot of...ah, sand," replied Philippe, who had to pause and think of the correct words.

"Sand? Is that all?" she asked, disappointed.

"It is possible to see many... *loups marins*," he added.

"Of course, the Grey seals. That's why they're there."

"It is possible also to see the bones of whales. And sometimes you will see...*un navire naufragé*," added Philippe.

"A what?"

"*Un navire naufragé.* I don't know the English."

"Neither do I but I'll get your dictionary. It's in my room." Andrea darted upstairs and ran back down with his French-English school dictionary, which she had borrowed for the summer.

"*Navire naufragé* means a shipwreck. Wow! That would be awesome!"

"*Anciens* shipwrecks. A long time ago. Me, I like that place very much. My father—before he is died—we go often in his boat but now...I did not see it for a long time," he concluded a bit sadly.

"Gee, that's too bad. But, hey, you know what? Maybe you should come too, seeing as you're not working right now. Karen and Tom wouldn't mind, I'll bet. You could probably help them out. They're taking down their camp next week," explained Andrea, hopeful that this would be a rare opportunity to get better acquainted with Philippe.

Philippe's eyes brightened and he put down his magazine. "I think that is a happy voyage for me," he smiled.

"*Will be* a happy voyage," Andrea corrected him. "*C'est au temps futur.*"

"Yes, the future," he grinned. "The happy future."

CHAPTER TEN

Le Petit Chevalier put-putted slowly away from the wharf. At the helm of the big dory sat Théophile Detcheverry, a hefty man with a large nose and a tiny grey beard that barely covered his chin. He had been a fisherman for most of his sixty-seven years but this summer had the less arduous job of ferrying weekly supplies to the two Canadian scientists camped on the shore of the Grand Barachois.

Andrea was beginning to feel quite at home in boats now, even though *Le Petit Chevalier* wasn't nearly as big as Uncle Cyril's scallop dragger. She crouched down in the bow of the open boat and zipped up her leather jacket. The breeze was chilly despite the sunshine.

The sunbeams on the waves created a dazzling pattern. Andrea gazed into the sombre green depths, hypnotized by the darting arrows of light which, in a peculiar way, reminded her of the twinkling lights in the big stores and office buildings in downtown Toronto at Christmas.

Toronto seemed so far away now. Andrea thought about the way things had been before her mother married Brad and before Brad got the crazy idea to go teaching school in Africa. She thought about her best friend from Willow Drive School and wondered what Suzy would be doing right then. Andrea had promised to write to Suzy, and here it was the end of August and she still hadn't found time to do it. She vowed she would do so as soon as she got back to Auberge Cécile. She had so many things to tell her.

Philippe was sitting in the stern of the boat alongside skipper Théophile. He was wearing a baggy, cable-knit sweater his mother had knitted. Navy blue suited him. He hadn't had a haircut all summer and his curly hair was getting rather long. He really was very cute, Andrea decided.

Occasionally he and the older man chatted quietly in French but most of the time Philippe seemed lost in his own thoughts as the old engine propelled the boat resolutely towards the mouth of the harbour. As they were passing a wharf in front of a windowless, concrete building, Théophile pointed towards it and began talking rapidly about a matter that obviously disturbed him.

"Regarde ce bâtiment, mademoiselle!" he shouted to Andrea over the thudding of the engine. *"Le frigorifique. Tout abandonné maintenant. C'est terrible, n'est-ce pas?"*

Andrea noticed the large, featureless building. It was a fish-freezing plant and had once been the busiest place in St. Pierre. Not now.

"Pas de morue," lamented Théophile, shaking his head sadly.

No more codfish. Andrea was beginning to understand the situation. A hundred men and women had once made their living cutting and packing tons of fish every day and now they were unemployed. Too many people had been taking too much fish from the entire Atlantic Ocean. It was no wonder the *St. Pierrais* were so possessive of the small ocean territory around their islands where they had mistakenly arrested Uncle Cyril.

The dory chugged past the flat island of Ile aux Marins and then the high island called Grand Colombier, a place where puffins built their nests. After that they were in open water, heading for the big islands of Langlade and Miquelon. Few people lived on Langlade, just summer cottagers and campers. Most of Miquelon was uninhabited, too, except for a small village at the north end. Ninety per cent of the people of St. Pierre and Miquelon lived in the town of St. Pierre.

Langlade and Miquelon were connected by a long isthmus known as La Dune. True to Philippe's description, there certainly was a lot of sand. Along both sides of the isthmus white, sandy beaches stretched on and on and on. *Le Petit Chevalier* travelled parallel to them for half an hour before finally reaching a narrow opening in the dunes leading into a vast, salt-water lagoon called Le Grand Barachois. This was where Tom and Karen had set up their camp.

The dory moved very slowly now as Théophile carefully steered it into the lagoon through a maze of channels and sand-bars. As they approached the far shore, they could see three small tents and Tom Horwood and Karen Corkum waving to them.

"Welcome to Grand Barachois!" called Tom.

Tom and Karen both had suntans. Tom had grown a beard. Karen looked relaxed and prettier now. Her long, dark brown hair was gathered at the nape of her neck with a blue plastic hair clip. Andrea remembered purchasing it and sending it up with the supplies several weeks earlier.

Théophile inched the bow of his boat into the sandy shore. Andrea and Philippe removed their shoes and waded ashore, making several trips to unload the cartons of food and other supplies.

Andrea felt sure Karen and Tom would be really pleased she had been able to find the right camera filter for them. She figured it might be a good idea to show it to them before she mentioned inviting Philippe to stay too.

"Terrific! You found one," exclaimed Karen, with a big smile.

"I had to go to four different shops but I finally got one, the last filter they had, too," Andrea explained smugly.

"Sure, that's okay," said Tom casually, when she cautiously told them about Philippe, "but he'll have to sleep in the tent with the camera equipment. The bed-and-breakfast accommodation around here isn't as good as it is in St. Pierre," he chuckled.

Indeed it wasn't. There were no buildings or any other signs of human life as far as the eye could see—just sand and tussock grass and surf and sky and birds.

The tide was falling so Théophile did not linger. He departed, and as soon as the sound of the boat's engine faded into the distance, a seal appeared in the channel close to the camp.

"Look!" shrieked Andrea, startled by the sudden appearance of the sleek black head that had emerged from the shallow water only a stone's throw from where she stood.

"Yep, there's old Sammy," said Tom.

"Sammy?" asked Andrea.

"We gave them names," explained Karen. "Just wait a moment and the next one you'll see will probably be Slippery. She's Sammy's wife—one of his wives. He always pops up first, then she follows."

Andrea sat down on the sand, fascinated. Sure enough, in a few minutes another gleaming, dark grey head appeared a dozen feet from Sammy. The two mammals stared at the four people on the shore for several moments, apparently as fascinated by the sight of human beings as Andrea was by the seals.

Karen handed Andrea her binoculars. She watched for a long time, then suddenly, as though a signal had been given, the seals disappeared below the surface of the water.

"They look like dogs—great big dogs without ears. And all those whiskers!" observed Andrea.

"They're a lot bigger than dogs," said Tom. "Sammy weighs at least three hundred pounds, Slippery somewhat less."

"Look, there's Sally," called Karen, pointing to yet another seal's head that had popped up in the water.

"Sally may be Sammy's other wife. Or she could be their daughter from last year. We're not certain."

Andrea watched Sally through the binoculars until the seal slid silently beneath the surface to some secret destination of her own.

"You know what I think?" said Andrea firmly. "I think it's really gross the way people club baby seals to death out on the ice in the winter. I saw it on TV one time."

"Those weren't Grey seals, though," explained Tom. "Grey seals don't whelp on the ice as a rule. What you saw on television were Harp seals. For the most part, Grey seals give birth to their young on offshore islands. They aren't slaughtered for their pelts the way the Harp seals are."

"I'm glad to hear that," said Andrea fervently.

"Mind you, the Grey seals have their enemies, too. Fishermen don't like them."

"Why not?"

"They see them as competition—for the fish. Fish stocks have been dwindling for quite a long time now. Some people prefer to blame the seals instead of mankind's greed."

"And speaking of fish, I think it's time we started making supper," interrupted Karen. "You must be starving. We'll be seeing lots more seals. Scruffy and Sebastian and Stanley haven't arrived yet but I expect they'll be along soon. They're a bunch of young bachelors. They like to go out roaming on a Saturday night."

"Like me," laughed Philippe.

Andrea laughed, too. However, this was one Saturday night he wouldn't be out clowning around with his soccer buddies. He had no choice but to stay right there in camp.

"Got a job for you two," added Karen. "How about gathering firewood—some driftwood from along the beach? Our propane supply is getting low so we have to cook over a camp-fire tonight. Hope you both like clam chowder!"

Andrea and Philippe wandered barefoot in the

white sand, picking up weathered sticks and boards.

"Qu'est-ce que c'est là-bas?" asked Andrea, pointing to something moving in the far distance.

"Ah! Chevaux sauvages," answered Philippe.

"Wild horses?"

"Oui. Ils habitent La Dune."

"Ils n'appartiennent à personne?"

"Personne."

"That's awesome," said Andrea, thrilled by the discovery that horses wandered around freely here and didn't belong to anyone but themselves. She watched the three grazing horses for several minutes until they eventually cantered off beyond the sandy horizon. Once again the landscape was still.

"Cherchons un navire naufragé," said Andrea.

"Okay," agreed Philippe. *"Quand j'étais petit il y a eu un grand naufragé près d'ici."*

They searched in every direction but there was no sign of a shipwreck from long ago. Where was it now? *"L'épave, où est-elle maintenant?"* she asked.

"Disparue. Au cours des grandes tempêtes d'hiver, le sable se déplace. La dune change de forme chaque année."

"Ooooh, wicked," Andrea exhaled with a small shiver, trying to imagine what this windswept place would look like during a ferocious winter storm when the sands shifted and mysterious things were unearthed while others disappeared.

They hiked back to the camp, clutching bundles of driftwood. Tom and Karen were organizing supper. Karen was tending the fire under a big kettle of chowder made from clams Tom had dug up on the beach that morning when the tide was out. Near the fire was a long, low table he had constructed from weathered boards he had found washed up on the shore earlier in the summer. Now he was busy setting out plastic dishes containing butter, cheese, pâté, canned sardines, hard-boiled eggs, and fresh French bread.

When everything was ready, the four of them sat cross-legged in the sand around the table. They ate and talked and laughed for a long time as the fire burned down, the sun set, and the western sky gradually changed from blue to the colour of apricots and peaches.

Philippe seemed more relaxed this evening than Andrea had ever seen him—and so were Karen and Tom, who seemed truly glad to have the young people there with them. As she stole a glance at Philippe's shadowed profile, it occurred to Andrea that this was the most romantic evening of her entire life. She wished it could last for ever.

"So, Phil, what do you think you'll do when you finish school?" Tom enquired.

"I think about the military, perhaps," replied Philippe. "There is not much work here now."

"The French military?" asked Tom.

"Of course. It is a possibility for *St. Pierrais*. But . . . I don't know. France is . . . *très* . . ."

"Very far," coached Andrea quietly.

"Yes, very far. Perhaps I do not be happy if I go."

Andrea decided not to correct his grammar this time. He was trying hard to express himself and doing very well, and she didn't want to discourage him. She glanced at him again in the glow from the embers of the camp-fire. She could picture him in a soldier's uniform, maybe one like the St. Pierre *gendarmes* wore. There might be medals on his chest, medals for bravery. And some kind of a smart cap— and then she suddenly realized he would be a zillion miles away in France. How would she ever have a chance to see him dressed in his uniform? Would he be coming back to St. Pierre? Would she?

"True," nodded Karen Corkum. "France is rather a long way. And it has a different lifestyle from here."

"My brother—he live in France," said Philippe. "He is a soldier. I have another brother—in Montreal."

Montreal. That sounded better to Andrea. Closer to home. She could visualize a trip to Montreal much more easily than a trip to France.

"I have one more brother. In Newfoundland," continued Philippe.

Better still, Andrea thought and then ventured to ask, *"As-tu faites un séjour chez ton frère en Terre-Neuve?"*

*"Pas encore. Mais à Noël nous irons à St. Jean, ma
mère et moi. Mon frère a épousé une jeune fille de Terre-
Neuve. Ils attendent un bébé bientôt."*

So Philippe and Cécile would be spending
Christmas in St. John's, Newfoundland—which
wasn't an impossible distance from Anderson's Arm.

Tom Horwood yawned. "Well, you young people
may have all kinds of energy to stay up talking all
night but I think we should turn in. Around here
we go to bed with the sun and get up with the sun.
No electric lights to distract us."

After they had cleaned up the camp-site and
washed the dishes, Andrea crawled into the little
pup tent that had been set up for her. She snuggled
into her sleeping bag and squirmed around, making
dents in the sand so she would be more comfortable. As she lay there, she wondered if this was
something like the place where her mother was
working in Africa. No, it would be hot there. Here it
was cool and there weren't any trees. There weren't
any snakes either, thank goodness.

She and Philippe were going to search for the
remains of an old shipwreck in the morning. Even
if they didn't find one, they could just sit and look
at the seals for hours. Maybe she ought to think
about studying marine biology. Maybe...lots of
things. Then she drifted off to sleep.

CHAPTER ELEVEN

 Andrea opened her eyes and stared groggily up at the green nylon above her head. Had she been dreaming? She was sure she had heard a loud, sharp bang, like a firecracker close at hand. She propped herself up on one elbow and listened intently for a moment. Then she wiggled out of her sleeping bag and crawled over to the door flap to look out. The eastern sky was streaked with the first light of dawn, the ocean was a sombre grey, and the surrounding landscape uniformly beige. It was incredibly quiet. There was a cool breeze and she began to shiver. She reached for her leather jacket and put it on over her pink pyjamas.

There was no sign of life from Tom and Karen's tent, nor from the small red one where Philippe slept alongside the camera equipment. It must have been a dream. Maybe, she yawned, she should just go back to bed.

Then she heard it again—this time a series of gunshots. What was going on? Suddenly Philippe bolted from the red tent, yanking on his blue jeans and sweater.

"Qu'est-ce qui arrive?" he blurted, catching sight of Andrea peering out of her tent.

"Je ne sais pas," Andrea replied, trembling more from fright than from the cold.

"C'était un coup de fusil?"

"Je pense que oui."

Now Tom emerged from the other tent, followed by a sleepy-looking Karen. They were both wearing striped pyjamas.

"What in hell? Is someone starting a war?" Tom spluttered.

Karen darted back into the tent to get a pair of binoculars. Then she scanned the cool, grey horizon. "Over there!" she pointed.

Near the entrance to Grand Barachois was a small boat with two people standing up in it. They were pointing guns at an unseen target.

"What the devil do they think they're doing?" asked Tom angrily. "This isn't hunting season."

"Look out there!" Andrea cried. "There's a bigger boat further out at sea."

They stared where Andrea was pointing. A vessel that looked like a long-liner appeared to be anchored about half a kilometre from the shore.

Bang! Bang! Bang! Bang!

"For the love of—*Get down! Get down!*" ordered Tom. "Those shots were in our direction!"

The four of them dropped to the sand.

"Ohmigosh! Is somebody trying to kill us?" whispered Andrea.

"No. I doubt they were aiming at us. Probably never imagined anyone was here but whatever they're shooting at is in this direction. What the dickens are they up to?" grumbled Tom angrily.

"We must go to the big dune...over there," said Philippe urgently. "There it is possible to see—"

"Good thinking, Phil. You two stay here. We'll check it out," Tom ordered.

Crouching low, Tom and Philippe sprinted the hundred yards to the dune and slipped behind it. After a minute or two, Tom waved to Karen and Andrea to join them. Soon they were all lying panting side by side on their stomachs just below the grassy crest of a sand dune where they had a clear view of the entire barachois.

Tom handed Philippe the binoculars. "Would you take a look and tell us if those guys are people you know? And that long-liner out there—whose boat is that?"

Philippe scanned the surface of the ocean.

"Maybe they're spies," Andrea suggested in a low voice.

"Ha!" chuckled Philippe. "What is it they spy here in this place?"

"I don't know. Maybe there's a secret rocket-launching site. Or there could be a neutron bomb testing range around here somewhere."

Philippe handed the binoculars back to Tom.

"Ah, Andrée," he grinned. *"Quelle imagination vive!* I think you see too much television, eh?" He reached over and tousled her hair which, Andrea realized, she hadn't even combed yet this morning.

"Is it anyone you recognize?" enquired Tom.

"Non," replied Philippe. "She is not from St. Pierre, this boat."

"Maybe a fishing vessel from Miquelon?" suggested Karen.

"Non," said Philippe. "There is no...*grand bateau de pêche*...like that in Miquelon."

Bang! Bang! Bang!

They ducked their heads and lay in fearful silence for a moment.

"They do not catch fish, this boat," observed Philippe as he peered over the crest of the dune. "There is no...*mouette*..."

"Mouette? What's that?" asked Andrea.

"It is birds who follow a fishing boat. Look... that bird there..."he pointed to one on the shore.

"Oh, a gull. A seagull," Andrea translated.

"Son of a gun! You're right!" cried Tom, noticing the absence of birds around the vessel. He knew that seagulls always follow a working fishing boat, waiting for scraps to be thrown overboard. "So just what are they up to?"

"Drug smugglers," Andrea speculated.

"I don't think so," said Tom. "Otherwise there

would be someone on shore to collect the stuff. There's not a soul around here, except us, of course. And what's more, smugglers wouldn't be firing off guns and making their presence known."

Bang! Bang!

"They weren't in our direction this time," observed Tom. "Whatever they're after is moving around."

The sun had risen and visibility was improving. By now the colour of the ocean was closer to blue than it was to grey. Andrea took her turn with the binoculars, aiming them alternately at the row-boat and then out to sea where the larger boat was anchored. Gradually the stern of the vessel faced the shore, and Andrea could see there was a name and a home port painted on it.

"I can almost read her name!" squealed Andrea, squinting into the binoculars. "Something with a lot of letters close together. Underneath it says... mmm...Port McLean or maybe Port McLeod... Port McSomething, N.S. Or is it N.B.? One or the other."

"Nova Scotia or New Brunswick. So they're Canadians, for heaven's sake," said Karen disapprovingly.

"Why on earth are they here?" Tom asked again.

Bang!

Seconds after the rifle shot, Andrea watched as

one of the men jumped out of the boat and waded through the shallow water alongside a sand-bar. At the end of it lay his quarry—a Grey seal, writhing in its death agony.

"Oh, no!" moaned Andrea, lowering the binoculars. "He's shot that seal!"

"Damn!" cried Karen.

"Damned idiots!" added Tom. "I should have guessed! They're bloody bounty hunters."

"He killed that seal!" Andrea wailed, tears streaming down her face.

"Now, now, Andrea, don't cry," said Karen, trying to comfort her with a hug, her own eyes wet with tears.

"'Bounty hunters'? What is that?" asked Philippe.

"Until recently in Canada there was a bounty—money, that is—paid by our government for every Grey seal that was killed. It was a measure that was supposed to protect fish stocks, the assumption being that the seals eat too much fish. It's still a contentious issue. And, as it turned out, fish stocks have declined anyway, regardless of how many seals there are."

"These men will take dead seals to Canada for money?" enquired Philippe.

"The bounty has been removed—only these yahoos don't seem to know that. The way it worked, they had to present the dead seal's jaw-bone to a Fisheries officer. Then they could collect fifty dollars. Of course there are people, regrettably, who are so bloodthirsty they want to kill seals anyway," Tom explained.

"Jaw-bone? *Qu'est-ce que c'est?*" Philippe asked Andrea.

"*La mâchoire,*" Andrea translated. "You mean they're going to...remove the jaw-bone?" She looked at Tom, horrified.

"Yup. Take a look," said Tom, clenching his teeth and offering her the binoculars. "They're doing it now."

"Oh, no! No! I won't look! I can't!" moaned Andrea, as more tears ran down her cheeks. "Which one is it? Is it Sammy, or Slippery or Sebastian?"

"There's no way of knowing right now," replied Karen sadly. "We'll find out later when that one doesn't show up."

"They might kill the others, too. Can't we stop them?" pleaded Andrea.

"I think not. Those men are armed, and damn careless, too! Idiots! They could easily kill one of us by accident," Tom growled.

"But this is not...*légitime,*" exclaimed Philippe. "They come to Miquelon and kill our seals. Those seals belong to us."

"Absolutely," agreed Karen.

"They must be stopped!" Philippe insisted.

"How? All we've got is a canoe," argued Tom.

"The French navy has a...*frégate*. It would not be a problem for them," noted Philippe.

"The French navy is a long way from here," said Tom.

"*Pas du tout!*" Philippe protested. "In St. Pierre right now there is a naval exercise. This *frégate*... she arrived yesterday."

"No kidding?"

"Yes, I saw it, too," added Andrea, "when we were on our way up here in Théophile's boat."

"Do you suppose," asked Tom, "that they would help? We might be able to reach them on the radio-phone."

"Why not?" Karen asked.

"Tell you what," said Tom. "Karen and I will stay here and keep an eye on these jerks. You two...go back to our tent where the radio-phone is and try to raise the authorities down in St. Pierre. I know it's awfully early and it's Sunday morning, but see if you can get hold of somebody. Try and persuade them to get the Fisheries patrol or somebody to come up here right away."

Hardly bothering to duck their heads, Andrea and Philippe raced across the expanse of sand between the look-out and Tom and Karen's tent. As they reached it, Andrea realized she was still wearing her pink pyjamas with her black leather jacket over them. Her clothes and hair were sprinkled with sand. What must Philippe think of her, looking like this? Of course, he was covered with sand, too. Well, there were other things to think about right now. How were they going to persuade the French navy to come to the rescue of a family of Grey seals?

CHAPTER TWELVE

"Allô Allô! St. Pierre Radio!" called Philippe impatiently, pressing the transmission switch on the microphone of the portable radio-telephone.

No reply.

"Oh, God, what if it's broken?" groaned Andrea, looking alarmed.

"Un moment...j'écoute...allô."

"St. Pierre ici," said a distant voice.

"C'est VOBW portatif. La Gendarmerie, s'il vous plaît."

The telephone connection was made immediately. Philippe was soon talking to a policeman at the other end of the line. At times Andrea could barely understand him as the volley of words bounced back and forth. *"Oui. Deux Canadiens. Oui, deux fusils. Nous les avons vus. Oui. Okay. Oui."*

"What did he say? What did he say?" Andrea was dying to know.

"It is...um...*illégal*..."

"Against the law."

"For Canadians to hunt in St. Pierre. He will ask the navy to help."

"Terrific!"

"But he does not know if they will do this. It is not the responsibility of the navy. Perhaps, because

197

the Fisheries patrol boat is, ah, rather slow to come here, then the navy may come."

"Come on, let's get back and tell Karen and Tom. Hurry."

As they left the tent, they heard a distant shot. They immediately dropped to the ground and began to crawl on their hands and knees. They hadn't gone far when Tom called out to them.

"It's okay. You can get up. The two guys are rowing out to the other boat."

"You mean they're escaping?" gasped Andrea.

"Did you get hold of anyone on the phone?"

"Yes, yes! Philippe asked the police to ask the navy and we think they might be coming," said Andrea triumphantly.

"But not certain," Philippe cautioned.

Tom shrugged. "Well, not much chance anyone could catch them before they leave St. Pierre territorial waters but at least they are on their way and good riddance to them. Let's get a fire built and make some breakfast. I don't know about the rest of you but I'm starving."

They all were. Andrea and Philippe quickly gathered more driftwood. Karen began assembling a frying pan, dishes, knives, and forks. Twenty minutes later, as they stood around waiting for the water to boil for coffee, Philippe suddenly called for silence.

"Ecoutez! Qu'est-ce que c'est que ça?"

Somewhere in the distance was a muffled thud-thud-thud-thud-thud-thud, accompanied by a high-pitched whine. The sound grew louder. Karen was the first to spot the source as she scanned the sky with her binoculars. A helicopter was skimming over the hills of Langlade and heading in their direction.

The two Canadian hunters were now back on board their long-liner and were hauling their skiff up on the deck. Andrea stood on the shore and watched them closely through the binoculars, still hoping she could make out the name of the ship in case that information would be useful to the police. However, within minutes, the small camouflage-coloured helicopter flew directly towards the vessel and hovered directly above.

"Hurray!" yelled Andrea. "They're going to arrest them!"

"Hold on," cautioned Tom. "Those guys aren't big international crooks, as far as we know. All they're guilty of is hunting illegally. It's one thing for the crew of the chopper to spot them and identify them and quite another matter to have them arrested. The important thing is to scare them off and make sure they don't come back."

"But they killed one of the seals you were studying!" Andrea protested indignantly.

"I know. And that's a real shame but it hardly warrants a chase on the high seas," Karen reasoned.

"Well, I think it does," Andrea insisted angrily. "Why should they get away with it? Why should any of those seals be killed at all?"

"Whoa, there," said Tom, trying to calm her. "Grey seals are not on the endangered list, you know. They're not about to become extinct. Even scientists have to kill them sometimes in order to study them properly. We don't like doing it, of course."

Andrea was in no mood to be reasonable. "I should hope you wouldn't like it! And as for killing them just for some bounty money, I think that's disgusting. Don't you want to punish them? That seal was like a friend of yours!"

She turned away from them and ran down to the edge of the shore where, her arms crossed tightly in front of her, she glared angrily out over the water as the helicopter flew in slow, menacing circles above the long-liner. "I hate you, you seal killers! I hate you!" she screamed, even though no one could hear her over the noise of the helicopter.

Philippe walked down to the shore and stood beside her, putting his hand on her shoulder. "Hey, Andrée, don't be angry like that," he said softly.

"I can't help it," she said firmly. "I hate people who kill!"

"Sure, but—come on with us. There is coffee ready."

"I hate coffee, too!" she snarled, with a sour face. Then Philippe winked at her. She couldn't help but smile back at him.

"Look at it this way," reasoned Tom, who was starting to fry some bacon in the iron frying pan, "those guys on board are undoubtedly scared witless right about now."

"I certainly hope so," agreed Andrea with a wicked grin. "I wouldn't mind if they were scared to death."

The helicopter swung away from the ship and headed towards the shore. Soon it was flying in a circle above their camp. The four of them waved excitedly at the pilot who landed not far from where they stood. The huge propeller blew sand in every direction before it gradually ground to a halt. Two young men in flight uniforms jumped out and ran towards them.

"Merci! Merci beaucoup!" shouted Tom Horwood.

His French really isn't very good, thought Andrea. He pronounced *"merci"* as if it was "mercy." At least he *is* trying though, she allowed.

The helicopter belonged to the French navy frigate that was moored in the harbour of St. Pierre. The crew had been preparing for a routine exercise that morning when the St. Pierre police asked their commander to investigate a foreign vessel off the coast of Miquelon. The pilot and the navigator had been challenged by the assignment and had carried it out with *élan*.

"We told those *matelots* that if they ever came back into these territorial waters, they would be arrested," said the navigator in excellent English.

"Oui, la Bastille!" the pilot admonished with mock authority, making everyone laugh at the prospect of sending two hunters off to the most formidable prison in France for having killed a seal.

"We gave them a shower to remember. Our downdraft blew sea water all over them. They will not return," proclaimed the young navigator.

Philippe was absolutely fascinated by the helicopter, and the pilot invited him to sit inside while he explained how it worked. Tom joined them and together they inspected all the dials, levers, lights, arrows, and buttons.

"Just look at us, Andrea," laughed Karen. "We're still in our pyjamas, except Philippe. Those airmen must think we've been having a pyjama party on the beach this morning! They'll never believe we're scientists who are serious about our work."

"I'm going into my tent to get dressed," said Andrea, suddenly self-conscious.

"Me too," added Karen, "and then we'll see about that breakfast. I'm famished. And you know what?"

"What?"

"It's Sunday. This is the day we have pancakes for breakfast—with maple syrup. And seeing as this is our final Sunday here, we have to finish off all the maple syrup today. No use carrying it back to Nova Scotia."

"Is there enough for them?" asked Andrea, tilting her head towards the two airmen.

"Sure. Go ahead and invite them. How often do they get asked to a breakfast party in a place like La Dune?"

"Okay, I will," said Andrea happily.

It was a breakfast none of them would forget. The pilot and the navigator were only a few years older than Philippe. It was their first visit to St. Pierre and Miquelon and they were curious about everything. They had never seen seals before and were fascinated when two of them appeared in the barachois close by. They were very interested in the scientific study that Karen and Tom were making. But what delighted them most was the maple syrup. They had never tasted it before. In France it was an expensive luxury. By the time they had finished their pancakes, there wasn't a drop left.

"*Sirop d'érable*," said the young pilot as he swished the last bit of pancake around on the Melmac plate. "*C'est merveilleux!*"

The helicopter crew didn't stay long as they had

to report back to their ship. They thanked their hosts for *"un bon souvenir de Miquelon."* Within one minute the gigantic blade began to whirl, again blowing sand all over their camp. The helicopter lifted noisily from the ground and soon disappeared into the southern sky.

"Well," declared Tom Horwood. "Unless we get any other unexpected company this morning, we might just possibly find time to start packing up our camp."

CHAPTER THIRTEEN

Philippe was engrossed in his motorcycle magazine again when Andrea came downstairs for breakfast. It was a different magazine this time but he evidently found it just as interesting as the last one. This was Andrea's final day at Auberge Cécile, at least for the summer. Already she was talking about returning next year—if Cécile asked her, if Aunt Pearl and Uncle Cyril didn't object, if her mom and Brad didn't have any more wacko ideas like all of them moving to Africa.

Tom Horwood and Karen Corkum had left the day before. They were pleased to have gathered so much information and hoped to come back next year, too, although that would depend on getting a government grant to pay for a second expedition.

It seemed possible that, by the following summer, Philippe might own a motorbike. Andrea could picture the two of them zipping around St. Pierre, stopping now and then at some little café for a cold drink. This was such a far-out place.

Andrea figured her mom would like it here. Maybe next summer, her mom could come, too, and take a course in French—she had often said she wished she knew more French. But that would probably mean that Brad would be coming, too.

Maybe that wasn't such a great idea. Maybe her mom and Brad would be happier in Africa. Or in Toronto.

"Andrée, promettras-tu de m'écrire s'il te plaît?" asked Cécile, looking a little sad.

"Oui, Cécile. Je te le promets," Andrea replied as she reached for another chunk of the French bread she loved. She would be happy to write to Cécile. She would miss her. Among the many things she would remember about this place was her trip to the bakery every morning. It had been her first job of the day to walk down to the centre of the town before breakfast as the community was coming to life. The bakery always smelled so delicious. She was going to miss a lot of things.

"Et toi, Philippe," Andrea teased, *"tu m'écriras, n'est-ce pas?"*

Philippe looked up at her and laughed in embarrassment. *"Mon anglais...pas bon,"* he apologized.

"Ecris en français," Andrea shrugged.

Philippe continued to look embarrassed and returned his gaze to the magazine. He had never, in his entire life, written to a girl.

When it was time to leave for the airport, Philippe offered to carry Andrea's duffle bag out to the Renault. Andrea was wearing her new purple sweatshirt with a map of St. Pierre and Miquelon on it. She felt sure it would be a big hit with the kids at

Rattling River High School where she would be a new student a few days from now.

Andrea was surprised that Philippe had decided to go to the airport with them. As the car pulled away from the curb, she looked back nostalgically at Auberge Cécile and silently said good-bye to the orange cat sitting on the fence.

Cécile steered a careful slalom course through the narrow streets of St. Pierre. As they passed the familiar houses and shops, Andrea glanced at them wistfully. They drove past the Gendarmerie National—the place where this adventure had begun so dismally only a couple of months earlier. She remembered how angry Uncle Cyril had been at being arrested by mistake, and how scared she and Jeff had been. Yet everything had turned out so well. She recalled something her uncle had often said: "Bad beginnings, good endings." She had never quite believed it until now but—was this the end of something or only the beginning?

All too soon the flight to St. John's was being called. Andrea hugged Cécile, who kept on chatting about the trip she and Philippe were planning to visit Philippe's brother and his family in Newfoundland at Christmas time. Cécile was determined to visit her new-found cousins, too—Pearl and Cyril, Jeff and Matthew . . . and Andrea, and lots of other yet unknown relatives in Anderson's Arm.

Philippe also gave Andrea a hug. And then, to her utter amazement, he kissed her goodbye, once on each cheek in the French way. "I *will* write to you," he said shyly. "I will write to you...in English."

"Et moi, je t'écrirai en français."

"Promise?" he winked.

"Je te le promets," she smiled.

She turned and walked out to the departure gate and then to the waiting plane.

Soon the French Isles would be behind her...but never to be forgotten.

LAST
SUMMER IN
LOUISBOURG

CHAPTER ONE

"I won!" Andrea shrieked the instant she hung up the phone. "I won! I won!" Overjoyed, she galloped down the stairs in her worn-out jeans and sweatshirt and bare feet. She didn't bother to comb her hair. There actually were occasions when it didn't matter what you looked like, and this was one of them.

"What is going on?" her mother called from the small room beside the kitchen, where she worked at her desk most evenings. She was a teacher, and she had lessons to prepare and papers to mark.

"Mom! You're never going to believe this." Andrea panted as she rushed into the room.

"Calm down. Believe what, sweetie?"

"I won!"

"Won what?"

"That contest. Remember? I wrote a history essay and my teacher, Mrs. Greenberg, entered it in that contest for students."

"And you won?" her mother asked incredulously.

"Yes, I did."

"Fantastic!" her mother cried, and hugged her daughter. "To tell the truth, I'd forgotten all about that contest."

"Me too. Well, almost. Actually, I'm not the only winner. There's one from each province and territory. I won the Ontario prize."

"Wait till we tell Brad," exclaimed her mother joyfully. "He'll be so proud of you."

Brad was down in the basement installing a workshop, a place where he could fiddle around with his power tools. He loved fixing things. Brad was Andrea's stepfather. He was okay, but he could never replace her real father, who had died when Andrea was a little girl. Her mother had married Brad a year and a half earlier and that had abruptly changed their lives. When Andrea and her mother lived in an apartment by themselves, life had been a lot simpler. She didn't have to share her mother with anyone. It was nice that Brad could fix faulty toasters and broken porch railings. If only he wasn't always barging into their lives with his own complicated plans.

Brad emerged from the basement with wood shavings clinging to his T-shirt and dust coating his glasses. He grinned when he heard the news. "Terrific, kiddo! Naturally we knew all along you were going to win...didn't we, honey?" He winked at Andrea's mother.

"You bet," she agreed. "So, what's the prize?"

"You'll never guess."

"Now let me see," pondered Brad. "What about a

gilt-edged, leather-bound edition of *The Life of Sir John A. Macdonald*?"

"Yuck," said Andrea. "Better than that."

"I thought you liked Sir John A. Macdonald. I thought he was one of your heroes," said her mother.

"Sort of."

"Because you share a birthday, right?"

Andrea Baxter and Canada's first prime minister had both been born on January the eleventh—about a century and a half apart. It was a rotten time of the year to have a birthday, Andrea had often complained. Always freezing cold, it was too soon after Christmas and New Year's for anyone to think about presents and parties again. The only good thing was that the principal of Willow Drive School always called an assembly to celebrate Sir John A's birthday and inevitably Andrea got some spin-off attention since it was her birthday too. She kept hoping the Canadian government would declare the day a national holiday, but so far that hadn't happened.

"I didn't write about Sir John A. Macdonald. I wrote about... don't you remember?"

Her mother thought for a moment. "Ah, yes, the Battle of the Plains of Abraham. I read it over before you submitted it. It was first-rate."

"So the prize has to be a trip to the Plains of Abraham, right?" Brad queried.

"You're close. It's a trip. But even better than that."

"Better? How?" asked her mother.

"Farther away."

"Farther away is better, is it?"

"I don't mean that. It's just that I always wanted to visit this place. There were pictures of it in a book at school. You see, the prize for each winner is a summer job with Parks Canada. The man who phoned to tell me I won asked me if I had a preference—like, did I want to see the Rocky Mountains or Quebec or Saskatchewan or whatever. So I told him I was born on the East Coast and I liked it there. He asked me if I spoke any French, and I told him I'd been in an immersion class for years and it was no problem. So he suggested the Fortress of Louisbourg on Cape Breton Island. And I said that would be awesome!"

"Louisbourg?" repeated her mother, looking startled. "Louisbourg!"

"Right, Mom. They have an incredible fortress there. It's an entire town that's been rebuilt just like the old days. It's something like Upper Canada Village, only bigger, and this one is French, and you get to wear old-fashioned clothes if you work there. Oh, I can hardly wait!" Andrea cried.

"You're going to spend an entire summer in... Louisbourg." There was no enthusiasm in her mother's voice. "It's...it's...so far away."

"Mu-um," grumbled Andrea, in the tone of voice she always used when she was fed up. "It isn't as far away as Newfoundland, and I've been there lots of times visiting our relatives."

"You don't have any aunts or uncles or cousins in Cape Breton, though, and Newfoundland and Cape Breton Island are not all that close together. I'm just concerned you might be...well, lonely if you go."

"*If* I go. What do you mean, 'if'? I already told them that I would take the job, that I really, really wanted to be there," Andrea protested.

"I'd certainly like more details about it," her mother insisted. "What if you run into difficulties? What if there are problems?"

"Mu-um! For Pete's sake! There won't be any problems. They said they'd arrange for a place for me to stay and everything. This is a job in a million. I absolutely have to go," Andrea pleaded.

"You earned it, kiddo, you really did." Brad chimed in. His wife shot him a dark look that said he had better keep out of this.

Andrea was surprised—and pleased—that he had spoken up on her behalf. Sometimes, she grudgingly acknowledged, Brad could be almost human, and she did have to admit that he had managed to make her mother a happier person than she had been. But he was always trying to change things. It had been his idea that they move out of their perfectly nice apartment in the Toronto suburb of Willowdale. Now they lived in a brick house in Trillium Woods, a far-too-small town beyond the boundary of Metropolitan Toronto. Out there everything seemed so far away—the mall, the new school she attended, the fitness centre where she swam, and, of course, Suzy, her best friend, whom she had had to leave behind in Willowdale. Now when she wanted to go anywhere she had to get her mom or Brad to drive her to the train station. As far as she could judge, nothing even vaguely interesting ever happened in Trillium Woods. Andrea was dying to get out of the place.

"Andrea," said her mother in the ultra-serious tone of voice she reserved for heavy discussions. "I know you deserve this prize. But it is a long way from home and you are only fifteen years old, and I need to know a few things before you go there all by yourself. I'll give Mrs. Greenberg a call. And I'd like to know the name of whoever is in charge of things at Parks Canada. Also, I want you to think it over for a few days. It might turn out you don't really want to go."

"*Mu-um*! How can you even think that? Of course I want to go. Where else am I going to find a summer job anyway?" Andrea groaned. What was all the fuss about? Last year her mother had gone off to Africa to teach school for six months, sending Andrea to Newfoundland to stay with her aunt and uncle. Her mother had always been proud of her own adventurous spirit. She said it ran in the family, and Andrea had it too. Now, all of a sudden, she was acting as if Andrea was a baby who couldn't look after herself.

"It's getting late and there's school tomorrow," her mother declared flatly, but added in her normal, kindly voice, "I know you're very excited, sweetheart, and truly it is wonderful news that you won this prize. You probably don't feel like sleeping but do try. I imagine tomorrow will turn out to be a very exciting day at school for you."

"Oh, Mom," Andrea grumbled, even as she gave her mother a goodnight hug and headed upstairs to her room.

"This proves conclusively, as we should already know, that war is a terrible thing. This battle should never, never have been fought. Nobody won. In the long run it didn't prove very much. There was plenty of space for everyone, as things turned out. General Wolfe and General Montcalm both died horrible deaths"—here Andrea paused dramatically as she emphasized the words "horrible deaths"—*"and so did many fine young soldiers. But worse than that,"* she continued passionately, *"it meant that there would be a legacy of*

bad will between the French and the English in Canada for many, many years to come. If that dreadful battle had never occurred, then we could have worked out our differences and lived together more harmoniously.

"In conclusion, I would like to say that war and battles are a waste of lives, time, and money. People should always sit down together and talk it over and work things out. That way the world would be a better place.

"Thank you very much."

Andrea sat down. Everyone in the assembly room clapped as she finished reading her prize-winning essay. She could feel her face turning the same shade of Desert Rose as her nail polish. She fidgeted in her chair and focused on the braided silver ring on her finger.

When the applause died down, Mrs. Greenberg, the teacher who had submitted her essay to the contest, stood up. She told the audience how proud the school was that one of their students had won this important prize. She announced that Andrea Baxter would be leaving in June to spend the summer working at the Fortress of Louisbourg on Cape Breton Island, Nova Scotia.

There was a moan of envy from her classmates. They were all hoping to get summer jobs—anywhere.

Mrs. Greenberg went on to remind the students that there were a lot of books in the library about

Canadian history. There would be another contest next year. It would be a good idea to begin preparing for it right away, as Andrea obviously had.

"Remember, it wasn't a matter of mere luck that Andrea won this contest. It was due to the effort she brought to the task," Mrs. Greenberg concluded.

Andrea squirmed and stared into the middle distance. She knew what the other kids would think of that. To her relief the bell rang. Assembly was over. Everyone got to their feet and shuffled noisily out of the auditorium.

CHAPTER TWO

"Andrea, you can still change your mind. You don't have to go if you don't want to."

"Mom. Honestly. You know how I feel."

Her mother sighed. "I'd feel much better about it if I could come with you."

The two of them were having breakfast in the sunny kitchen. Andrea couldn't finish eating hers, she was so excited. This was the day she was leaving for Cape Breton Island.

"I'm going to be perfectly okay. I like travelling, remember?" She couldn't figure out why her mother had turned into such a worry-wart all of a sudden. "I get on the train and then we take off. It's like an airplane, only it stays on the ground."

"But you have to change trains in Montreal and wait an hour or more for the train to the Maritimes. Stay in the station and don't talk to any strangers."

"I never do," Andrea reminded her fretful mother. "I've got a book I'm supposed to read, *A Guide to the Fortress of Louisbourg*. When that's finished, I've got my stereo with two new tapes," she said, patting her bulging duffle bag.

"I wish I hadn't agreed to do a summer course," her mother lamented. Having spent six months teaching in West Africa, she and Brad had agreed to instruct a number of other teachers who were going to work overseas.

"Aw, Mom, you'll enjoy it. You always do."

"I'll miss you."

It was embarrassing the way her mother got sentimental at times like this. Andrea would make plans to go somewhere and then, when it was time to leave, you'd think it was the end of the world.

"I'm coming back. It's only a summer job," she said reassuringly, giving her mother a big farewell hug.

Her mother drove her to Guildwood station, where the train to Montreal made a brief stop. Andrea climbed aboard quickly, gave a final wave goodbye, then headed down the aisle looking for a seat. She wanted to sit beside the window, but the coach was almost full. She finally spotted a window seat but had to climb over a long-legged, sloppily dressed man who appeared to be asleep. He stirred and grunted and then ignored her as she brushed past him and sat down.

The train gathered speed and Andrea stared out the window while the hot, leafy suburbs of Toronto rolled by. The houses thinned out and they passed a golf course and then were in wooded countryside. Here and there she caught a glimpse of the pale water of Lake Ontario under a hazy, humid sky. She began to daydream about the ocean, and about Louisbourg. What was it going to be like, really?

Her reverie was interrupted by the conductor striding along the aisle asking to see everyone's tickets. Andrea dug hers out of the pocket of her duffle bag and handed it to him.

"Truro," muttered the conductor. "Truro. So you're going all the way to Truro, Nova Scotia," he said as he handed her the remainder of her multi-paged ticket.

"I'm going to Sydney," Andrea corrected.

"So you are. But Truro is where you get off the train and catch the bus for Sydney. You have a separate ticket for that. See, there it is." He pointed it out.

After a while another man came along the aisle with a trolley containing food and beverages. Andrea ordered a tuna sandwich and some ginger ale. The fellow beside her woke up and ordered some sandwiches too.

"Jeez. Railway food!" he grumbled as the train was whizzing past a town named Trenton Junction. Andrea thought the sandwich didn't taste too bad, but this grumpy, unshaven guy in the faded grey sweatshirt and stained blue jeans continued to complain, even as he wolfed down the sandwiches.

"So, where you off to?" he asked Andrea when he had finished.

"Louisbourg. That's on Cape Breton Island. I'm going to Sydney first. Somebody's meeting me there," she added, just so he wouldn't think she was alone in the world.

"Huh, Sydney. Armpit of the earth. Me, I'm headin' for Cape Breton too. Glace Bay. Had it up to here with Upper Canada," he complained.

Andrea wasn't sure if he was referring to Upper Canada Village or Upper Canada College, but decided not to ask. He seemed to be in a bad mood.

"I've got a summer job in Louisbourg," she offered, and then wondered if she should have told him that much about herself.

"One of the lucky ones, are ya?"

"Guess so."

"That's your home, Louisbourg?"

"No, I live...near Toronto."

"And you got a job in Louisbourg? You takin' a job away from some Maritimer? Holy shit!"

"Actually, I'm from the East Coast originally. I was born in Newfoundland," Andrea shot back.

"Hah, a goofy Newfie," he snorted.

Andrea felt a rush of anger. "If you must know, the reason I got this job was because I won a contest, an essay contest about Canadian history. The prize was a summer job with Parks Canada," she told him tartly. That should put him in his place.

"So you're a smart ass too!" he guffawed.

"And you're a stupid jerk," she thought, but didn't say it.

Her mother had been right, Andrea thought. She should not talk to strangers. Who wanted to listen to this guy's insults? She vowed she wouldn't speak another word to him. She hauled her book out of her bag and began to read it as the train was pulling into the station at Belleville. She concentrated on the book for the rest of the afternoon until the train reached Montreal.

"The aim of the Fortress of Louisbourg is to portray a moment in time: the summer of 1744 when the fortress was nearly complete and the town had yet to suffer bombardment and conquest. Archaeologists have exca-vated the remains of the original buildings. The historical staff has assembled evidence for every aspect of Louisbourg life, the buildings and their uses, the goods that filled them, the people who lived here, the society and economy that shaped them.

"The Fortress of Louisbourg continues to train and employ workers in building skills once thought extinct, in craft industries, even in eighteenth-century tailoring and deportment. Soldiers and families in period dress renew the activities of Louisbourg's people."

There was a different atmosphere on board the overnight train to the Maritimes, and Andrea saw no more of her former seat mate. Her ticket entitled her to a lower berth. A friendly porter explained how he would turn her seat into a bed while she was eating dinner. In the dining car another cordial man, who appeared to be in charge of things, ushered her to a table where three women were already seated.

"Hello there," one of them said, reaching for a dinner roll and a pat of butter. Andrea only nodded. She wasn't interested in getting involved in another conversation with strangers. For quite a while she simply listened to them. They all knew one another, that was certain, and they were very chummy with two men sitting at the table across the aisle. All three women wore a lot of eye make-up and huge, dangling earrings.

"They're our brothers," one of them remarked in an aside to Andrea as the conversation bounced back and forth between the two tables. "Bill and Gord."

"And we're sisters," added another one. So this was an entire family of brothers and sisters all going somewhere together. Andrea wondered where they were going, and finally got up her courage to ask.

"Cornerbrook, Newfoundland," they replied. "That's where we belong, originally, but none of us lives there now. I live in Toronto. My sister here lives in Vancouver. This other one lives in Atlanta. Bill lives in Sudbury and Gord lives in Brantford."

"Is this a family reunion or something?"

"No, dear, we're going home to bury our father," explained the lady from Atlanta solemnly.

"Oh, I'm sorry," offered Andrea, feeling embarrassed.

"Don't you fret, girl," said the Vancouver sister. "You couldn't have known that. And where are you off to, all by yourself?"

Andrea decided she could tell them where she was going. She also told them that she, too, came from Newfoundland, that her parents had brought her to Toronto as a small child but she had returned to visit Newfoundland several times.

After that her companions treated her like one of their own, and the meal they had together became great fun. It wasn't until the main course was being served that Andrea realized Gord was blind. His brother helped him out by reading the menu or placing his hand on his coffee cup or cutting his steak for him. Apart from that, Gord chatted and joked with his sisters and managed to eat his dinner without any problems.

"And who is the young lady at the other table talking with my sisters?" Gord asked, picking up on the sound of Andrea's voice.

"My name is Andrea. Andrea Baxter," she replied a little shyly, not knowing precisely how to handle this situation.

"I hope you have a good journey, Andrea," he said, looking in her direction but not seeing her. "And remember, us Newfs have to stick together!"

When the meal ended, Andrea paid her bill and got up to return to her reserved seat. "Now, my dear, if you get lonesome, we're going to have a little game of cards back there in the club car. You come and join us, why don't you?" invited the sister who lived in Toronto.

"Um...thanks a lot, but I really ought to go to bed. I have a lower berth," Andrea explained, then wondered if she should have mentioned where she was going to sleep. Who were you supposed to trust? These people were so nice...but...

"Well, girl, if you change your mind..."

"Thank you."

Andrea returned to her place in car number 1603 to find the double seat had been transformed into a bed totally enclosed by heavy, dark green curtains. Inside, it was as private as a tree-house and as dark as a coalmine. Andrea located the switch and turned on the light. The porter had lowered the window blind, but, after putting on her pyjamas, she raised it, then switched out the light. For a long time she stared out the window as the darkening countryside sped by. Here and there she could see lights from lonely looking farmhouses. Every so often the train whizzed through a small Quebec village or town. At highway crossings she could hear the muffled ding-ding-ding-ding-ding-ding of the warning signal. How many times had she been in her mother's car when they had stopped at a level crossing to wait for a train to pass by? It was fascinating to be inside the train at night, in one's own private space, looking out at the world. Andrea wasn't the least bit sleepy. She decided to unpack her stereo. What better place and time to listen to her new tapes?

The melancholy voice of her favourite singer seemed to suit the black landscape. For a long time the train travelled through a forest with no lights to be seen anywhere. After a while they passed into another farming region. Then Andrea began to see large buildings—warehouses and factories—and dimly lit streets and alleys with wires overhead. All the signs were in French. The train slowed and at ten o'clock squealed to a full stop.

Beyond the railway tracks Andrea noticed a body of shimmering water. There, on the other side of the wide St. Lawrence River, stood an illuminated Quebec City. Windows in the tall buildings glittered against a navy blue sky. She could see the turreted roof of the Château Frontenac dominating the skyline of the lower town. It looked like a huge fairy castle from one of her childhood story books.

She yanked off her stereo earpiece as she suddenly realized where she was. "That's it! That's where the battle took place, up there above the old city! I can see the Plains of Abraham where Wolfe and Montcalm fought!"

It was an incredible moment—but there was no one with whom to share it. She felt sad and alone. She wished her best friend, Suzy, was with her. Or even her teacher, Mrs. Greenberg. For a moment she considered getting dressed and walking back to the mysterious club car, wherever that was, and joining the chummy family from Cornerbrook. She envied them, travelling together and having fun, even if they were going to a funeral. The trouble was she didn't want to play cards. She wasn't very good at it. If she interrupted their game to tell them she had just seen the Plains of Abraham, where the famous battle was fought, what would they say? "So what?" Would they laugh at her? They might even call her a smart ass.

Ten minutes later there was a hissing sound, followed by a cloud of steam rising outside the window of her lower berth. As the train dragged its great weight into motion Andrea caught the name on the station: LÉVIS. She pressed her nose against the window and watched the enchanted city across the river disappear from view. She put her stereo away, pulled the crisp, white sheet and the beige wool blanket around her shoulders, and snuggled down. She had stopped feeling lonely. The rhythmic beat of the train wheels on the tracks lulled her to sleep. Tomorrow morning she would wake up somewhere else.

CHAPTER THREE

"You must be Andrea Baxter," declared the smiling young woman who approached her at the Sydney bus station. "You look just the way I pictured you from your letter. Isn't that amazing? I'm Jackie Cormier. Welcome to Cape Breton!"

Andrea managed a weak smile, more of relief than joy. She was enormously grateful that someone was actually here to meet her, as had been promised. For the final hour of the long bus trip from Truro she had worried about what she would do if no one showed up. What if she found herself all alone in Sydney, Nova Scotia, late at night in a place she had never been before? She was feeling disoriented under the glaring lights amid a crowd of strangers. It had been a long journey, twenty-five hours on the train and another five on the bus.

Jackie helped Andrea carry her luggage out to the parking lot, where she stowed it in the back seat of her bright blue Pontiac Firefly. Andrea gradually began to relax. From the outset Jackie seemed like the sort of person you could trust, a down-to-earth woman who wore a sporty red raincoat and tiny gold earrings in her pierced ears. She was slender, and was the same height as Andrea, five feet five. Her hair was a nondescript shade of brown and had been cut dramatically short, a style that suited her heart-shaped face and her mirthful blue eyes.

Fine, silvery rain began to fall as Jackie drove out of the city towards Louisbourg, half an hour away. She was a cheerful, talkative person and during the journey Andrea learned that Jackie was a public-relations officer at the fortress. She worked there all year round. Apparently there was a lot of work to do, even when the place was closed to the public for the winter.

Jackie had always lived in the present-day town of Louisbourg, which was near the fortress. She was twenty-six years old and married to Steve, a heli-copter pilot, who was away in Labrador all summer. She was the mother of a little boy named Kenzie, who had just turned five.

By the time they pulled up outside the Northeast Bed and Breakfast in Louisbourg, Andrea felt a lot more at ease. Jackie was going to be her supervisor for the next two and a half months and, barring some unforeseen quirk in Jackie's personality, she was sure they would get along.

Andrea got out of the car and stretched, then looked around at the town of Louisbourg—as much of it as she could see under the street lights. There was a gift shop across the street, a gas station next to that, and a motel farther along. None of it looked the least bit interesting.

"I live around the corner," said Jackie. "See that white house up the hill there? That's mine," she pointed.

"So where's the fortress?" Andrea asked.

"Over there, beyond the town, way across the harbour," Jackie gestured. "I'm sure you must be dying to see it, and you will—tomorrow. Right now you need to get settled in your new home and meet your roommate."

Andrea followed Jackie in the front door of the Northeast Bed and Breakfast. It was a tall, frame house, painted dark green with white trim. It was very quiet inside, as if everyone had gone to bed.

"This is my Aunt Roberta's home. She'll be asleep by now. She only rents out the two rooms—yours and one other, so even at the height of the tourist season there won't be too much of a line-up for the bathroom," Jackie explained as they climbed the creaky stairs. At the end of a dark hallway was a partly open door and a lighted room beyond. Jackie tapped and they walked in.

"Justine, here's your roommate, Andrea Baxter. Andrea, this is Justine Marchand," Jackie introduced them.

Justine was tall, with shoulder-length dark hair and dark brown eyes. She was dressed in pyjamas with a pattern of zebras all over them.

"Oh, I am so glad you got here. I've been waiting

and waiting and waiting!" she exclaimed with as much enthusiasm as if she'd been waiting for the Queen.

"Have you been here a long time?" asked Andrea, tossing her duffle bag on the floor.

"Ever since Sunday. But now I won't have to sleep in this room all by myself. You want to know something? I've never slept in a room alone before, never ever, until I came here."

Andrea hardly knew how to reply. She had always had a room to herself. "You must have a sister," she said.

"I've got two sisters. And a brother. Sylvie is my twin sister. Then there's my little sister, Holly. She's only ten. My brother, Marc, is seventeen. Sylvie and I've always, always shared a room and for a long time Holly was in with us too, but then my dad built an upstairs on our house and Marc moved his room up there and Holly moved into Marc's room. We have bunks, Sylvie and I," Justine rambled on, apparently in an enormous hurry to tell Andrea all the details of her life.

"So, does your twin sister look just like you?"

"No way. We're not identical. We're fraternal twins. Sylvie is, oh, she has reddish sort of hair, only hers is really long."

"I'm letting mine grow," said Andrea, trying to get a word in.

"And she has greenish-grey eyes. And she's not as tall as I am. And she's fat. At least, I tell her she's fat. I bet she weighs eight or nine pounds more than I do," continued Justine with a grin.

"I'll guarantee she doesn't like it when you call her fat!"

"She gets so mad. She throws pillows at me sometimes. Mom gets mad at both of us when the feathers fly around. What about you, Andrea? How many brothers and sisters have you got?"

"None. I'm an only child," Andrea admitted defensively. She often wished she did have a sister or a brother.

"Oh," was Justine's only comment.

"I am an only child too, Andrea. I know what it's like," said Jackie kindly.

"I've got some cousins, in Newfoundland," Andrea said, trying to make her family situation sound less bleak. "I go there to visit them. Quite often."

"I've got a lot of cousins too. Really a lot. They're nearly all in Cape Breton, except for four who moved to Alberta."

"Now then," Jackie interrupted firmly. "I'm sure you two have a lot to talk about, but it's very late. There's going to be plenty of time to get acquainted tomorrow. You'll need your sleep. We get up early around here, don't we, Justine?"

"Tell me about it," groaned Justine, climbing into her bed. There were twin beds and both had quilts. Justine had a green one with a design of interlocking circles. Andrea's bed had a yellow one with a design of tulips and leaves.

When the lights were out and the girls were supposed to be asleep, Justine leaned over and whispered, "Andrea, are you awake?"

"Yes."

"Do you know what we could do tomorrow?"

"What?"

"We can go down the road and get some pop and chips. I know a place. We can walk there. It only takes about five minutes. Wanna go?"

"I guess so," replied Andrea cautiously. "But I want to see the fortress tomorrow."

"Oh, did you never see it?"

"How could I? I've never been here before."

"Well, I saw it plenty of times. Even before I came to work here."

"Where do you live?"

"River Bourgeois."

Andrea had never heard of the place, but she didn't want to sound stupid by asking too many questions. "I'm from Toronto—well, close to Toronto—and that's a long way from here."

"Don't worry. You'll see the fortress all right. You'll get sick of it before you know it. What I meant was we could go for some pop and stuff after we get off work, around five, okay?"

"Sure. Sounds neat," replied Andrea.

"Okay. G'night," said Justine.

Andrea was exhausted, but she had trouble falling asleep right away. So much had happened in a short time. Here she was in a strange room in an unfamiliar town with this bubbly roommate who was apparently more interested in going somewhere for a snack than she was in the Fortress of Louisbourg. Andrea hoped they would get along, but at that moment she wasn't exactly sure.

CHAPTER FOUR

Justine turned out to be one of those people who could bounce out of bed in the morning with the energy of a wind-up toy. Andrea wasn't like that. She usually woke sluggishly, wishing she could sleep for another hour. Today she was glad her roommate was so alert. Andrea had a hundred questions. Where did they get their breakfast? How would they find their way to the fortress? She didn't even know what time they were supposed to start work.

They dressed, then Andrea followed Justine down the stairs to the dining room, where the ingredients for breakfast were spread out on a large table. There was no one else in the room. A few minutes later Roberta MacNeil cautiously opened the kitchen door and peered in. She had frizzy grey hair and wore a flowery apron around her ample waist.

"Good morning," said Andrea, her mouth full of toast.

"So you're the new girl, are you?"

"Yes, I am," Andrea answered, thinking that was a pretty dumb question. What would Mrs. MacNeil have done if she had replied that she'd been here for weeks?

Mrs. MacNeil had nothing else to say. She returned to the kitchen, leaving the girls by themselves.

"Never mind her," whispered Justine. "She keeps to herself a lot."

Maybe just as well, thought Andrea.

After breakfast they headed towards the fortress on foot. "You can't possibly get lost in Louisbourg," Justine reassured her. "There's only the main street and then it becomes the highway and then it ends at the fortress."

"How far is it?" Andrea wanted to know. She couldn't see any trace of the place. By then they had reached the edge of the town and there were no more houses or stores. The road ahead led through a forest of stunted spruce tress.

"Couple of miles. Couple of kilometres maybe. I don't know. I never have to walk the whole way. Somebody always picks me up," Justine explained nonchalantly.

Andrea shot a sideways glance at Justine. A pickup? Her mother had always told her never to get into a car with strangers. Never, ever. Not that she needed her mother to remind her. There were enough scary stories in the news to warn her of the dire consequences.

Less than a minute later a grey truck, driven by a middle-aged man, pulled up and stopped beside them. Justine greeted the man by name and climbed in, followed by a reluctant Andrea. After a few words with the driver about someone they both knew Justine, said, "Joe, this is Andrea who's starting work today."

"Hello there," Joe greeted her warmly. Andrea responded with an uncertain "Hi," wondering who Joe was. Their journey didn't last long. The road ended in a huge car park. There were only a few cars in it at this time of the morning. They got out and walked towards a modern building with huge glass doors and a sign that said VISITOR RECEPTION CENTRE.

"Not that way," directed Justine, as Andrea headed for the door. "We're not supposed to go in there. That's for the public. We're staff."

Andrea followed her around to the side of the building, where a bus stood waiting with both doors open. Along with Joe and several other men and women, the girls filed in and soon the bus was heading down a narrow road.

"Doesn't anyone come to work in their own cars?" asked Andrea, thinking of Jackie's nifty little car from the night before.

"They don't allow cars anywhere near the fortress," explained Justine. "It would spoil the look of things. See? There it is over there."

Last night's rain had dwindled to a mist, out of

which, on the far side of the bay, rose a fortress town from another age. Andrea could not take her eyes off the hazy panorama of gleaming slate roofs, tall brick chimneys, soaring spires, and massive grey stone walls. It was hard to believe that what she was seeing was a replica of a town that had stood here on this bleak, windswept peninsula beside the Atlantic Ocean nearly three hundred years ago. It seemed like pure magic to Andrea.

As the bus rolled along Justine chatted with another girl who was sitting across the aisle, a giggling conversation about someone who had recently cut her long hair short then dyed it hot pink. Andrea wished they would shut up. Their outbursts of laughter were spoiling her special moment. She continued to gaze out the bus window, enchanted by the vision of another world.

The bus stopped at a circular drive, and everyone got out and began walking along a broad pathway towards a wooden drawbridge that spanned a narrow river. On the far side Andrea recognized the Dauphin Gate, consisting of two massive stone towers with a huge wooden door between them. She had read that the original Dauphin Gate had been built to keep out the dreaded English. Andrea's ancestors had been English people who migrated to Newfoundland about the same time that the French were building this great fort in the New World. It gave her a strange feeling to realize that her people would not have been welcome here, that they might have been imprisoned or even killed. Why, she wondered, had the French and the English always been fighting? And why did they still seem to have trouble getting along?

The girls walked past two young men dressed in baggy blue-and-grey uniforms. Their role was that of eighteenth-century French soldiers, but they were still part of the twentieth century. One was sipping coffee from a styrofoam cup and the other was drinking Diet Pepsi out of a can. Their flintlock muskets were propped against the wall along with their tricorn hats.

"Hi, Dave! Hi, Jimmy!" called Justine.

"Have a nice day!" one of them replied.

"Break a leg!" added the other.

The girls continued along a gravel path beside the high, impenetrable wall that had once defended the people of this garrison against their enemies. How futile it seemed nowadays in a world full of aircraft and bombs and missiles. Yet how imposing it still looked. Andrea realized that no matter how many pictures one saw of a place, it was always a surprise when you finally got there. You could feel it then, as well as see it. Of course, the book of fortress photographs she had seen in her school library had not included the sound of the waves lapping in Louisbourg Harbour, the smell of salt water, or the wild voices of the seagulls. It took Andrea a moment or two to realize that something was missing. Then she got it. There were no power lines or telephone poles cluttering the horizon and no cars or trucks to dominate the scene.

They entered a labyrinth of orderly streets and stone buildings within the walls. Andrea had begun to imagine that she was sliding back in time, picturing herself as a resident of this place, when Justine stopped in front of a tall wooden fence and pushed open a well-disguised secret door.

"C'mon. Follow me," she directed.

"What is this?"

"It's Lartigue House. It's where we get into our costumes."

"What did you call it again?"

"Lartigue. It's named after the family who built the original house. All the houses here are named after the colonists who lived in them in 1744. That was the last peaceful year. After that the English attacked and things were never the same again."

"Couldn't we look around a bit more first?" Andrea asked.

"We're not supposed to walk around unless we're wearing our costumes. Besides, you've got the whole summer to see all the stuff. You'll get bored with it soon enough. Just follow me."

They entered an enclosed yard and walked around to the back door of an ancient-looking house. But it only looked old from the outside. Inside they found themselves in a large room lined with lockers—exactly the same kind that lined the halls in the school Andrea attended in Ontario.

"Mine's number ten and Jackie said yours is number thirteen," stated Justine as she hastily pulled off her T-shirt and jeans and shoved them in her locker. She grabbed a long-sleeved white blouse from a hanger and wriggled it over her head. Then she stepped into an ankle-length, olive-green skirt that fastened with a drawstring at the waist. Finally she tied a cotton apron over the skirt. Andrea sat and watched as her roommate transformed herself into a maiden from another time.

Jackie Cormier arrived just then, carrying an almost identical costume. The only difference was that the coarse, woollen skirt was a faded shade of dark blue.

"These ought to fit you, Andrea. But I forgot to ask your shoe size, so I brought three pairs for you to try."

"Size seven and a half," said Andrea as she examined the unattractive shoes she would have to wear. They were flat, black slippers with a strap across the instep that fastened with a button, like babies' shoes. The toes were broad and square.

"How do you tell left from right?" she asked as she thrust her foot into one of them.

"You don't," laughed Jackie. "They were the same back then. Believe it or not, poor people sometimes bought their shoes one at a time. Shoes used to be an expensive luxury for ordinary folks."

"They still are," Andrea remarked, remembering how much her new winter boots had cost last year.

"These aren't as comfy as sneakers, but you'll get used to them," said Justine stoically as she buttoned hers. Then she helped Andrea into her costume. Andrea felt slightly ridiculous. There was something about long skirts that always made her feel like a little girl, as if it were Hallowe'en or she were making a game of trying on her mother's clothes.

"Very nice," nodded Jackie approvingly. "You suit the role. Now don't forget your bonnet."

Andrea had been fingering the white cotton bonnet. She was not sure which way it was supposed to sit on her head, and anyway she was hoping she could get away without wearing it at all. She didn't like wearing hats of any kind and this one was downright silly. It looked more like a large handkerchief than a hat.

"I bet you don't know why we have to wear these bonnets, do you?" teased Justine as she stood in front of the mirror adjusting hers.

"No, why?"

"Because we've got lice!" squealed Justine.

"The bonnet," explained Jackie, "was supposed to keep the lice at home, if you see what I mean. Thank goodness we have ways to get rid of them nowadays. Apparently everybody had them back then."

Voices and footsteps signalled the arrival of more people. A small boy and girl scrambled noisily into the locker room, followed by their mother.

"Good morning, Brittany. Good morning, Scott," Jackie greeted the children.

"Sorry we're a bit late," the mother apologized.

"We coulda got here faster, but Scott wouldn't eat his cereal," grumbled Brittany, who had blonde pigtails and looked about eight years old.

"I did so eat my cereal," protested her younger brother loudly.

"No quarrelling," their mother ordered.

"Children, I want you to meet Andrea. She's going to be working with you," said Jackie.

"Say hello," urged their mother.

"H'lo," they mumbled, glancing briefly at Andrea.

Andrea shook their hands and tried to look serious about her new responsibilities. The job she shared with Justine was the supervision of these, and other, children. Every day twelve youngsters helped to recreate life as it had been lived in 1744 in the Fortress of Louisbourg. They ranged in age from five to twelve and were members of a corps of junior volunteers who lived in nearby communities. Although they only "performed" during the summer months when the fortress was open to the public, they met regularly throughout the winter with instructors who taught them the children's games, music, dances, and handicrafts of eighteenth-century France.

Andrea and Justine were there to help them get into their costumes, to supervise games and lunches and snack times, to make sure they wore their capes on rainy days, and to keep track of the musical instruments they played, as well as the handmade dolls and the partly finished embroidery. Things had to keep running on time, whether it was the daily performance of a folk-dance or being dispatched home on the bus at the end of the day.

The little girls wore costumes almost the same as those worn by Andrea and Justine. The boys wore white shirts with baggy pants, rigid wooden shoes, and black tricorn hats. Even the littlest boys had to wear those preposterous hats. Andrea wondered if she was going to have trouble persuading them to keep their hats on.

"It's the little kids who really bring this place to life," Jackie declared, as several more of them arrived. "I know you're going to enjoy working with them, Andrea, but since this is your first day here I suggest you take a look around and become familiar with your new surroundings. Justine can show you about. I'll keep an eye on the youngsters for now."

Nothing could have pleased Andrea more. Jackie was turning out to be a pal—one of those people who sensed what you needed before you got up your nerve to ask. Andrea put on her idiotic bonnet and buttoned her baby-doll shoes. The two girls quickly left the building and hurried out through the secret door in the fence.

Chapter Five

By the time they reached the centre of the town, the first bus-load of visitors had arrived. Andrea barely noticed them. She was absorbed by the atmosphere of this ancient town with its walled gardens, beckoning doorways, and quaint dormer windows. Except for the tourists in their modern summer clothes, she really did feel as if she had stepped back into another age. It took a while for her to realize that the tourists were staring at her as well as at the buildings. Of course. She and Justine were as other-worldly in appearance as the make-believe soldiers at the gate. At first she felt self-conscious. A young couple with a baby in a stroller paused to look her over. A pair of grey-haired women grinned at her and snapped a photograph. What was she supposed to do? Smile back or what?

"You sort of ignore them," said Justine with a shrug. After one week on the job, Justine was already indifferent to the curious stares. "Working here is something like being in a play. We're part of the cast, but we're still ourselves, if you get what I mean. If somebody asks us a question we answer them, but otherwise we just go on about our business."

Andrea followed Justine past a long, wooden

building with neat, shuttered windows. "So, I hear you won a writing contest," Justine remarked.

"Hmm mm," Andrea acknowledged as casually as she could, uncertain whether her achievement would make Justine admire her or hate her. "That's how I got this job. The winners were offered summer jobs with Parks Canada."

"What a brain," Justine said in a voice that was neither praising nor condemning.

"I chose to come here. It's where I most wanted to be. So, what about you? How did you get the job?" Andrea asked.

"I heard about it because one of my cousins worked here a few years ago. So I applied. I guess I got lucky, because they hired me."

"Are you in French immersion?" Andrea asked.

"No, I want to specialize in science."

"Do you speak French at all?"

"Sure I do. Back home just about everybody speaks French as well as English. My great-grandfather spoke only French, but I didn't know him because he died before I was born. Now, my grandfather, he switches back and forth between English and French. But my mom...Hey, look where we are! Perfect timing," proclaimed Justine, abruptly changing the subject.

Andrea followed her down a lane leading into a yard, then in through the back door of a building. It was dim and warm inside and smelled delicious. This was the town bakery, known as the King's Bakery because the King of France had owned it, along with almost everything else in Louisbourg. As her eyes adjusted to the gloom, Andrea could see two men dressed in loose, white shirts and baggy pants, hauling loaves of fresh bread from an enormous stone oven. One of them was Joe, the man who had given them a ride earlier that morning. Joe was stacking dozens of loaves onto racks where they would cool. The other man poked a long-handled shovel into the interior of the great wall oven to retrieve more round loaves. They were twice as big as the loaves people buy in supermarkets now.

"Mmmm. Do I ever love the smell of fresh bread." Andrea sighed.

"Joe! Joe!" called Justine. "Can we have some, please?"

Joe looked up and recognized them. His face, hair, and clothes were dusted with flour. He ambled across the room with two chunks of warm bread and gave them to the girls. "There you go, eating up all the profits again," he chuckled.

"What did he mean?" asked Andrea as they headed down the street again, munching as they went.

"They sell this bread to the visitors," explained Justine.

"Maybe we shouldn't be eating it."

"Are you crazy? They've got tons of the stuff. They bake it every day. Anyway, I know Joe. I go to the same high school as his daughter. They're from L'Ardoise, not far from where I live."

"Where else can we go?" asked Andrea, wanting to see as much as possible.

"Well...let's see..." pondered Justine. "We could go and look at the parade square. There might be some soldiers hanging around. Or maybe the stables...that's kind of fun. Or the storehouse. Wait till you see the storehouse. You know, back when people really lived here, they brought over absolutely every single thing they needed from France so they could live as if they were in a town back home. You'd think they were heading into outer space; as if there was nothing here that anyone could use."

"So just what is that?" asked Andrea, pointing to an object in a doorway that had obviously not been imported from France in some other century.

"That? That's a movie camera. Did you never see one before? It's for making films," replied Justine, giving Andrea a sarcastic smile.

"I know that," Andrea laughed impatiently. "I mean, what's it doing here?"

"A bunch of people from away—from the States or England or some place—are making a movie. It's a story about the olden days. They got permission to film it here because, with all these authentic buildings and everything, it makes it look real," Justine explained.

A nice-looking young guy, wearing black sunglasses, a plaid shirt, and faded jeans, emerged from the doorway, hoisted the camera and tripod onto his shoulder, and marched off down the street.

"Let's follow him," suggested Justine mischievously.

Keeping a discreet distance, the girls scurried along the street and turned a corner just in time to see the cameraman disappear through an archway and enter a doorway. A few seconds later they quietly opened the door and went inside. They could hear footsteps ascending a flight of stairs followed by the sound of a door being closed. They waited for a few minutes and climbed the stairs. At the top the closed door bore a sign that said NOT OPEN TO THE PUBLIC.

"Heck, we're not the public. We're staff," reasoned Justine as she cautiously pushed the heavy door open.

Andrea was not comfortable with Justine's boldness. She knew they weren't supposed to be there. She didn't want to get into trouble the very first day of her new job.

They found themselves in a large and elegant room that was a complete contrast to the pioneer atmosphere of the bakery. Here they were surrounded by antique French furniture embellished with silk upholstery and gilt. There was a large, multi-coloured oriental rug on the floor. Damask draperies the colour of rubies framed the elegant, tiny-paned windows.

"Hey, I like this," whispered Andrea.

"It's the governor's suite," said Justine in a hushed voice.

They could hear voices coming from the next room. They tiptoed to a doorway and peered in. The adjoining room was even larger and every bit as luxurious. At the far end, under a blaze of lights, stood a cluster of cameras and sound equipment, along with a group of people whose attention was focused on two actors, a man and a woman, who were looking intently into each other's eyes.

The man was dressed in a dark velvet jacket and a pale shirt with lace frills at the neck and wrists. His skin-tight white pants looked as if they would split if he sat down.

Perched on a dainty little chair, the woman was wearing a dress Andrea would have died for. It was made of some silky material the colour of roses and the long, puffed skirt cascaded over the floor. Her lace-trimmed bodice was cut so low in front that you could see...well, just about everything. Her hair, Andrea concluded, couldn't possibly have been real. It was as pale as a mushroom and piled up high in the shape of a haystack.

Andrea and Justine huddled together behind the folds of the draperies and kept as still as a pair of porcelain mice. They knew they weren't supposed to be there, but this was altogether too exciting to miss. A bearded man kept interrupting the male actor and making him say his lines over and over. At long last he apparently got it right because the gorgeous lady stood up, picked up her accordion-pleated fan, flicked it flirtatiously below her eyes, then glided gracefully away from her suitor and all the cameras and lights.

"That's a take!" called the bearded man who seemed to be in charge of things.

Andrea and Justine exchanged glances. Justine jerked her head in the direction of the door. This was obviously the right time to leave, while there was some commotion among the crew and the actors. They were nearly at the door when they heard a man's voice call out, "Hold on there!" They turned around to see the bearded man almost running towards them.

"Uh oh." Andrea gulped.

"I'm outta here," blurted Justine.

"Young ladies!" The man greeted them. "I want to talk to you."

"Sorry," Andrea apologized. "We just wanted to watch."

"And you enjoyed watching us at work, did you?" he asked.

The girls nodded.

"Well, I was watching you...out of the corner of my eye. You looked rather...appropriate...just the way a couple of servants might look if they happened to be eavesdropping on a conversation."

Both girls looked embarrassed. They really had been eavesdropping. And they had been caught.

"It just so happens we're looking for someone about your age and appearance to play a small role in this film. I don't know if this is your cup of tea but, in case you'd care to give it a whirl...well, here's my card. I'm the director of this film," he explained in a rapid-fire British accent.

Andrea and Justine read the card, CHRISTOPHER GRUNDY, DIRECTOR, then looked at one another in amazement. They had expected a bawling out, at the very least.

"Well...thank you. That sounds...um...interesting," said Andrea, who was too surprised to know what else to say.

"We'd have to ask our supervisor," added Justine cautiously. "You see, our real job is to keep an eye on the little kids and help with the games and things, and wander around and look as if we lived here in the old days."

"Precisely what I have in mind," he agreed. He

was a thin man with a thin face, and he wore a thick sweater of ivory-coloured wool. He pointed towards the busy crew. "That's my assistant over there. Let us know fairly soon if you'd like to be involved."

Andrea glanced across the room to see a muscular young man in a black T-shirt coiling a length of black cable. He had a long pony-tail the colour of the fur on an Irish setter. He appeared to be sharing some sort of joke with the glamorous star in the divine dress. She didn't look quite so elegant now. She had taken off her outrageous wig and her own hair was a tangled mess. Meanwhile, the director was writing something down in his notebook. He ripped out the page and handed it to Andrea. "This is my assistant's name and phone number."

The paper read, "Penny Goodman."

"Penny?" questioned Andrea. "That guy's name is Penny?"

"I beg your pardon?" exclaimed Christopher Grundy. "I hasten to assure you that Penny is decidedly a female. There she is. Over there, beside the armoire."

Andrea had been looking at the wrong person. Penny was a shapely woman in beige slacks, a navy turtleneck, and horn-rimmed glasses. She was busy writing something in a notebook on her clipboard.

"Oops," laughed Andrea. "I thought you meant

him, that guy over there, the one with the long hair."

"No, no. That's Calvin. He's the gaffer. Do tell us your decision as soon as possible, won't you?" he said commandingly and then turned and walked away to rejoin his crew. Andrea watched him go, then her gaze drifted back to Calvin and his copper-coloured hair. It couldn't be his real colour, could it?

As they descended the stairs, Andrea asked Justine, "What's a gaffer?"

"Haven't a clue."

The two of them hurried out of the building and rushed back towards Lartigue House. They didn't stop smiling. They could hardly believe their good luck.

Chapter Six

Justine said she would ask permission for them to be in the film, but when it came right down to doing it she lost her nerve. "You ask, okay?" she pleaded, tossing the responsibility to Andrea. "I'll bet you're good at that kind of thing."

"Not especially," Andrea protested, but she mustered her courage and went to the administration office. It was located in Dugas House, a building that, from the outside, looked like a typical eighteenth-century French colonial home. Inside, it was a different story. Instead of the sparse, wooden furniture and open fireplaces that had sustained French families so long ago, this building was furnished with steel desks, swivel chairs, a row of gleaming filing cabinets, a computer, a fax machine, and several telephones. This was where decisions were made about the day-to-day concerns of running the Fortress of Louisbourg and where Jackie Cormier's office was.

Jackie listened carefully while Andrea described how she and Justine had been asked to play a role in the film. "Would it be all right if we accepted?" she asked tentatively.

There was a thoughtful pause while Jackie tapped her pen on her desk. "I don't see why not," she replied. "Film is another way of promoting the fortress, after all. As long as this won't take too much time away from your regular work..."

"They didn't say how long it would take."

"Tell me about it," said Jackie, nodding wearily. "Film makers seldom do know how long anything's going to take. I've worked with them before."

"All we have to do is stand behind some drapes and secretly listen to the governor's conversation with his fiancée. That shouldn't take very long," Andrea reasoned.

"That depends," said Jackie, raising a sceptical eyebrow, "on the length of the conversation. I hope it'll be fascinating."

"Well, it's not," replied Andrea. "We've already heard it. The governor had to repeat it over and over and over. It got boring."

"So you really were eavesdropping, were you?"

"Ohmigosh, no. It's just that we had to keep quiet while they were rehearsing. We couldn't help overhearing them," Andrea explained in a hurry.

"I'm sure it's not a state secret. It's part of the script. Okay, you and Justine go ahead. Sounds as if it could be fun."

Andrea left Jackie's office almost dancing with excitement. She and Justine really were going to act in a film, a major film, not a school play. She could hardly wait to tell Justine the good news.

A week later the two girls were called back to the governor's suite. The first person they saw was Calvin with the mahogany hair and the black clothes. He was up on a stepladder, tinkering with a tall light standard. Whatever it was that a gaffer did, it had something to do with wiring and lights.

"Um...hi," said Andrea. "We're going to be in the movie. We're supposed to see Penny Goodman about it."

"Well, ah declare," said Calvin, as he gave them both the once-over. "This's a day ah'll surely remember." He spoke in a slow, almost musical, accent of the sort you hear in old movies about cowboys and horses. Calvin's dark eyes darted from one girl to the other. His one gold earring was as flashy as his smile. "Ah'll go find Penny for you. Just who-all do ah say is he-ah?"

"Andrea and Justine."

"Andrea and Justine," he repeated carefully, as if their names were of great significance. "Don't y'all go 'way now."

He was back in two minutes, accompanied by a harassed-looking Penny Goodman carrying her clipboard. She glanced at the girls, but her mind was obviously on something else. "Be with you in a minute," she announced, and strode towards one of the cameramen, launching into an energetic discussion with him. When she came back, she seemed distracted. "Your costumes are okay, but you need make-up. Downstairs, to the left. And tell Charlene to make it snappy. We're behind schedule."

The make-up artist worked in a cramped room with one small window, a room normally used for storing fortress furniture. Tables and chairs had been shoved against a wall to make space for a couple of bright lights, a big mirror, a wheeled cart full of make-up, and a bulky reclining chair. In it was the actor who played the governor, still in white tights and velvet jacket. A cotton cape was draped around his shoulders. Charlene, a plump woman in a pink smock, was leaning over his face and brushing powder over his closed eyelids. Andrea had never seen a man's face covered in make-up before.

Charlene had chocolate-coloured skin and a halo of thick black hair. She glanced at Andrea and Justine and said, "Oh, Lordy, don't tell me there's two of you. I thought there was only one more."

The governor opened his powdered eyelids and looked over at them. "Good morning, ladies," he greeted them, oozing the artificial charm trained actors seem able to project even first thing in the morning.

"Lean back," ordered Charlene and brushed mascara on his eyelashes. Then she flicked off the make-up cape and announced, "You're done. Who's next?"

"You go first," said Andrea, nudging Justine.

"No, you," protested Justine.

"I want to watch how she does it," Andrea insisted.

Justine wiggled herself into the big chair. Charlene wrapped the make-up cape around her shoulders, then she stood back and took a long, analytical look at Justine's face before getting to work applying creams and powders in a subdued rainbow of pastel shades. Justine began to look older and considerably more glamorous. Charlene put the final touches to her work of art with a swoosh of mascara and a dab of bright lipstick. She stepped back to inspect her creation and nodded approvingly.

"What about your hair?" she enquired.

"What about it?" asked Justine. She was admiring her brand-new image in the mirror. She ran her fingers through her hair and patted it into shape.

"Oh, now I remember," said Charlene. "You two are going to wear some kind of hats, right?"

"Our bonnets," replied Andrea, pulling hers out of her pocket. "It's because we've got lice!"

"Lice!" cried Charlene. "You better not."

Andrea was next. After Charlene had worked her magic Andrea took a long look at herself in the mirror, wondering if she could pass for eighteen. Maybe nineteen. Would her friends be able to recognize her when the film was shown? She hoped her name would be listed in the cast. Justine finally dragged her away from her daydreams, worried that they were going to be late.

"Mah eyes are buggin' outta mah head," declared Calvin approvingly as he viewed the girls from halfway up the stepladder. "Li'l dahlins," he sang out, as if it was a fragment of some song he knew.

Andrea tried not to smile in case it left lines in her make-up. No guy had ever called her "darling" before.

At the other end of the drawing room the governor, whose real-life name was Brock Rutherford, sat uncomfortably on the little curved chair that his true love usually occupied. He was wearing glasses and reading a copy of the *Halifax Chronicle-Herald*. His screen fiancée, whose real name was Deborah Cluett, was again dressed in the divine gown and the towering white wig. She was standing by an open window with her elbows on the sill—smoking a cigarette!

"Eww. Disgusting," muttered Andrea.

Justine nodded and then said, "That Calvin guy has a funny accent."

"He's from the States," Andrea explained.

"Way down yonder y'awl," mimicked Justine, trying to imitate him without much success.

"Do you think he's cute?" Andrea asked.

They stood watching him while he adjusted a light reflector. Justine considered the matter for a minute. "Sort of. Not exactly. I don't like his hair."

"Let's move it!" ordered Penny. She positioned the two girls in the doorway while she gave instructions about the way they were to look as they spied on the governor and his fiancée. She coached them on the expressions they should wear when they glanced at one another with their shared secret.

"You're frightened by what you've heard and seen," she emphasized. "Remember, you are servants. No status. No job security. If you get caught listening in on the boss, it's..." she demonstrated by pulling her index finger across her throat as if it was a knife. "So you're curious, but you're also very nervous. Got it?"

The girls nodded, already looking nervous.

Penny stepped off to one side. The governor and his lady returned to their proper places, without the cigarette, the eyeglasses, or the newspaper.

"My heart is yours, my own sweet love."

"I pledge you mine."

"Then shall we rendezvous this very night?"

"Oh yes, my dearest."

"Oh, yuck," thought Andrea to herself. Did people ever really say this kind of thing to one another? Even if it was the eighteenth century it still sounded absurd. She would have laughed out loud except that the cameras were now pointing in her direction. She acted surprised. She acted alarmed. She exchanged a knowing look with Justine before the two of them nervously inched their way back behind the drapery.

"Cut!" called the director. "That's the right idea. Now, next time it would be better if you, ah... Anita..." He pointed to Andrea. He had forgotten her name. "Could you stand just a little to the left of the door? And you...ah..." He pointed at Justine and didn't even attempt her name. "Ah... you could look a bit less startled. Not quite so much expression."

They did the scene again. And again and again. In the end it took over an hour for them to create the precise mood the director wanted. By the time they were finished Andrea was weary and hot and Justine was in an irritable mood. Their heavy clothes were damp and their make-up felt sticky as they endured the heat from the lights. They were relieved when they were finally thanked and told they could leave.

"Y'all don't have to hurry away now," suggested Calvin, smiling at Andrea as he gathered up an electric cable.

"We want to get out of our costumes. We're awfully hot," Andrea complained.

"Then we can get some pop," added Justine.

"That's a mighty fine idea," Calvin agreed. "Ah was wonderin' where a fella goes aroun' he-ah for refreshment. Maybe ah could buy you a Pepsi. Maybe ah'll call you up sometime."

Andrea tried not to look surprised. Was this guy asking both of them to go out with him? Or just one? Which one?

"'Low me to introduce mahself. Calvin Jefferson Lee. Ah'm the gaffer. New to these parts. Come from Alabama."

"Oh," remarked Justine, who couldn't think of anything to say. She had never met anyone from Alabama before. Nor had Andrea.

"Sure...we could go out...sometime," replied Andrea uncertainly.

"And you are Miss Andrea...?"

Andrea suppressed a giggle. "Miss" for heaven's sake. It was almost as old-fashioned as the governor's dialogue. "Baxter," she finally managed. "Andrea Baxter."

"I'm Justine Marchand," Justine announced. "We'd better go now. We room together at the Northeast Bed and Breakfast."

When they were aboard the bus heading back to town, Andrea asked her roommate, "Think I should go out with him?"

"Up to you."

"He is cute, isn't he?"

"I think he's kind of old for you."

"How old is he?"

"Ask him."

"I can't."

"I wouldn't worry about it. He might never call anyhow."

"I don't care," Andrea lied.

"Let's go for some pop," suggested Justine a few minutes later as they trudged up the main road of the real-life town of Louisbourg.

"Right now?"

"Sure. They're gonna die up at the store when they see us made up like this."

"Uh oh. The make-up. Maybe we should go home first and wash it off," suggested Andrea, suddenly aware of how unnatural they must look.

"Who cares?" shrugged Justine. "I just want to see the look on that guy's face when we walk in there like this."

"What guy?" asked Andrea.

"You know."

"No, I don't."

"He works there sometimes."

"Oh, that guy. Curly hair. Wears those round glasses. Never smiles. Right?"

"Cory is his name."

"You like him, don't you?"

"I never said that."

"You do so like him."

"I never said... all I said was I wanted to... oh, never mind. I just want a Coke, okay?"

"Let's go."

When they reached the store, it was to discover that Cory was not working that day. Vivian, the woman who owned the store, was behind the counter instead. She greeted them cheerfully and asked them where they were going that evening, seeing that their faces were so lavishly made up. That only added to Justine's disappointment. They weren't going anywhere. By then Andrea merely felt self-conscious. Theatrical make-up simply didn't look right when you were wearing a sweat-shirt that said BEAVER CANOE.

Disheartened that Cory was not around, Justine downed her Coke in a hurry. Andrea gulped a 7-Up and bought a chocolate bar, and they left. Justine was silent as they walked back. It wasn't until they were in the bathroom washing away the final traces of their brief acting career that her downcast mood began to improve.

"So, ah yew goin' to go ay-out with him... Calvin Jeff-ah-son Lee?" she asked, mocking his accent.

"Don't bug me. I dunno."

"I just thought of something. When he sees you

without your make-up and your fortress costume, he might think you're...too young or something."

"I'm not too young," Andrea almost shouted.

"Just kidding."

"Besides, I can always make myself look older."

"How?"

"I'll get a grey wig, and a walking cane, Aunt Roberta's orthopaedic shoes, and my mom's reading glasses and..."

"And he'll think he's going out on a date with his grandmother," giggled Justine.

"Right."

"I dare you."

"Well, he has to ask first."

CHAPTER SEVEN

 There was a knock on the bedroom door. "Phone call for Andrea," announced Roberta, who then clumped heavily back down the stairs. Andrea opened her eyes and looked at her alarm clock. It was 7:20 a.m. Why would he call her at this unromantic hour of the day? She got up, yanked her bathrobe over her pyjamas, dashed into the hall, and picked up the phone.

"Hi," she said, hoping she sounded as if she had been awake for ages.

"Hi, sweetie," came the voice of her mother.

"Mom!" she exclaimed. "It's awfully early."

"It is. And it's even an hour earlier in Ontario, but I just felt like calling you before the day got started. I miss you, you know. Sometimes I worry about you. I know that's silly but..."

"I'm fine, Mom. Honestly. I've been meaning to write to you. It's just that I've been busy, very busy," Andrea yawned. It was an effort to think of anything interesting to say when she had been awake for only a couple of minutes. For a while she simply listened as her mother chatted.

"How do you like your new job?"

"I like my job. I like my boss. I like my roommate.

But the big news is that I got to play a part in a movie."

"A movie?"

"Yes, a film is being shot in the Fortress of Louisbourg because the story is set way back in history and the fortress looks absolutely right for that. Justine, my roommate, was in it too. We were supposed to be servants. It wasn't a very big role."

"How wonderful! When can I see it?"

"Not for quite a while. They're still working on it. And we're back to our real jobs," Andrea explained, a bit wistfully.

"What's the weather like down there?" her mother asked. She always asked that.

Andrea hadn't even looked outdoors yet. She went to the top of the stairs, where she could see the sky through a small window. It was beginning to rain. "It's raining, Mom," she replied dismally, not looking forward with any joy to the prospect of a damp day full of restless little kids and no likelihood of seeing Calvin.

"Too bad. The sun's shining here."

"Anyway, Mom, I'd better go. I have to get dressed and then eat and get to work. I promise I'll write and tell you more about it, okay?"

"Okay. Take care. Stay out of trouble."

"Mu-um. Stop worrying about me."

"Brad sends his love."

"Thanks for calling."

"Bye."

Andrea and Justine were gulping a fast breakfast when Jackie Cormier dropped by to offer them a lift to work. By then a steady rain was pelting down. When they reached the fortress parking area, the girls climbed out of the car, but Jackie remained inside, along with her five-year-old son, Kenzie.

"Aren't you coming with us?" asked Andrea.

"I'll be along later. I'm going to Sydney first to see my mother. She's in a nursing home there."

"Oh. Too bad."

"It is. She's got Alzheimer's disease. She has good days and bad days. It's hard for us sometimes, especially for Kenzie. He never knows whether his grandma will recognize him or not."

Andrea thought about how sad that must be. Her own mother was still young and healthy enough to worry about her.

"Anyway," Jackie continued, "I'll be back soon. And I'm looking forward to a relatively quiet day without that film crew in my hair. They always seem to need something—permission for this or that, or else they want to borrow things, or rearrange the furniture. Today they're spending the entire day filming in the chapel."

"Is that so? Thanks for the ride, Jackie," Andrea called as she swung the car door shut. She ran to catch up with Justine, who was already on board the bus.

The volunteer children soon began to arrive in plastic raincoats and wet sneakers. They donned their costumes and prepared for a day that promised indoor activities only. There would be many games of checkers. Some of the girls would work on their embroidery. There might even be a session of blowing bubbles through the stalks of angelica plants, a simple pastime that the colonial children had invented using the tough, celery-like stalks of a flowering plant that grew in their gardens.

However, Andrea had a plan of her own. Once the children were dressed in their costumes, she sprang it on them.

"Kids! I've got an idea for this morning. Instead of just hanging around and doing handicrafts, I thought it would be fun if we walked up to the chapel for a while."

Justine stared at her in utter surprise. "In the rain? Are you crazy? Why on earth do you want to do that?"

"Because...the chapel is so beautiful. It's peaceful and it's...I can't explain...I was just in the mood for..."

"For praying?"

"Wouldn't you like to go? You're a Catholic, aren't you?"

"Yes, but we don't usually go to church on Tuesdays."

"Well, it wouldn't hurt. I bet the kids would like it for a change. Okay, who wants to come with me to the chapel?" Andrea asked enthusiastically.

A chorus of agreement greeted the idea of going somewhere. Justine made no further comment. Possibly Andrea had a serious problem, she thought, or a terrible secret she couldn't discuss with anyone. Maybe she needed to sit in the chapel and meditate, although why she would want to do so with a dozen young children tagging along was something of a mystery. They wrapped the children in their capes and hats and soon they were all trudging through the drizzle towards the chapel.

When they reached the chapel, everyone except Andrea was surprised to see that the little church was anything but a haven of tranquillity. Andrea managed to look appropriately amazed at the blaze of lights, the camera equipment, and the glamorous Deborah Cluett standing outside the door, dressed to kill, and—wouldn't you know it—smoking a cigarette.

"Hi there!" she greeted them, as if they were old friends. "This is my wedding day. Would you like to watch me get married?" she invited, as she butted her cigarette on the wet ground underneath a dainty white shoe. Her wedding dress was even more spectacular than the dress she had worn the previous day. It was the ivory colour of old lace, with an embroidered bodice and a long, full skirt that billowed out over a hooped petticoat. A delicate veil hung from the top of her wig to her smooth shoulders. Andrea would have given a lot to try on that costume. She wondered where it was kept when Deborah wasn't wearing it.

"Sure is a beautiful dress," Andrea managed to say.

"Yes, but I wish it was more comfortable. It has a whalebone corset inside the waist, and I can hardly breathe it's so tight," Deborah complained.

The bride returned to the chapel, while an entourage of children and Andrea and Justine stood and watched from the doorway. Deborah took her place in front of the altar, while her attentive audience stood silently against the back wall.

"Andrea," whispered Justine sympathetically, "it's not very peaceful here right now. We can come back some other time."

"It's fine. Really," Andrea reassured her, then turned to the children. "Now not a peep out of anyone, understand? This is a wedding, and if we're very quiet we can watch them film it."

In front of the altar stood a gaunt-looking actor

dressed as a priest. He was being fussed over by Charlene, the make-up artist, who kept dabbing more powder on his bald head. Nearby Mr. Grundy, the director, was engaged in some sort of argument with a frowning Penny Goodman. Deborah, the bride, was sitting on a folding chair blotting her hairline with a paper towel and complaining about her itchy wig. The governor, who was about to marry her, was immaculately dressed in a royal blue brocade coat and those same clingy white tights. However, he looked as if he couldn't have cared less about the wedding. He was sitting on the top step of the pulpit, leafing through a sports magazine. Near him stood Calvin Jefferson Lee. He was looking in the opposite direction, as if something were about to happen in the farthest corner of the chapel.

Justine nudged Andrea and whispered, "They certainly didn't waste any time getting married, did they? They only fell in love on Friday and here they are getting married on Tuesday."

"Honestly!" giggled Andrea. "They don't film scenes in the sequence that the audience sees them. In the story, there could have been a long time, maybe a whole year, between when they first met and when they finally got married. They're probably filming this wedding today because it's raining and they can't work outside."

"I know that!" said Justine. "I was making a joke."

Christopher Grundy heard the buzz of conversation and squinted past the bright lights to see who it was. Andrea was silent immediately and her face turned pink with embarrassment. Only a minute earlier she had been admonishing the children to keep quiet and now she and Justine were the ones to be caught making a noise.

"Oh, it's you." He gave a slight wave. "Don't go away. I want to talk to you."

Andrea and Justine exchanged an apprehensive look. Mr. Grundy continued talking to Penny until they had apparently resolved their problem. Then he spent another couple of minutes explaining something to the priest.

"I'm going to re-name Mr. Grundy 'Mr. Grumpy,'" Andrea announced quietly. "That guy never smiles."

"Grumpy Grundy," echoed Justine with a smirk.

Just then he turned and strode to the doorway where Andrea and Justine were surrounded by a huddle of children in damp capes. "The very girls I wanted to see," he greeted them. "It appears we have another role for you in this film sometime soon. Are you interested?"

Too surprised to speak, Andrea and Justine nodded their heads.

"Splendid. Let's see now...you are Anna and you...ah...are Christine," he ventured.

"Andrea," corrected Andrea.

"Justine," corrected Justine.

"You'll be hearing from us. Penny's got your names written down somewhere," he said, and promptly returned to the altar to have a few words with the restless bride.

"Gawd," Deborah groaned loudly. "This damn dress is so uncomfortable. I can't wait to get it off."

"Not till after the weddin', Deborah dahlin'," joked Calvin Jefferson Lee.

"From the top!" shouted the director imperiously. Calvin and the rest of the crew stepped off to one side. The bride and groom took their places beside each other. The priest opened his prayer book and read something in Latin. The filming began.

By the time the third take was completed, the youngest children were starting to shuffle their feet and whisper among themselves. Reluctantly, Andrea herded them all outdoors. It was better to leave now, before they were asked to leave. She was annoyed that Calvin hadn't even noticed she had been there. However, she had seen him. What's more, she was now going to play an additional role in the film. He wouldn't have any choice but to notice her next time.

"Isn't it wild?" giggled Justine as they all hurried along the road in the dwindling rain. "Maybe they really are in love."

"Of course they're not," Andrea insisted.

"Could be," Justine persisted.

"I happen to know that Brock Rutherford is already married to someone else. They're just acting."

"Actors get divorced any time they feel like it, and then they get married to somebody else. Everyone knows that," Justine declared.

"Not all of them. And I'll tell you something, if I ever get married—and I'm not sure I'm going to—it will be for keeps," Andrea said emphatically.

"Same here," echoed Justine. "But if I were Deborah Cluett, I wouldn't want to marry that guy anyway. He's much too old for her."

"You want to marry Cory up at the store."

"Oh shut up."

CHAPTER EIGHT

 The following day was as bright as the previous one had been dreary. A brisk west wind banished the clouds and rain. A galaxy of waving wild flowers could be seen in the fields surrounding the walled town. On days like this the sea was the colour of sapphires, a fathomless, deep blue, broken only by the bursting white spray where distant waves collided with offshore rocky islands. Even if there had been no Fortress of Louisbourg, Andrea imagined that it would have been a fulfilling experience for tourists just to stare at the ever-changing Atlantic Ocean. She never got tired of looking at it herself.

Andrea turned back towards the town, where a bus-load of visitors could be seen crossing the drawbridge by the Dauphin Gate. Suddenly she noticed Justine in front of Lartigue House. She was talking to a nice-looking guy, chatting to him in a way that suggested she knew him, that he was more than a visitor asking for directions. Did she have a crush on someone else? What about Cory? Andrea ambled slowly towards them, curious to get a better look at whoever he was. Eventually Justine saw her and waved enthusiastically.

"Andrea, come on over!"

Andrea approached nonchalantly, not wanting to appear too eager.

"Surprise, surprise. This is my brother Marc. Marc, this is Andrea."

"H'lo there," said Marc shyly, with a quick half-smile.

"Hi," Andrea greeted him. Marc was a large, imposing-looking fellow, dressed in a new pair of jeans and an oversized, white T-shirt. He had short, dark hair, the same colour as Justine's. He had dimples when he smiled.

"So guess what?" asked Justine, without stopping long enough for Andrea to guess anything. "Marc drove up to Sydney airport to pick up a couple of exchange students from Quebec and it turned out they missed their connecting flight out of Halifax, so now they won't get here until this afternoon on another flight. Meanwhile, Marc had to hang around, so that's why he came over here."

"Helps to pass the time," explained Marc.

"Well, yeah, there's lots to see," Andrea agreed.

"You gonna stay for lunch?" Justine wanted to know.

"Nah, I better be on my way. I can get a sandwich at the airport," said Marc.

"Anyway, we should go too. Almost performance time. I'll see you in a few weeks," concluded Justine.

"See ya," said Marc, and then, as he walked away, he turned and added, "Nice to meet you."

"Same here." Andrea smiled.

Every morning at 11:30 when the weather was fine the children performed for fortress visitors. A trio of boys played tunes on a recorder, a drum, and a tambourine, while a circle of girls danced a traditional French step vaguely similar to the square dancing of today. Visitors loved it. They always gathered around to watch and to take lots of photographs.

One sunny morning it dawned on Andrea that this little performance hadn't been invented for tourists. This had been the reality in the days before people had television or videos or amplified music. In this distant outpost people had had to rely on themselves for entertainment. It occurred to her that little children would have enjoyed this uncomplicated dance and simple music the way they enjoyed taped music and movies today. Was it possible they could have enjoyed it more? In this fortress community the performers and the audience would have been acquainted with one another. If anyone had a special talent, then everyone else would have known about it. No one would have had to wait a lifetime to be discovered.

"You want to know something?" Andrea confided to Justine as they observed the children. "I once thought about becoming a video star—well, maybe not a star exactly, but doing some professional acting or singing."

"You did? So did I," admitted Justine.

"I was in a play at school," Andrea reminisced. "It was called *Lady Windermere's Fan*. It was a lot of work, but I didn't mind because I enjoyed doing it. There were four performances, and after the last one there was a terrific party. I didn't get to bed until two o'clock in the morning."

"I was in a play at school too. It was a drama to teach kids to take care of their teeth. I played the part of the toothbrush," Justine said proudly.

Andrea made no comment. That didn't sound like a very interesting part, pretending to be a toothbrush.

"The trouble is my mom doesn't think that acting is a good career choice. She says there aren't that many jobs around. So I thought about it for a while and decided I'd be an airline flight attendant. I love to travel."

"I changed my plans too," Justine agreed. "What I really like best in the world is animals. So I've decided to become a veterinarian."

"I love animals too. I wish I had a dog. I might be getting one in the fall."

"We've got a dog. And three cats. And seven cows. And twenty-two hens. And a pig," counted Justine.

"You're lucky. I wish we had room for lots and lots of animals."

"Do you want to come home with me sometime? You could see our dog and meet everyone. In August there's going to be a big party on my birthday. And my twin sister's birthday too, of course."

"Sure. I'd like that," said Andrea enthusiastically.

"We can catch the bus from Sydney. It only takes about an hour from there."

The children completed their little show and the tourists clapped enthusiastically before dispersing to see other things. Andrea glanced along the quay and her heart suddenly skipped a beat. Calvin Jefferson Lee was striding towards them, his long hair blowing in the wind.

"Found you at last," he said breathlessly to Andrea, as if he had been looking for her all his life.

"We haven't exactly been hiding," Justine remarked quickly.

"Ah been lookin' for Andrea Baxter all over this burg, and he-ah she is, ta-dum!"

A shiver ran down Andrea's spine. "What's up?" she asked as calmly as if Calvin searching for her was an everyday occurrence.

"Penny Goodman wants to see you. Over on the parade square."

"Now?"

"Right now."

"Just me?"

"Just you."

So Calvin was only the messenger.

"It's almost lunchtime," Andrea protested. "We have to supervise."

"You'd better go. I'll watch the kids till you get back," Justine volunteered, but without a smile.

Andrea had to walk faster than usual to keep up with Calvin, who charged through the crowds with a long, loping stride. He was a lot taller than she was.

For a time he didn't say a word. Finally he remarked, "I s'pose you got a boyfriend back home?"

Andrea wasn't sure how to reply. Would he be impressed if she said she did have one? Would he think there was something wrong with her if she didn't? She decided the truth was the best choice.

"Not at the moment."

"A purty gal like you and you haven't got a guy!" said Calvin in mock horror. "Why, ah might have a chance after all."

"Who knows?" said Andrea as casually as she could, tossing her head in a way she hoped would tell him she wasn't tripping over her shoelaces to go out with him.

When they reached the main intersection of the town, Calvin turned the corner to the left. "Ah'm off to see a man about a hoss," he chuckled.

What did he mean? Was that some kind of code meaning he had to go to the bathroom, or was he...

"We gotta hire a pony from the stable for tomorrow's shootin'. S'long, dahlin'."

Andrea continued up the road by herself. When she reached the parade square, she couldn't see Penny Goodman anywhere. The place was deserted except for Grumpy Grundy way down at the far end. He waved and beckoned her to join him.

"Hello there, Angela. Just the girl I wanted to see!"

"It's Andrea."

"Of course it is. I need a word with you without your friend...what's-her-name."

"Justine."

"Right. I'll be brief. It now appears that we have a more expanded role coming up. The lady's maid is going to be somewhat more significant to the plot. We've revised the script, and we have a scene where the maidservant will be transporting an important secret message. It calls for dramatic looks—bewilderment, fear, relief—the sort of thing that you do rather well, if I may say so. Do you think you could handle this role?"

Andrea swallowed and thought about it for two seconds. "I think so."

"Sorry we don't have another role for your friend. Josephine's quite good, but—"

"Justine."

"You have what we're looking for."

His cellular phone rang, and he reached into his briefcase to retrieve it. It was a call from Penny Goodman, who was supervising a scene in the garden behind the engineer's house. "Yes, Penny. Yes, she's right here and we've discussed the part. I believe she intends to do it." He looked Andrea in the eye and nodded his head, asking for confirmation. Andrea nodded back.

"A done deal then," he told Penny, and continued to talk to her about production details. After a while he perched the phone on his shoulder and said, "Thank you for coming by, Amanda. We'll be in touch."

"I'm Andrea."

"So you are."

When the day's work was over, Andrea and Justine caught the bus back to town. As usual they walked to Vivian's store for some pop. It gave them something to do before supper and, of course, Justine had a chance to see Cory—if he happened to be on duty that day. She never knew for sure.

"I phoned home," said Justine, "and my brother Marc said he'd come up and get us in the car when we get our days off in August. That way we won't have to wait around for the bus."

"Sounds great," Andrea agreed.

"And I was thinking. I might even invite one or two kids from around here. It's my birthday, after all."

"Cory. Cory. Cory," teased Andrea.

Justine blushed. "Shut up," she muttered, and changed the subject. "So what did Penny want? Do we have to do that stupid scene over again?"

"No, we don't. Actually, Penny wasn't there. Just Grumpy."

"Oh, him. What did he have to say?"

"Nothing really...except there's another scene to do."

"Ohhh. Gimme a break," groaned Justine. "All those hot lights. All that waiting around. All that make-up. I can't STAND it," she proclaimed in mock dismay, holding the back of her hand to her forehead and looking up towards the sky.

"Actually...as it happens...this time there's only one part...for one servant...for me," Andrea explained haltingly.

"Oh," said Justine frostily, and didn't utter another word until they arrived at Vivian's store. Luckily Cory was behind the counter and that thawed Justine's icy mood. The girls were the only customers, so there was time to chat. And, as it turned out, there was a lot to talk about. The big news was that there had been a robbery at a convenience store in the town of Dominion, not far away. Cory had just heard all about it from the guy who drove the bread-delivery truck.

"The police figure the man was mainly after cigarettes," he explained earnestly. "He took nineteen cartons of them and also stole twenty-five videos, along with all the money in the cash drawer."

"How did he get in?" Andrea wanted to know.

"They think that maybe he hid, that he was inside the building at closing time. The fellow on duty that night had to step outside because there's a gas pump out in front. A couple of cars came by for gas just before he closed the store. Somebody could have walked in and hidden in a cupboard maybe."

"Scary," commented Justine, sipping her Coke very, very slowly.

Another customer came in, and Cory got busy slicing baloney, cutting a chunk of cheese, and signing out a video.

"We'd better go," Andrea suggested.

"How's everything up at the fortress?" enquired Cory as they headed for the door.

"Come and see for yourself," Justine suggested coyly.

"I might," agreed Cory with a hint of a smile.

As they walked back, Justine became quiet again. The two girls ate their supper in silence and after that Justine slumped in a chair in front of the television, watching a re-run of "North of 60." Andrea went upstairs and washed her hair. Justine was obviously hurt that she hadn't been asked to play another role in the film and Andrea had. It wasn't my fault, Andrea reasoned. I wasn't the person who made that decision. Why does she have to take it out on me with her big sulk?

When they were getting ready for bed, Justine announced importantly, "As soon as I finish grade twelve I'm going to apply."

"Apply what?"

"Apply to the University of Prince Edward Island, to the veterinary college there."

"Terrific," Andrea said enthusiastically, and listened patiently as Justine mentioned the high marks she always got in science and talked about her interest in farm animals. At least Justine was speaking to her.

They got into their beds and Andrea leaned over to turn out the light. "Hey, Juss, when did you say your brother was coming to get us?"

"He'll let us know," she yawned, and then turned her back on Andrea and snuggled her head into her pillow.

"G'night, Juss."

Justine didn't say anything.

Andrea lay awake for a long time.

CHAPTER NINE

 "Get set! Now RUUUUUN!" bellowed Grumpy Grundy.

Andrea hoisted her long skirt just above her ankles, not too far above them, but exactly the way Penny had demonstrated. Then she darted fairly gracefully down the gradual slope of the parade square. As she reached Maison de la Plagne she paused and glanced back with a well-rehearsed anxious expression on her face. Then she disappeared around the corner.

By the time the morning's work was over, Andrea had run down that same slope and around that same corner a total of nine times. How could such an uncomplicated scene possibly have so many variations, particularly as she wasn't required to speak one single word? She ran and ran and ran. Grumpy was turning out to be an insufferable perfectionist. He rarely appeared to be pleased with anything that Andrea or the other actors did. If it hadn't been time to break for lunch, Andrea felt sure she would have been asked to run down that boring parade square a tenth time, an eleventh time, a twelfth time...

Everyone in the film crew was entitled to a one-hour break for lunch. They carted their equipment to a nearby building then drifted away. Andrea watched them, hoping for a glimpse of Calvin, but he wasn't among them. It must have been his day off. Just her luck. She returned to the staff lunchroom, where Justine and twelve little children were sitting around the table eating their sandwiches. Justine greeted Andrea with an impassive "Hi" and not another word. She didn't enquire about the morning film shoot. She didn't ask about Calvin. She didn't ask about anything. She focused her attention on the children and made sure they cleaned up the mess after they had eaten.

After a while Andrea felt courageous enough to ask, "Hey, Juss, are you going up to the store for some pop after work?"

"I'll see," replied Justine stiffly.

Andrea could feel a knot tightening in her stomach. It became an effort to swallow her peanut butter sandwich. In the end she couldn't finish it. She was in no mood to work on the film that afternoon, but she knew she had to. It was a good thing the script didn't call for smiles or laughter. She could never have managed that, not today. In her next scene, during which she was still fleeing across town with her secret message, she had to portray fear, to look as if she thought she was being pursued by someone dangerous. She had spent a lot of time in front of the bathroom mirror every night for two weeks past, practising expressions of fear, anxiety, and exhaustion. She had wisely locked the bathroom door in case Justine barged in and observed what she was doing.

By the middle of the afternoon it wasn't a challenge to look exhausted. Eventually she was rescued by the weather. This particular scene had to be filmed in fog. There had been lots of that in the morning, but by three o'clock the wind had shifted and, to the delight of everyone except Christopher Grundy, the sun began to shine. Completion of the scene was postponed until the next foggy day.

Andrea returned to her regular job for the rest of the afternoon. Jackie was generous in letting her take part in the film, but Andrea never imagined that it would occupy so much time. Justine had taken most of the children for a walk among the ruins beyond the fortress, so Andrea didn't have much to do. She used the time to tidy the costume cupboard and then she caught an early bus to town. She was relieved to get back ahead of Justine so she could wash off every trace of the theatrical make-up before her roommate came home. When Justine did return she was still aloof, but Andrea was determined not to let it get to her. Together they walked to the store in gloomy silence while Andrea prayed silently that Cory would be on duty when they got there.

And he was. However, there were five other customers in the store, so he was kept busy ringing up sales, stuffing things into plastic bags, checking out videos, and selling lottery tickets. One by one the customers left, all except one fellow who slouched against the pop cooler while he read a magazine from the rack.

Andrea finished her 7-Up and tossed the can into the garbage pail. Justine, who could sip a Coke more slowly than anyone else in the world, stopped reading the community notices on the bulletin board and meandered back towards the counter where Cory was finally alone, arranging a stack of videos on a shelf.

Andrea thoughtfully kept her distance. She knew what it meant to Justine to have a private chat with Cory, even though her moody friend always insisted she didn't give a hoot. She did so. Andrea walked over to the magazine rack, selected a copy of *Canadian Living*, and pretended to be reading an article describing how to dry wildflowers, a subject that didn't interest her at all. She was really listening to Justine talking to Cory, telling him something that one of the tourists had said to her that day.

"...no kidding. That's what he asked. He wanted to know why didn't they build this fortress over near the Bras d'Or lakes instead of here, because

there isn't as much fog over there. Also—get this—
he said it would have been handier to the
Trans-Canada Highway as well."

"Jeez," Cory guffawed. "So what did you say?"

"I told him there was no highway in 1717, the
year that the king of France decided to build here. I
mean, they hadn't even invented cars then. People
travelled in ships. Louisbourg has an awesome harbour. I pointed to it, but the fog was so thick this
morning we couldn't see it."

"Some people!" Cory snorted.

"Dumb de-dumb dumb," trilled Justine.

Andrea turned to put the magazine back on the
rack. She'd learned everything she needed to know
about dried flower arrangements. She headed back
to the counter, paid Cory for her pop, then tactfully
suggested to Justine that they would miss their supper if they didn't head back.

Justine swallowed the last drop of her Coke, paid
for it, and left the store reluctantly. At least by then
she was in a better mood, almost her normal self.

Next morning there was another early phone call
for Andrea. She put on her bathrobe, padded out
into the hall, and picked up the phone. It was
Penny Goodman.

"Andrea? You do know how to swim, don't
you?"

What kind of a question was that so early in the day?

"Sure, Penny," she replied. "I took lessons for ages. I got my intermediate badge, and I even started working on my senior's. Why?"

"More script revisions. We've got a scene coming up that requires filming you in some sort of boat. There's no danger, of course, but we just wanted to be sure you could swim if you had to. Are you comfortable about being in a boat in the harbour?"

"You bet. My uncle in Newfoundland has a fishing boat, and last summer I spent a lot of time in it. And before that there was another time..."

"Great," Penny cut her off. "Just what we wanted to hear. I'll get back to you. Bye."

When Andrea arrived at the locker room that morning, she found Kenzie Cormier and another little boy fighting on the locker room floor.

"Kenzie! Scott! You boys stop it this minute!" she shouted, yanking them apart.

"He took my shoes!" accused Scott fiercely.

"I never did!" Kenzie loudly insisted.

"Boys! Stop it! The shoes are all the same anyway. Maybe Kenzie put yours on by mistake," Andrea consoled.

"He did it on purpose," protested Scott.

"I doubt that very much," Andrea said firmly. "Kenzie, if those happen to be Scott's shoes, I want you to give them back and then you and I will find another pair for you, okay?"

Grudgingly Kenzie kicked off the wooden shoes and left them on the floor for Scott. He followed Andrea downstairs in his stocking feet. Having just turned five, Kenzie was the youngest member of the entire volunteer corps. He spent Wednesdays and Fridays at the fortress. The other weekdays he stayed with a babysitter in town. He was quite a handful, although Andrea wouldn't have admitted that to Jackie. She didn't want her boss to think she couldn't cope with any child in her charge, especially not Jackie's son.

Andrea hunted around in the costume cupboard and found another pair of wooden sabots that almost fitted Kenzie. She stuffed some straw into the toes of the rigid shoes, using the same method that fortress dwellers had once used to ensure a good fit. She got him into his costume in time to join the other children. Kenzie spent the next half hour running after a couple of the bigger boys who were playing hoop and stick. This was another game that had been played by children who grew up here long ago. The only people who played it nowadays were the volunteer corps at the fortress. All they needed was a simple wooden hoop, the kind that was once used by barrel makers, and a stick. The object was to keep the hoop rolling as long as possible by prodding it with the stick. A lot of running was required to prevent the hoop from falling over. It was the perfect game for overly energetic little boys.

Andrea watched as the children darted along the quayside, laughing and shouting as the hoops continued on their wobbly courses. At moments like this, she sometimes indulged in a daydream that she was actually living her life here that last, peaceful summer back in 1744. The longer she worked here the more she thought about that distant world when there had been no cars, no radios, no computers, no telephones, no washing machines, no hair-dryers, no pop music, no magazines. They didn't even have organized sports in those days, unless hoop and stick could be classified as a sport. There were very few books. Only the children of wealthy parents learned how to read. School was a luxury, the way ballet classes and riding lessons were today.

She liked to fantasize about living in a place where there were no schools. Imagine—never having to pay attention to a teacher or do your homework. But what would she have been doing instead? On a summer day like this, keeping an eye on children playing wasn't a bad way to pass the time. Yet it wouldn't all have been like this. She would have had to spend many hours scrubbing, knitting, and sewing—work that was now done by machines. There were some real disadvantages too, like head lice and scratchy clothes, and sleeping on a mattress stuffed with straw, not to mention the absence of certain things, like antibiotics and anaesthetics if you became ill.

There was one other thing that Andrea couldn't quite picture for herself. Young women were sometimes married at her age. They might even be mothers by the time they were fifteen. A wife. A mother. Could she possibly...? Well, someday. Not yet.

Her fantasy came to an abrupt end with the pitiful sound of Kenzie bawling his eyes out. He was lying on the ground, clutching his knee and making a terrible fuss. Andrea rushed over, stood him up, and inspected his bleeding knee.

"I f-f-fell down!" he wailed.

"Come on," she said, putting her arm around him. "It'll be okay. We'll go and wash this off and get you a nice Band-Aid."

"'kay," he sobbed and limped after her, tears streaming down his face.

There was a first-aid kit in the staff room for minor emergencies like this. Andrea dabbed his knee with a wet cloth, then covered the scrape with three Band-Aids. Kenzie finally stopped crying. He liked Band-Aids.

"Want my mommy," he demanded solemnly.

"She's over in her office. Let's go and show her your new Band-Aids."

Jackie gave her little boy a hug and told him how brave he was. She even found a toffee in her desk drawer, which cheered him up. As Andrea and Kenzie were about to leave, Jackie said, "I guess you heard what happened up the road last night?"

"No, what?"

"That little shop... in town here..."

"Vivian's?"

"Yes, that's the one. They were robbed."

"Robbed!" cried Andrea. "When?"

"I haven't got the whole story. It happened at closing time. There was a fellow on duty..."

"Cory!" exclaimed Andrea.

"That's the name. He was alone there. He was held up at knife point."

"Ohmigosh! Is he okay?"

"Yes, he's okay. A bit shaken up, but he wasn't hurt."

"Poor Cory," Andrea stammered.

"I didn't realize you knew him," said Jackie.

"I don't. Not really. Justine does."

Andrea could hardly wait to tell Justine. She would have run all the way back to the hoop-and-stick game, but Kenzie was still hurting and limping and making the most of his injury.

Justine was busy supervising a game of ninepins by the time Andrea found her.

"Justine, wait till I tell you!" Andrea called.

"What?"

"Cory was held up at knife point last night at the store!"

"You're kidding!" gasped Justine.

"It's true. I just heard it from Jackie."

"Oh my God! Is he okay?"

"Yes, he is." Andrea relished being the bearer of dramatic news. "It seems that it happened when he was closing the store," she added.

"Did anything get stolen?"

"I don't know. I only heard about it a few minutes ago from Jackie, and she'd just heard it from somebody else," Andrea explained.

"We've got to go there as soon as we can," said Justine urgently.

"Right after work."

CHAPTER TEN

The two girls jumped off the bus and ran all the way to Vivian's store. They were out of breath by the time they charged through the doorway. Vivian was behind the counter, facing a clutch of customers who were listening intently as she described the alarming events of the previous night.

"Cory couldn't say for sure if it was a knife or some other sort of weapon. It was sharp and was pushed into the middle of his back. Poor kid. He must have been terrified," said Vivian sympathetically.

"So then what happened...after he nearly got stabbed?" asked a tall lady in a denim jacket.

"He was forced to open the cash drawer. The thief took all the money, then he forced Cory across the store and shoved him into the cold cupboard. That's where we put the fruit and vegetables at night. The burglar locked him in. The thing is, there's a lock on the outside of that door but normally we never use it. Apparently this fellow was familiar enough with the building and that's why the police suspect he'd been in the store before."

"How long was Cory in the cupboard?" asked Justine anxiously.

"Till nearly midnight. When his parents realized

he wasn't home and it was that late, they came looking for him," Vivian replied.

"What's the world coming to?" asked a heavy man in a navy blue T-shirt.

"Makes you wonder," Vivian sighed. "We get quite a few strangers in here in the summertime with all the visitors coming and going from the fortress. There's no way we can remember every single person who shops here."

"Is Cory all right now?" Justine enquired earnestly.

"He's fine, thank God. I told him to take a few days off. What a brave boy. You girls should go over to his house and say hello. I bet he'd appreciate a visit," Vivian suggested.

"His house?" repeated Justine. Somehow she hadn't given any thought to Cory's other life in a house where he presumably lived with his family. All she had ever seen or known of Cory Rankin was right here in this store.

"Good idea," said Andrea enthusiastically, giving Justine a quick jab with her elbow. "Now which is his house? I forget."

"Just up the road there. The yellow one right across from the seniors' home," Vivian gestured.

"Oh, sure. Let's go, Juss," Andrea directed, as she ushered her surprised friend out of the store. They hadn't even had time for a Coke.

At the yellow house they stood looking at the door for a long minute. It was Andrea who finally knocked. Justine was too nervous to do it.

Someone called, "Come in."

They timidly opened the screen door and found themselves in a large kitchen. Cory was sitting at the kitchen table, along with a lady who surely had to be his mother. When he saw who the visitors were, he looked a bit startled.

"Hi. How's it goin'?" he enquired.

"That's exactly what we came to ask you," laughed Andrea.

"Vivian said we should come over," Justine explained quickly, to justify being so bold as to track Cory right into his home.

He looked perfectly all right. Apart from a piece of masking tape around the bridge of his glasses, no one would have guessed the ordeal he had endured.

"Sit down, girls. I'll put the kettle on for some tea," invited Cory's mother. "You're the girls who stay over at the bed and breakfast, aren't you? And you both work up at the fortress?"

"That's right, Mrs. Rankin. I'm Andrea. This is Justine. We heard about the robbery, so we came over to see if Cory was okay."

"Isn't it dreadful? I can hardly believe it," clucked Mrs. Rankin, who was a small woman with short, dark hair and a round face. She wore baggy blue jeans and a red T-shirt with the words SPORTY FORTY printed on it. "A robbery right here in Louisbourg. It just proves you don't know who's out there. I never did like the idea of Cory being over at the store late at night. I don't want him working there in the evenings any more; not on his own."

"Aw, Mom," grumbled Cory.

"The police have been here. Twice now," his mother added.

"What did they ask you, Cory?" Justine wanted to know.

"Oh, a lot of things. Did I see the guy's face? What kind of clothes was he wearing? Was he tall or short? What age was he? Had I ever seen the guy in the store before?"

"Had you?"

"No. Trouble was, I didn't really see his face at all. He snuck up behind me while I was putting the oranges and celery and stuff away for the night. He poked something sharp in my back and ordered me to open the cash drawer. He grabbed all the money, then he pushed me across the store so hard it knocked off my glasses. I don't have very good eyesight without them, so all I could say for sure was that he was wearing jeans and sneakers and a baseball cap pulled down around his eyebrows."

"Which sounds like just about every guy in the country," remarked Andrea.

"Did he steal anything else?" asked Justine, eager for every detail.

"All the cigarettes. Fifteen cartons."

"Ewww. Gross," commented Andrea.

"And on top of that he took my Walkman, which was lying on the counter, and that makes me really mad," said Cory angrily.

"Now, Cory, dear, we can get you another," consoled his mother as she got up to make the tea.

It didn't take Justine very long to return to her chatty self once her astonishment at being inside Cory's home wore off. Cory's mother was the sort of woman who made people feel at home, and Cory, despite his recent ordeal, turned out to be a more relaxed person in his own home than he was when he was working at the store.

"So, how do you like Louisbourg?" he asked them both.

"The town or the fortress?" countered Andrea.

"The town."

"Suits me okay," replied Justine.

"Me too," Andrea said with a nod.

"Not much goin' on here," Cory lamented, "unless getting robbed is your idea of a good time."

Both girls giggled a bit and then Justine remarked, "There's not much excitement where I come from either."

"Where's that?"

"River Bourgeois."

"Oh yeah, I've heard of it. But I was never there. They say it's pretty nice."

"It is. Actually..." Justine began, "if you wanted to see it for yourself you could...you could come to my birthday party next week. Andrea's coming too. My brother's coming up to get us so you could get a ride. And you could stay overnight because Marc has space in his room for a camp bed."

"But what would your parents say about that?" asked Mrs. Rankin. "I think you'd better ask them first."

"Oh, my mom and dad wouldn't mind. I'll check first, but I know they like me to bring my friends home. Mom always says we're less likely to get into trouble if we're at home," explained Justine.

"I'm sure she's right," said Mrs. Rankin.

"Mmm," muttered Cory uncertainly. "I dunno if I can go."

"I'm really looking forward to it," said Andrea persuasively.

"Cory, why don't you go too? It would be good for you to get away from all this fuss for a while, to take your mind off the robbery," suggested his mother.

"The robbery's history," declared Cory firmly. There was a long pause before he said anything else. He didn't want anyone to think he had been bothered by what had happened to him...nor that he was going to take his mother's advice. Finally he sighed and shrugged and said, "Might be fun. Why not?"

Justine flashed a wide smile and then, in case she appeared overly enthusiastic, she assumed a matter-of-fact expression and hoped she sounded businesslike.

"Okay. I'll let you know what time my brother's coming. We'd better go now. Thanks for the tea," she said.

"Yes, thanks," added Andrea as they got up to leave.

Justine didn't stop talking all the way back to the Northeast Bed and Breakfast. Andrea had never seen her in such a good mood.

CHAPTER ELEVEN

"You expect me to play my part in this?" Andrea exclaimed, looking down in mild horror at a slender birch-bark canoe lying half in and half out of the water.

"What's your problem? I thought you said some uncle of yours owned a boat and you loved it," countered Penny as she surveyed the stony shore where the scene would be filmed.

"My uncle has a big scallop-fishing boat. It's got a cabin and an engine, and places to sleep and cook and everything. It's not a bit like this."

"Don't get your shirt in a knot. You won't be in it for long. With any luck we can get the entire shoot done today, as long as the fog hangs around. What's more, we have an experienced paddler among our crew and he's volunteered to teach you how to paddle it. Here he comes now. So get busy and practise. We start work this afternoon."

Penny rushed away and Andrea turned around to see who her instructor would be. Her mouth fell open. Calvin Jefferson Lee was approaching her. Was this her lucky day or what?

"Miss Andrea! Good mawnin'!" he greeted her, lifting his floppy canvas hat in a mock gesture of southern courtesy, as if he were acting in *Gone with the Wind.* Sometimes Calvin seemed to be coming from another planet. "Back when ah was a student..." he began, as if that part of his life were ancient history. How old was he anyway? "Ah taught youngsters at a summer camp how to paddle a canoe. So far's ah know nary a one of 'em has drowned. Now then, you watch me real close and heed what ah'm sayin'. You're goin' to catch on real quick 'cause you're smart as a mockin'bird and twice as purty." He winked at her.

Andrea could feel her heart pounding. "I can handle it," she replied bravely, hoping the apprehension wasn't evident in her voice.

Calvin turned out to be a patient teacher. First he demonstrated how to crouch down and grasp both gunnels before setting foot in the canoe. They got in and Calvin paddled away from the shore. Kneeling behind Andrea, he reached around and gently closed a hand over hers as he showed her the correct way to hold the paddle, how to propel the canoe straight ahead, how to turn, and how to stop. His arms felt incredibly strong.

After that he watched from the stern seat while Andrea paddled alone. He reminded her more than once that she must never stand up in a canoe, no matter what. He even described a manoeuvre to get back into the canoe if she happened to fall overboard, but reassured her that

that wasn't going to happen as long as she remembered her lessons.

The fog became thicker and for a while they couldn't even see the nearby shore.

"I had the idea they hired stunt people to do scenes like this," Andrea remarked, to let him know she knew a thing or two about making movies.

Calvin gave a quiet, throaty chuckle. "Never fe-ah, dahlin'. The crew's gonna be practically 'longside, just inches away from the sweet sound of your paddle dippin' in the water. Don't you worry that purty l'il head of yours."

There was that word again. Purty.

But Andrea did worry—not about falling overboard and drowning—she was a good swimmer. She was more concerned about making a fool of herself in front of Calvin.

"You're gettin' the hang of it now," he said approvingly. Throughout the lesson he had been facing her back. She wondered if he had merely been watching the way she paddled or if he had actually noticed her. For all she knew he might have been staring off into space. Now Calvin steered the canoe back to the shore, where they got out and together lifted the little craft above the high tide line. The enchanted lesson was over. The fog was lifting a little. Calvin returned to his real work of setting up lighting systems for the film.

Andrea had to return to her real world too. She headed back toward Lartigue House, wishing she could share her excitement with Justine. Imagine— a whole hour with Calvin! But she knew that if she mentioned her role in the film again, it would send Justine into another long sulk.

Maybe she could phone Suzy, back in Toronto. No, that wasn't possible. Suzy was up north at her parents' summer cottage, where they didn't have a phone. She could phone her mother but that wasn't such a hot idea. How could she tell her mother she had just spent an hour with a guy she wanted to spend all day with? She couldn't. If only there was somebody to share her joy.

Even if Justine had been a willing listener, there wasn't a hope of talking to her that day. In the staff lunch room Justine was now centre stage. Everyone wanted to hear all the details of the robbery at Vivian's store. Andrea was getting a little bored listening to the story over and over, but Justine obviously loved describing it.

"The robber stole mostly the same things— money, cigarettes, and videos," Justine continued knowingly. "And the thing that made Cory so mad was the guy stole his Walkman. Anyway, his grandmother is going to buy him a new stereo on Friday, when she gets her pension cheque."

"How do you know that?" enquired Andrea.

"I know a few things you don't," said Justine smugly.

Penny Goodman appeared at the door of the lunch room looking for Andrea. "Of all the rotten luck," she grumbled. "The sun is starting to shine. Just when we need the fog, the damn stuff disappears. This afternoon's shoot is cancelled. I'll call you when we need you."

Nothing could have pleased Andrea more. Calvin wouldn't be working either. There might be time for another canoe lesson. Maybe he would even ask her out.

Next morning at 7:00 there was a phone call for Andrea. "Damnation," she muttered as she hauled herself out of bed and into her bathrobe. "Why does my mother always phone me at this ungodly hour?"

It was Penny Goodman. "Perfect day," she stated. "There's fog everywhere and the forecast says it's going to last. We start the canoe shoot at 9:00 sharp."

"But I can't work today," Andrea protested. "Today and tomorrow are my days off. I'm going to River Bourgeois with Justine. It's her birthday."

"You've got to work today," Penny insisted. "We're running weeks behind schedule. We've had far too many delays already, what with the weather and everything else. We've got a deadline, you know! This is show business, not a teddy bear's picnic! Do you want this part or not?" she bellowed into the phone. She sounded really angry.

"But..." stammered Andrea.

"I'm sending a car for you in an hour. Make-up first, then I'll meet you on the quay. Don't be late." She hung up.

Andrea went back into the bedroom and sat down heavily on the edge of her bed.

"Happy birthday, Justine. But I can't go with you today," she lamented, tears welling up in her eyes. "I have to stay here and work on that stupid film."

Justine was about to brush her hair but stopped in mid-air. "That's the pits," she grumbled sympathetically. "Everyone at home wants you to come."

"They do?"

"Yeah. And especially my brother Marc. He keeps asking me about you. Anyway, I'll bring you back a piece of birthday cake. Mom always bakes two—one for me and one for Sylvie."

"Thanks a million," said Andrea joylessly. A piece of cake would be nice, but it wasn't going to compensate for this lost opportunity to see Justine in her own home among her family and friends... and to see her brother again.

CHAPTER TWELVE

 The Frederic Gate was a huge wooden structure that dominated the waterfront of the fortress. Square and solid, and as tall as a barn, it framed an enormous archway, a replica of the one through which sailors from all over the world had once passed as they unloaded cargoes from sailing ships. It had been the commercial centre of this community, a gathering place for colonists eager for news from the rest of the world.

Nothing significant happened here now, but tourists liked to have their photographs taken standing in front of it. Andrea had memorized the facts about this imposing landmark so that she could answer questions when visitors asked. However, today she didn't want to talk to anyone; she thought she was going to cry. Justine and Cory had already left for a fun weekend in River Bourgeois. Andrea was still uncertain about her ability to paddle that wobbly canoe on her own. Calvin had not volunteered to give her a second lesson yesterday, and today he was nowhere to be seen. Several other crew members were there, setting up their equipment, but not him. Didn't they need a gaffer today? Where was he?

Grumpy Grundy came striding out of the fog

towards her, waving a friendly greeting. He seemed to be in an uncharacteristically good mood. "Yon rising star appeareth," he proclaimed as if he were on a stage.

"She braveth the winds of change
And the tide of time,
Her secret held against her gentle breast
And courageous heart."

What's with this guy? Andrea wondered. He's the director, but he acts like a frustrated actor. What was he rambling on about anyway? The secret note, which was the reason—in the film—that she was making this canoe trip, was in the pocket of her skirt and not against her... honestly, what an idiot.

"I want to see a smile on that pretty face," he continued, this time in his normal voice. "Just think, ah, Adriana, you could be nominated for Best Supporting Actress for this role. Stranger things have happened. You're a talented young lady, you..."

"My name is Andrea!" she almost shouted.

"So it is. Let's get to work. We'll begin with you paddling away from us, glancing back once or twice with your dark, anxious look. You're concerned that someone may be following you."

"The cameraman will be, that's for sure," Andrea muttered under her breath.

"After that," he instructed, "keep on paddling out towards the centre of the bay. We'll do a second shoot there, only from a launch instead of the shore. And remember, if you feel uneasy about anything just give us a shout."

"I'll do that," said Andrea coolly.

Charlene appeared with her portable make-up kit. She dabbed more powder on Andrea's face, aimed hair spray on her bangs, and twisted a few curls with a butane curling iron.

"What's the matter with you today, honey?" she asked. "You look like you've lost your last friend."

"I probably have," Andrea agreed gloomily.

"I don't believe it. You cheer up now, you hear? This film's nearly done. I want outta here as much as you do."

"All I wanted was my two days off to go to River Bourgeois."

"Where?"

"Where Justine lives. You remember her. We did a scene together in the governor's drawing room."

"Now don't you fret. There's gonna be other times to visit with your friends. You got your whole life ahead of you."

"If I haven't screwed it up," Andrea lamented.

Charlene merely smiled.

"We haven't got all day!" shouted Grumpy Grundy from the water's edge, where he was holding the canoe in place with his foot.

Andrea grasped the gunnels, placed one foot in

the middle of the canoe, and with the other shoved it away from the shore. It was tricky to manoeuvre her way into a canoe when she was wearing a long skirt. Cautiously she settled into the stern seat and slowly paddled away. She soon discovered that it wasn't as easy to keep the canoe moving in a straight line this time. The tide was going out and the current tended to pull the canoe to the left. She paddled hard to the right and, after every third or fourth stroke, looked back through the foggy murk towards the camera with her much-practised expression of anxiety. Finally she heard the welcome word "Cut!"

"Stay there, Andrea," called Penny.

Andrea sat very still in the canoe in the fog. The sound of voices carried clearly in this kind of weather, and she could hear the crew talking among themselves as they loaded film equipment into a motor launch. After a while she heard the motor start. They were heading her way.

The thing about fog is that it doesn't stay still for long. Today, it wafted back and forth across the bay. One minute Andrea could see the shore and the next minute she couldn't.

"As long as it doesn't blow away altogether," Andrea prayed, because if it did she would have to do this scene over again another day.

The launch with the crew and cameras pulled up beside her.

"Okay, brave little courier," ordered Penny, "now we want to see you paddling purposefully in the direction of the lighthouse."

"But I can't see the lighthouse. The fog's too thick," Andrea complained.

"Of course you can't see the lighthouse and we don't want to either. It hadn't been built in the eighteenth century, remember? Just paddle in that direction."

Andrea paddled diligently into the grey and blurry distance. Stroke. Stroke. Stroke. Another stroke. Then a backward glance. More strokes. More backward glances. Surely she had paddled and glanced backward long enough by now.

"I am royally fed up," Andrea muttered through clenched teeth. "I have had enough. I am—"

Abruptly she realized that the engine in the launch had stopped and the crew might be able to hear her. She turned around to see what was happening. Had they changed their minds again? She could see only a dark blur in the fog where the boat ought to be.

"Andrea! Can you hear me?" came the distant voice of Penny Goodman.

"I hear you," yelled Andrea.

"Something's wrong with this blasted engine. Better come over here till we get it fixed!"

Andrea dipped the paddle in the water and

started to steer the canoe in a wide arc. She soon realized she had pulled too far to the right, so she switched the paddle to the other side and stroked hard to the left.

"Dammit," she muttered. Now she was too far to the left. She switched the paddle again, trying to remember something in Calvin's instructions about a "J" stroke. What had he said? Turning a canoe around was not as easy as it looked. She switched to the other side again and then—hoops!—the paddle slipped right out of her hands and was floating away from the canoe!

She bent over and reached out to grab it, stretching her fingers to the limit, but the infuriating paddle floated away from her. She leaned out farther...just a little more...a little more...and then had to pull back a split second before the canoe would have overturned.

How humiliating! She turned to see if anyone was watching her, but the launch had completely disappeared into the fog.

Now what? The launch was back there somewhere and for a moment Andrea considered jumping overboard and swimming towards it. She was confident about her ability to swim, but how far away were they anyway? And of course she was wearing her costume! Maybe, if she took off her cape and chemise and skirt, she could jump in wearing only her bra and panties. She decided against that. It would be altogether too embarrassing to be seen by the whole crew in her underwear. Besides, the water was awfully cold, even though it was August. What if she got a cramp? She would drown for sure, because no one could see where she was. A shiver ran down her spine as the paddle drifted out of sight into the mist.

"Aaandreeeaah!" The voice sounded a hundred miles away. "Where aaaaaare yooooou?"

"Heeeeere!"

"Stay there. We're...fix...engine..." The voice died away into the clammy silence.

"Okaaaaay!" hollered Andrea. There was absolutely nothing else she could do. She was so angry at her own clumsiness. What was Calvin going to think when he heard about this? His pupil had failed. She felt so helpless and so silly and she couldn't stop shivering. She clutched her woollen cape tightly around her shoulders. What a ridiculous predicament this was. There was nothing to do and nothing to look at even. It was just as well she didn't realize the tide was gradually carrying the canoe out to sea.

Andrea began to wonder what time it was. She had had to leave her wrist-watch behind because, in the era of the film, watches had yet to be invented. It felt as if she had been drifting in the canoe for hours.

There was only one distraction—the seagulls. Every once in a while a gull glided by like a ghost. She had never taken much notice of these commonplace birds before. They had always been just part of the scenery. Now they were company. She began counting every gull, a game she used to play with her mother whenever they made a long car journey and counted the number of cows they saw, or horses, or barns, or red cars. It made the time pass more quickly. One gull, two gulls, three gulls, four... After a while—and she had no idea how long—she was up to sixteen. She also noticed for the first time that some gulls had black backs and grey fronts and some had white fronts and grey backs. Were they different species altogether? Next time she was near a library she would go in and ask for a book about birds and find out. Then she began to wonder if she ever would be in a library again.

It slowly dawned on her that a really long time had gone by. Where on earth was she—no, not on the earth, on the ocean? Where was everyone else? Had they gone ashore and abandoned her? What would her mother do when her only daughter didn't come home? Would she be angry at Andrea's stupidity? No, she would be heartbroken.

"Oh, why did I want this dumb job anyway?" Andrea sobbed, tears streaming down her face. "I

wish I wasn't here. I wish I was at Justine's party."
She wept until the whole canoe shook.

The fog was growing thicker. Then finally she heard something besides the screeching of the gulls. It was a motor, but one with an entirely different sound from the launch carrying the film crew. Now she was really afraid. Whoever was driving this motor boat didn't know she was out here. They wouldn't be able to see her until they got very close, and they might easily smash into the canoe and break it into splinters. She could be hurled into the ocean, bleeding and possibly unconscious.

She sat bolt upright, uncertain what to do. Maybe she should scream, but if she did would anyone hear her? If she stood up and waved her arms she would be more visible. But no, she remembered she must never stand up in a canoe. Those were Calvin's ironbound instructions.

The sound of the engine had become a deep, sullen roar. Andrea crouched down in the canoe, gripping the gunnels so hard her hands were turning white. But what was the point of that? It would be better to shout and scream. There was a remote chance someone might hear her.

"Hey! I'm over here!" she hollered into the grey distance. "Here I am!" she screamed, sitting bolt upright, waving her cape. If only the cape hadn't been brown. If it was yellow or red the people in the boat might notice something before they smashed into her. "I'm over here!" she screeched, her throat hurting from the effort. But she could still hear the boat heading towards her.

Then, all of a sudden, the threatening roar stopped, diminishing to a low purr. Staring into the fog, Andrea saw a dim shape beginning to emerge. It grew larger until she could see the bow of a boat as big as her uncle's inching through the murk towards her.

Someone had seen her! She resisted the urge to jump to her feet, but the tears began again. This time they were tears of joy. Moments later a big grey boat slowed to a stop alongside the canoe and a smiling face looked out of the wheelhouse window.

"Hi there, young lady. Need a ride?"

CHAPTER THIRTEEN

A broad-shouldered Mountie held a coiled rope in his hands. He hurled it towards Andrea, and she grabbed it. He pulled the canoe alongside and tied it securely to his boat, then he reached out a hand to help Andrea climb aboard.

"You okay? I've got blankets on board, and a first-aid kit, and food and water," he offered. He wore a badge on his shirt that said D. ORZE-CHOWSKI.

"I am absolutely fine, thanks," insisted Andrea shakily.

A flicker of a smile crossed the Mountie's face, then he started the engine. "So, looks as if you were up the creek without a paddle, eh?"

"It's not a creek. It's an ocean. The paddle slipped out of my hands when I was switching sides. I tried and tried to reach it, but it kept floating away. I was so darn mad," Andrea admitted.

"So that's what happened. Your pals were sure worried about you. They couldn't get their engine going, and they didn't have a clue where you'd got to. That's when they called us. How long were you out here?"

"I don't know. It felt like forever."

"Were you scared?"

"No. Well, maybe. Just a bit."

"Luckily our radar picked you up. The tide had carried you a fair distance out of the harbour. Bet you didn't want to spend the night out there, did you?"

"No."

"And where is your life jacket, young lady? There are water safety rules, as I am sure you are aware."

"I couldn't carry one because they hadn't been invented in the eighteenth century," Andrea explained.

He glanced at her with a puzzled expression.

"What kind of an excuse is that? That was then and this is now."

"You don't understand. We were filming. I'm in a movie. It was a scene where I had to paddle across the bay carrying an important secret letter in my pocket. I had to paddle and paddle and keep looking back anxiously to make sure no one had seen me," Andrea continued.

"They sure in heck wouldn't. Not in this fog."

"A life jacket would have looked all wrong historically. The film has to appear authentic," Andrea stated emphatically.

"Yeah, but they didn't have movie cameras back in those days either, did they?"

"Well, no," Andrea conceded. This guy was missing the point. Historic films weren't about cameras; they were about history.

"Guess that explains why you're not exactly dressed for canoeing in the North Atlantic."

Andrea had forgotten how incongruous she must have looked, sitting in a canoe dressed in a long-sleeved white shirt, a bonnet, an ankle-length skirt, and a woollen cape, all soaked by the fog. She took off her bonnet and then ran her hand lightly across her cheek, suddenly conscious of the make-up she was wearing. She was worried that the mascara had started to run while she had been crying.

"So, I've rescued a movie star, have I?" enquired the constable, one eye on her and the other on his radar screen.

"I'm not a star. I don't speak one word in this film. I'm supposed to be a lady's maid," Andrea said, a little apologetically.

"You've got to start somewhere. Maybe next time you'll get a bigger role," he consoled her.

"I don't think so. I don't like the film business all that much. What I'm really doing is working at the Fortress of Louisbourg for the summer. It was just a fluke that I was asked to play a role in this film."

By this time they could see the misty outline of the shore. In a few more minutes the Mountie cut the engine and eased the boat alongside Louisbourg's public wharf, where a crowd had gathered. When they saw Andrea standing beside the policeman people began to cheer. Andrea climbed up on the dock and Penny Goodman rushed towards her and surprised her with a hug. Jackie Cormier was there too and she gave Andrea an even bigger hug. Even Grumpy Grundy patted her shoulder and actually smiled at her for the first time since she had met him.

"Spot of bad luck," he said kindly, "but all's well that ends well."

"Honestly, I was fine. I lost the paddle, that's all," Andrea shrugged, trying to make light of her ordeal. She was embarrassed at all the fuss, although she was glad they cared. People had worried about her, but she was ashamed that she hadn't handled the canoe properly. She looked around to see if Calvin was there, but fortunately, this time, he wasn't.

"I'll be on my way then," said Constable Orzechowski.

"Thanks a lot for rescuing me," said Andrea, amid a chorus of gratitude from everyone else.

"All in a day's work."

Jackie Cormier offered Andrea a ride back to town. Andrea climbed into her car and for a long time didn't say a thing. She felt she had ruined everything—her final scene in the canoe, the chance to attend Justine's party, and, even worse, a chance to impress Calvin by showing that she was one heck of a paddler. She wasn't. Nothing had worked out the way she had hoped.

"You weren't frightened, were you, Andrea?" asked Jackie.

"Nope. Just mad at myself."

"I know the feeling," Jackie sympathized. "I didn't realize what had happened. I was simply driving by...on my way back from visiting Mom in Sydney. I could see all these film people gathered together down at the wharf, so I parked and got out, curious to find out what was going on. That was when someone told me. You were adrift somewhere in a canoe and they had called an R.C.M.P. rescue unit to find you...they hoped! Luckily, they had just got news that you were on board the police boat and you would be there soon. What a relief!"

"No big deal," Andrea shrugged. "It's not as if there was a terrible storm or anything. The ocean was as calm as a cup of tea. It was...boring, that's all. But it was starting to get kind of cold out there."

"I'll bet."

Andrea didn't want to talk about it any more. She wanted to forget the whole episode, and she hoped everyone else would too. She just stared out the window. Then her eye caught the name on an envelope on the dashboard of the car. It was addressed to Mrs. John A. MacDonald.

"Hey, how about that?" Andrea asked brightly.

"A letter for the wife of the first prime minister of Canada."

"What?"

"It says 'Mrs. John A. MacDonald.'"

"Oh," laughed Jackie. "That's my mom. I have to deal with her mail. It's one of those government forms that have to be filled out."

"Your name used to be MacDonald? So you're not French then," Andrea remarked. "I just assumed you were. Jacqueline Cormier. It sounds... well... French."

"Who knows what anyone is, really? I was named Jacqueline after my dad. He was John Alan MacDonald, but everyone knew him as Jack."

"Maybe you're distantly related to Sir John A. Macdonald."

Jackie chuckled. "I don't think so."

"I guess there are a lot of MacDonalds all over the place."

"Tell me about it," said Jackie. "The MacDonald clan wouldn't dare hold a reunion. There isn't a building big enough in the world to hold us all. Did you ever look at the Sydney–Glace Bay phone book? You've never seen so many MacDonalds. And it's the same in a lot of places across Canada."

Andrea returned to her room. She felt depressed. It was Saturday night and she was alone and she didn't have anything to do. She thought she might phone somebody, but she got as far as the telephone in the hall and was too discouraged to pick it up. Idly, she leafed through the phone book and, sure enough, there were three full pages of people whose last name was MacDonald, or McDonald. Forty-one of them bore the first name John.

As she stood there the phone rang. It was Justine.

"Hi, Juss! How's your birthday party?" Andrea asked wistfully.

"Fab-U-luss! Lots of kids are here. Mom and Dad gave me new sneakers for my birthday. Sylvie got some too, of course. So what have you been up to?"

"Actually, quite a lot. I'll tell you about it sometime," replied Andrea.

"Hang on a minute. Marc wants to talk to you."

There was a pause, then Justine's brother spoke. "How's it goin'? Too bad you missed the party."

"Sure is. Wish I was there."

"I was just thinkin'..."

"What?"

"I'm comin' up tomorrow to drive Justine and Cory back."

"Uh huh."

"Maybe I'll see ya when I get there?"

"Well...okay. If you bring some of that birthday cake...then we could go out for some pop or something."

"Sounds good to me. See ya then."

"See ya," echoed Andrea, hoping she sounded as cool as the Atlantic fog. The truth was she suddenly felt as bright as sunshine. She was delighted. Marc was obviously a quiet guy...but...maybe quiet guys were all right. Tomorrow she would find out.

CHAPTER FOURTEEN

The next day the film crew began packing up. The shoot was finally complete. Men and women were busy dismantling lights, coiling cables, and hauling crates of equipment towards a fleet of trucks parked near the bus depot.

Andrea had decided not to take the day off after all. She didn't feel like spending it alone. She kept an eye on the film crew from time to time, wondering if Calvin might appear. Where had he been anyway during her ordeal on the water? Had what happened to her—as well as what might have happened—mattered to him at all? Did he care if she was alive or dead? "Filmmakers," she thought bitterly, "who needs them anyway?" She switched her thoughts to Marc Marchand, whom she would meet later that day. He sounded a whole lot nicer.

She was glad to be back at her regular job. There was something reassuring about the routine of shepherding the children around, organizing games, and chatting with the tourists. From now on, no one was going to make her spend her time running down some stupid hill or paddling around in a fog. When she happened to see Penny Goodman in the distance marching along purposefully, Andrea felt relieved to know she would no longer have to take orders from her. It crossed her mind that Penny might know where Calvin was today...but, no, she wasn't going to ask.

Penny spotted her. "Andrea! Just the person I was looking for. You've got a surprise visitor. Up in the visitors' rest building."

"Is that so?" Andrea replied, trying to sound as calm as she could. So, Marc Marchand had arrived, and quite a bit earlier than she had expected.

"I've just come from there," added Penny. "I think you should hurry over right away."

"Okay," Andrea agreed.

"And, by the way, thank you, Andrea," said Penny. "You've been a trouper. Who knows, maybe the next time we're working on a film up here in Canada we'll call on you again."

"Maybe," Andrea muttered as she turned and headed up the road. Yeah, Penny, maybe lots of things. Maybe life would be normal again. Maybe Justine would give up sulking. Maybe there would be another chance to visit River Bourgeois. Maybe Marc would turn out to be...She suddenly felt so light-hearted that she abandoned her dignity and ran the final block towards the building. She stopped long enough outside the door to smooth her hair and make sure her bonnet was in place, then she strode in. She was totally unprepared for what she found. There stood her mother.

"Mom!"

"Sweetie!" she cried and held out her arms to give her astonished daughter a hug.

"Mom. What...I didn't know you were coming," Andrea gasped.

"Surprise, surprise! I finished teaching my course and...I don't know...I just felt it was the right time for a little trip. There was an airline seat sale... so here I am."

Andrea didn't know what to say. The surprise of discovering her mother here in the fortress left her speechless. Finally she managed to ask, "How did you get in? How did you find me?"

"Easy enough. I just bought a ticket like any other tourist. I wasn't sure how I was going to find you actually, until I noticed a woman carrying a clipboard. She looked as if she worked here, so I simply asked her if she knew you. And she did. She said she'd keep an eye out for you. Is she your boss?"

"No, that's Penny. She's part of the film crew. She's not my boss. I like my boss. Penny's sort of... well, she'll be leaving soon. How long are you going to stay, Mom?"

"A little while. I've got a room at the Foxberry Inn. It's quite nice. But I'll tell you what would be even nicer—why don't I take you to lunch? I made some enquiries and they recommended Hôtel de la Marine, right here in the fortress. Apparently you have to eat the sort of food they ate two hundred and something years ago. Sounds like fun. Have you tried it?"

"Gosh no. We bring sandwiches and eat in the employees' lunchroom. I'm not sure if I'm allowed to eat in any of the restaurants here."

"Could you ask someone for permission?"

"I guess I could phone the office."

Andrea called Jackie Cormier and explained that her mother had arrived out of the blue and asked if the two of them could have lunch together in a fortress restaurant.

"That's a happy surprise," exclaimed Jackie. "Actually, staff members aren't supposed to eat there, but we'll make an exception. Attendance is low today, so I'm sure there'll be room. I'd like to meet your mother. If I have any spare time I'll drop by and say hello."

At Hôtel de la Marine the diners sat on backless stools at wooden tables covered with white table-cloths made of coarse linen. They were served a hearty soup in wide bowls that were reproductions of the pottery that had been used there in 1744. Andrea's mother ordered a glass of wine, which came in a thick, green-tinted glass. The waitresses wore the same kind of clothes as Andrea: long, dark skirts with pale aprons, and white shirts and bonnets. The smiling woman who served them was about the same age as Andrea's mother. She greeted Andrea like an old friend.

"Sounds like you had quite a time of it yesterday," she remarked.

"Oh, that," shrugged Andrea. It hadn't occurred to her that everyone who worked at the fortress would have heard about her escapade in the canoe and her rescue by the police. News travels fast.

"What happened yesterday?" asked her mother.

"Oh, nothing much. This is my mother." Andrea turned and introduced her to the waitress. "She just got here, all the way from Toronto."

"Is that right? You must be really pleased to see your daughter."

"I certainly am."

Andrea didn't want her mother to find out she had been stranded in a canoe in the fog and had had to be rescued. Her mother was always worrying about dreadful things happening anyway. The waitress was about to add something, but Andrea interrupted her by asking questions about the soup and how it was made, anything to change the subject until this too-friendly woman would go away.

"What did happen to you yesterday?" her mother asked for the second time, once the waitress had left.

"Um . . . remember I told you I was playing a part, a very small part, in a film."

"I remember."

"Well, we did the final shoot yesterday. I had to paddle a canoe and—silly me—the paddle slipped out of my hands. They had to come and get me. No big deal."

Her mother looked alarmed.

"I was only out here in the harbour. There's no way you can get lost or blown away or anything," Andrea insisted.

"That would depend," said her mother sternly, "on the visibility, the direction of the wind, and the tide. I know about these things. I'm from Newfoundland, remember?"

"Yes, Mom, I remember. Anyway, the filming is over. I won't be playing any more roles."

"Imagine, my daughter in a movie! I can hardly wait to see it. Was it fun?"

"Well, at times it was. The first day they put all that make-up on us and we hardly recognized ourselves in the mirror. That was wild. And then they coached us on what expressions to use so we would look as if we were eavesdropping. That was something else because that's the reason they noticed us in the first place. We really were trying to listen in."

"What was the story all about?"

"Actually, it was sort of stupid. It's some kind of love story. The guy who played the lead was a jerk. The director was always in a bad mood. Penny, his assistant—the one you met—was always bugging me about something. It took forever to get anything done. I enjoyed it, but I don't think I want a career in film."

"You do know that nothing gets accomplished without effort. These people obviously had a lot of work to organize. It can't have been easy for them." Her mother took a sip of her wine.

Andrea glanced past her mother's shoulder to see two people coming through the doorway of the restaurant. One was Calvin Jefferson Lee, and right beside him, holding his hand, was smiling, gorgeous Deborah Cluett, minus the monstrous wig and the lavish clothes. She wore pale blue jeans and a clingy white T-shirt. Her blond hair was short and windblown. She looked a lot younger and a lot prettier than when she had been made-up and dressed for the film.

"Andrea, what is it? You look as if you've seen a ghost," said her mother, turning around to see what was behind her.

Andrea couldn't take her eyes off the pair as they were ushered to a table on the other side of the room. Calvin and Deborah! Was this their first date? It didn't appear to be. They were sharing a laugh about something and looking directly into each other's eyes. How long had this been going on? Andrea felt as if she'd been hit by a truck.

Would they notice her? she wondered. What would be worse: to be seen there, with her mother of all people, or not to be noticed at all?

"It's nothing, Mom. Just some people I know. They're eating here too."

Her mother leaned towards her, suddenly looking very serious.

"Andrea," she began in a solemn tone. "I have something I want to tell you. Something very important."

"I know, Mom. Perseverance and patience. I realize how hard all those people had to work to get the movie made. I know about putting one hundred per cent into whatever I do. You've told me before." Andrea sighed.

"No, not that, sweetie, though I'm glad you remember. I have something else on my mind. And it's not altogether easy for me to say it."

Andrea stopped staring at Calvin and Deborah long enough to catch the look on her mother's face. This was no pep talk about getting things done. It dawned on her that something awful might be happening. What?

"Mom," she began cautiously, "are you and Brad splitting up?"

Her mother burst into a brief laugh but quickly returned to the earnestness of a moment earlier. "No, no, no. Brad and I are just fine. And he sends you his love. You mean a lot to him. I know it has been an adjustment for you...trying to accept a stepfather. But don't worry, Brad and I plan to stay together. Did I tell you Brad put up that new wallpaper you wanted in your room?"

"He did?" Andrea brightened.

"He sure did. But this isn't what I want to talk about right now. I want to tell you something that you might not—"

"Well, would you look who's he-ah!" called Calvin in a loud, you-all drawl that could be heard right across the restaurant.

Andrea blushed. He finally had noticed her.

"Hi," responded Andrea weakly, waving the fingers of her right hand.

Calvin and Deborah got up and came over. "This's a pleasure," said Calvin warmly. "Ah was sayin' to Debbie how ah hoped we'd get a chance to say goodbye to you 'fore we left."

So he called her Debbie, did he? Andrea swallowed and tried not to show her feelings. "I guess you're outta here soon, eh?" she said.

"Tomorrow morning." Debbie smiled, looking relieved.

"Um...this is my mother," Andrea explained reluctantly.

Her mother smiled and shook hands with them. There was an exchange of friendly greetings. Where are you from? How long are you staying? What a lovely daughter you have!

Andrea felt diminished, as if she had turned into a little girl again, stranded in the midst of a bunch of people talking over her head. They seemed so old. How old was Deborah anyway? She had heard that Calvin was supposed to be about twenty, but Deborah—Debbie—had to be older than that. She was too old for Calvin. But what did it matter to Andrea? They were probably an item. They were leaving Louisbourg, leaving Canada, leaving her behind.

"I like your friends," her mother remarked after Calvin and Deborah had returned to their table.

"Not friends exactly. We worked together on the film. They're okay," Andrea admitted grudgingly.

"I suppose you've made quite a few friends here?"

"A few."

"And maybe a boyfriend?"

"Not really."

"No?"

"No."

"Now then, Andrea. As I started to say, there's something I've been meaning to tell you..."

Just at this moment the cheery waitress returned with the rest of their meal and plonked down two heavy plates laden with a mixture of boiled cabbage and turnips and small chunks of beef.

"Bon appetit!" She smiled, busying herself clearing the plates and the crumbs from the table beside them.

"I'd call this a Jiggs' dinner," remarked Andrea's mother.

"It's supposed to be French, Mom."

"Call it what you like. We ate it in Newfoundland too. This is what I grew up on."

As long as the waitress remained within earshot, Andrea's mother made no further attempt at disclosing whatever it was she wanted to tell her daughter. Andrea sensed it was bad news of some kind, and she didn't want to hear it. Not now. She had had enough bad news for one day: Calvin and Deborah. How come she hadn't heard about them before? Every once in a while she shot a furtive glance at the couple on the far side of the room, looking at one another with those lovey-dovey eyes, those happy smiles, and the shared laughs.

"Sorry, we're full right now," she heard the waitress say to someone at the door. "If you'll wait in the hallway, it shouldn't be too long."

"I've only come to deliver a message." Andrea recognized Justine's voice. "And there she is, right over there."

"Oh, Juss."

"I'm sorry to interrupt your meal, Andrea, but..."

"That's okay. This is my mother. Mom, this is my roommate, Justine."

"Hello," said Justine hurriedly. "Jackie told me where you were. There's someone waiting to see you, like, right now. It's Marc," Justine continued breathlessly.

"Who's Marc?" asked her mother.

"Marc's my brother," explained Justine. "He's outside. He just wants to say hi to Andrea. He was hoping to stay for a while, but it turns out he has to go back right away."

"Oh. Too bad," said Andrea, trying not to sound crestfallen as she got up from her chair.

"I hope you won't be gone long," cautioned her mother.

"Not a chance," said Andrea glumly.

Marc Marchand was in front of the restaurant, shuffling his feet on the dusty surface of the road. When he saw Andrea, he held out a plastic supermarket bag with a small package in it. "Here's your piece of cake. Hope you like chocolate," he offered.

"Sure. Thanks," Andrea replied without enthusiasm. She didn't give a hoot about the birthday cake. It had only been an excuse to get together but evidently that wasn't going to happen now.

"I have to get back home or else my dad's gonna kill me," said Marc half-jokingly.

"Why is that?"

"Because of the scallops."

"The scallops?"

"Yeah. See, we're starting a scallop farm and the first couple of years it takes a lot of work, and right now is the season when we all pitch in and help," he explained.

"A farm for scallops," Andrea mused. She could only remember Justine talking about cows and pigs. "I thought they caught scallops in the ocean."

"Oh, sure they do. But that's doing it the hard way. This new way they grow in cages made of net, deep down in the water. You can bring in a lot more of them...eventually."

"No kidding," remarked Andrea, trying to sound interested, even though she didn't really understand what he was talking about.

"So, um, enjoy your cake..."

"Sure."

"And...Justine was saying that maybe when you're finished working here, at the end of summer, maybe you'll come home then...with her...for a visit."

"Sounds neat. I can meet your dog and all those hens and cows. And see those scallops running around the farm," she quipped.

Marc laughed. He seemed to like her sense of humour. "Shellfish don't run. But I'd better. See ya."

"See ya," Andrea repeated as she turned to go

back into the restaurant. In her absence Justine had occupied her empty chair. She and her mother were chatting away like old friends. Justine, Andrea figured, was probably telling her mother the story of her life. Whatever she was saying, it was making her mother smile. Her frown had disappeared and she looked as if she was enjoying herself. The bad news she was planning to tell Andrea would obviously have to wait.

Chapter Fifteen

That evening Andrea and her mother ate their supper in a little café next door to the inn. There were only three other customers, and her mother had deliberately chosen a table near the back, as far away from the other people as they could sit. They both ordered cheeseburgers and fries.

Andrea concentrated on making her meal last as long as possible, hoping to delay the inevitable. What was her mother going to tell her? Did they have to move again? That would be a royal pain, now that she had finally made some friends at her new school. Maybe her mother had lost her job. Maybe Brad had lost his. Were they going to be poor and hungry? Maybe it was even worse than that. Maybe her mother had been diagnosed with a fatal disease. She didn't look sick. She just looked very, very serious.

"Andrea, do you remember me telling you that I worked in a fish-packing plant a long time ago?"

"Sure, Mom, I remember," Andrea replied, a bit wearily. Why did her mother want to reminisce about that? What more could she say about packing fish except that it had been a cold place to work, and hard on her hands and feet. Andrea had heard all this before.

"I never told you where it was, did I?"

Andrea thought about it for a moment. She had never heard the name of the place. It hardly mattered. She shook her head.

"It was in North Sydney," said her mother.

Andrea looked up, only a bit surprised. Her mother came from Anderson's Arm, Newfoundland. But everyone knew Newfoundlanders sometimes had to go elsewhere to work. That was the way things were.

"I stayed over here for a year or so. It wasn't the best year of my life, as I think I've told you. I wasn't much older than you are now. When it was all over, I went back home to Anderson's Arm. I returned to high school and a year later I graduated. I've never regretted that."

"I know, Mom," nodded Andrea. She had heard that piece of advice before too. Maybe a hundred times.

"But there's one thing I've never told you, and I'm going to tell you now," her mother continued, taking a deep breath and twisting her napkin.

Andrea looked at her mother's face apprehensively. "What?" she dared to ask.

"I...I had a baby...that year," her mother said, getting the words out with difficulty.

"What?" blurted Andrea.

"It's true. A baby girl was born to me shortly

before I returned home to Newfoundland. I ... I gave her up for adoption. There just wasn't any other choice ... for me ... then."

Andrea was dumbfounded. She couldn't think of anything appropriate to say. What does someone say when struck by a thunderbolt? Her mother had had a baby when she was, what, sixteen or seventeen years old. Why was she telling her about it now? That baby would be a grown-up person now. That baby ... that woman ... Andrea suddenly realized, would be her half-sister. A sister! She had always wanted a sister. Somewhere—out there in the world—she had one. It was all too much! She began to laugh uncontrollably. Then she choked and almost cried, while her mother sat across the table from her, biting her lower lip and looking guilty.

"Andrea, I ... "

"Mom. Mom," Andrea hiccuped. "It's okay, really. You just told me I've got a sister. It isn't funny, I know, but ... somehow ... it is kind of amazing. I always wanted a sister. I mean, I'll never know her, but just the idea of it ... "

"I hope you're not angry," said her mother in an uncertain voice.

"No way, Mom. Why would I be? I'm glad you finally told me. And I'll tell you something. You can trust me, I won't tell a soul," Andrea promised.

"It doesn't have to be a secret any more."

"Really? Does Brad know?" Andrea asked.

"Yes, I've told him. He doesn't have a problem with it."

Andrea thought about that for a minute. Was everyone going to know about this? Was this a good idea? "Did my father know?" she asked.

"No. Albert didn't know. I didn't tell him. There didn't seem to be any reason to talk about it. We had you. We were a happy family. But, as the years go by, things change. You see... I now know where my first daughter is. I know her name. I came here to find her. She lives right here in Louisbourg."

"Here? Oh my gawww..."

"I know. It really is incredible. That's why, when I heard you were coming here to work, I was, well, uncomfortable. I didn't like the idea of you coming to Cape Breton Island on your own, because of what had happened to me."

"Oh, Mom," Andrea sighed.

"You see, I had applied to an agency to try find my lost child a couple of years ago. You can make contact only if both the mother and the child make an application. It's been just a few months since she applied too, and I discovered where she lived. The name of this place has been in my mind so much."

"What's her name?" asked Andrea, suddenly curious.

"Eleanor."

Andrea repeated the name. Eleanor. My sister, Eleanor. Somehow she couldn't suppress more laughter, even though this wasn't funny either. Right here in this town she had a real, live sister named Eleanor. "What's her last name?"

"MacDonald."

"Oh, Mom!" cried Andrea, convulsed with untimely mirth. "You won't believe how many people there are around here named MacDonald. There are thousands of them, columns and columns in the phone book. How on earth are you going to find Eleanor MacDonald?"

"Actually, that was the name of the family who adopted her. She has since been married, and she goes by her husband's name."

"What's that?"

"Cormier. Her full name is Eleanor Jacqueline MacDonald Cormier. And I intend to find her."

Andrea gasped and clapped her hand over her mouth. For the longest time she couldn't utter a word.

CHAPTER SIXTEEN

 "Andrea! This is a nice surprise. Come on in," invited Jackie Cormier hospitably. "I was just putting Kenzie to bed. It's story time, and you know how kids are about their bedtime stories. Make yourself at home, and I'll be with you shortly."

Andrea entered the kitchen uneasily and sat on the edge of a chair. She could feel her heart pounding as she rehearsed in her mind what she had come to tell Jackie. This had to be the most intense experience of her life, and probably it soon would be the same for Jackie too. How do you tell someone this kind of news?

It had fallen to Andrea to do it when her mother totally lost her cool after Andrea explained that she and Jackie Cormier had been working together all summer.

"Break the ice for me. Please," her mother had asked. "You already know her and I don't. I'm scared. What if it turns out she hates me because I had to give her up?"

"All right," Andrea agreed soothingly, confident that Jackie would be truly happy to finally meet her birth mother. But now, sitting in this friendly kitchen, she wasn't quite so sure.

She could hear Jackie's voice reading to her

son. It must have been amusing because every now and then Kenzie burst out laughing. Kenzie, she suddenly realized, was related to her too. She was—what—his aunt? His half-aunt? Aunt Andrea.

The story lasted about five more minutes. For Andrea, it seemed like five hours. Finally Jackie tip-toed down the darkened hall and emerged into the bright kitchen.

"I would have thought you and your mother might be out seeing the sights somewhere tonight," Jackie said.

"No," replied Andrea solemnly.

"Can I make you a cup of tea?" offered Jackie.

"I have to talk to you, Jackie. It's pretty serious."

Jackie immediately sat down across the table and gave Andrea her full attention. "Is something wrong?" she asked earnestly.

"Nothing's wrong. And this is not about me. It's about you."

"Me?"

"Jackie, I need to know something."

"What?"

"Is your full name Eleanor Jacqueline?" asked Andrea, trying to quell the tremor in her voice.

"Yes," Jackie nodded, looking perplexed.

"And you did tell me you were a MacDonald before you got married?"

"Yes," replied Jackie, wondering why any of this mattered to Andrea.

"Then I'll just come right out and say it," said Andrea, clearing her throat. "Jackie, do you know you are adopted?"

Jackie leaned back and started to giggle, relieved that she wasn't about to hear some disturbing news. Finally she stopped and said, "Oh, Andrea, I am sorry. I didn't mean to make light of what you told me. It's just that... of course I know I'm adopted. I've always known that. My parents married late in life. They couldn't have kids of their own, so they chose me. Mom used to tell me about it from as far back as I can remember. She often described how they went to the hospital in North Sydney and there I was—just eight days old—and she always said that the minute she laid eyes on me she knew I was... I was... destined to be her little girl."

Suddenly a tear ran down Jackie's cheek. She wiped it away and got up to find a tissue.

"Forgive me," she said as she blew her nose. "It's just that it's a bit rough right now. Dad died three years ago and now that Mom has Alzheimer's... she isn't her real self." Her voice trailed off into some far-away, sad place in her personal history.

"I'm really sorry, Jackie," consoled Andrea.

Jackie regained her composure. "So how did you

hear this? Not that it's a secret. I suppose Aunt Roberta told you, did she?"

"No, she never talks to us much."

Jackie shook her head. "Poor old Roberta. She never was very friendly."

"There's something else, now that I know your full name..." Andrea ventured.

"And what's that?"

"I know that you applied to find your birth mother."

Jackie's expression changed abruptly, her eyes narrowing. "How did you...? The only person who knows that is Steve. You surely didn't talk to him. He's been away all summer. Who...?"

Andrea could feel her heart pounding again. She felt as if she was losing her voice. She cleared her throat and began. "The reason I know about your search for your real mother...is...because your mother and my mother are...is...the same person."

Jackie stared at her in wide-eyed disbelief.

"Honestly! I'm not making this up. I only found out about it today. From my mom."

"Your mother is my mother?" gasped an incredulous Jackie.

"That's it," Andrea confirmed.

Jackie stared at Andrea hard for a few seconds, and it seemed as if she was going to start laughing again. Then she started shaking with sobs, and tears began rolling down her face. Suddenly Andrea wished she hadn't told her. Maybe someone from the agency should have written her a letter. Perhaps this kind of information was too overwhelming for anyone to cope with face to face. However, Jackie quickly regained her composure and spoke almost in her normal voice.

"Where is she? I want to see her."

Andrea got to her feet, shaking with relief. "She's sitting on your front steps. Can I invite her in?"

CHAPTER SEVENTEEN

 At first none of them knew what to say. These three women, who all had eyes the same shade of blue, and various shades of brown hair, could only smile at one another and go through the motions of perfunctory hugs. The mother of both Jackie and Andrea was the first to speak.

"I'm Doris. Doris Marie Goodyear Baxter Osborne," she announced, reciting her given names, her maiden name, the name of her dead husband, and the name of her living husband. Andrea had never heard her mother introduce herself that way to anyone before. Couldn't she simply have said, "Hello, I'm your mother," or something like that?

"I'm Jackie..." Jackie began, and then lost her voice and couldn't finish saying her own name.

"You're Eleanor Jacqueline. I've wanted to meet you again, well, all of your life and a big chunk of mine. I didn't know your name until a few months ago. I can't tell you what it means to me that I've found..." Then she lost it. She couldn't finish the sentence as tears began to stream down her face. Andrea hunted through her pockets for a tissue but didn't find one. This was so unlike her mother, who had never been at a loss for words. Jackie got a box of tissues from the bathroom and handed it to the distraught woman who had not seen her since she had given her up twenty-six years earlier. Jackie looked shaken too. She hadn't had time to prepare for this. She had to wipe a tear from her eye too. That was when Andrea noticed how much Jackie's eyes and eyebrows resembled those of her mother. Maybe that was why she had warmed to Jackie right from the start. There had been something familiar about her expression, something reassuring about her attitude, characteristics she couldn't have identified until this very moment.

Jackie finally managed to say, "Why don't I put the kettle on, and we'll have a cup of tea?"

"That would be l-lovely, th-thanks," stuttered Doris in a weak, little voice that Andrea wasn't accustomed to hear coming from her in-charge mother, a woman who had been a level-headed school-teacher for many years.

"Andrea, you could take your mother...ah, Doris...um, our mother..." suggested Jackie, who didn't quite know how to address her newfound parent, "down the hall and have a look in at Kenzie. He's asleep now, but when he wakes up in the morning I'll tell him his new grandmother came to see him."

Andrea was jolted again. It hadn't crossed her mind until that very moment that her own mother was somebody's grandmother. Grandmothers were old. Her mother was far too young for this.

The prospect of seeing her grandson improved Doris's composure. She stopped crying and blew her nose. She walked down the hall with Andrea to stand in the doorway of Kenzie's bedroom. The little boy was sleeping soundly beside his teddy bear. Doris didn't say a word; she just fixed her gaze on his face. Andrea wanted to say, "Wait till you see him when he's wide awake. He's not the little angel he looks right now." But she said nothing. There would be plenty of time for her mother to get acquainted when Kenzie was awake the next day. And the next. And the next. Jackie and Kenzie were family now. From now on they would be part of one another's lives.

Andrea, Jackie, and Doris sat down around the kitchen table, glancing uneasily at one another. Jackie, who had not been expecting company, apologized that all she had to offer were store-bought cookies kept in the cupboard for Kenzie. Nobody cared.

At first it was not easy for Jackie and Doris to talk to each other, so Andrea, the one person they had in common, became the focus of their conversation. Jackie began describing what a fine young person Andrea was and how she put such energy into her summer job and how well she had accepted the challenge of acting in the film. Andrea squirmed. This sounded too much like a school report.

The phone in the hall rang, and Jackie went to answer it.

"Hi, darling," they heard her say. It was her husband calling from some distant place in Labrador. Steve seemed to be doing most of the talking because all they heard from Jackie was an occasional "Sure...great...mm hmm...okay." Then, "Steve, honey, I'd better go," they heard. "You see...my mother's here." There was a pause. "No, not Mom. My birth mother." There was another pause while Steve, who must have been as astonished as Jackie had been, tried to digest this startling news. "I'll tell you all about it when you get home. Lots of love, hon. 'Bye now.

"That was Steve," Jackie explained unnecessarily as she returned to the kitchen. "And guess what? He figures he'll be home in a couple of weeks. Winter comes early in northern Labrador and the job he's on is gearing down for the season, so his work is nearly over. He's a helicopter pilot, working with a team of geologists."

Andrea hadn't thought about Steve at all. She knew he existed, but Steve was just a name and a face in photographs in Jackie's house. An absent husband. Now, abruptly, he had become a relative, some kind of brother-in-law.

Jackie sat down and sipped her tea, looking very serious. "There's one thing we haven't mentioned," she said quietly. "Who was my father?"

There seemed to be no end to revelations on this extraordinary day. Andrea didn't really want to hear any more. She didn't want to think about whoever he was, the man who had been her mother's long-ago boyfriend. But she realized Jackie had a right to know.

Doris pulled herself up in her chair, cleared her throat, and spoke in a small but calm voice. "He came from Quebec, Jackie. He was third mate on a ship bringing iron ore from Sept-Isles to Sydney. I met him at a dance in a union hall. After that we went out on dates whenever his ship was in port." She hesitated.

"Go on," urged Jackie, eager for more information.

"Well, there isn't a lot to tell, except that I thought I was in love...at the time. It turned out neither of us were. After a while he quit his job on the ship, and he never came back to Sydney. He had often talked about moving to Montreal. I guess he did. I suppose I could have written to him, tried to find him somehow, but I...well, I didn't. He never knew about you."

Jackie didn't say anything for quite a while. Neither did Andrea. She sat there trying to imagine her mother's terrible situation all those years ago. What must it have been like, finding herself pregnant and having her boyfriend sail away and never return?

"What was his name?" asked Jackie.

"Pierre Bélanger."

"Bélanger," pronounced Jackie slowly. "Bélanger," she repeated. Then her expression brightened. "So it turns out I'm actually French after all. Wait till I tell Steve!"

"Only half French," noted Doris with a cautious little smile. "The other half comes from Newfoundland."

"Maybe I'll find him someday," mused Jackie.

"Maybe so," said Doris sadly. "But I was in Montreal on a holiday once and I looked in the phone book and, well, you can't imagine how many people there are named Bélanger in Montreal."

"I suppose it's like all the MacDonalds in the Cape Breton phone book."

"Yes. So you'll probably have to settle for just me. And Andrea."

Jackie stood up, came around the table, and gave them each a kiss.

"You'll do." She smiled. "You'll do just fine."

CHAPTER EIGHTEEN

RR1, Trillium Woods
Ontario L1A 0X0

Dear Jackie,

Mom and Brad and I are really happy that you and Kenzie and Steve are coming here to spend Christmas with us. I thought I'd drop you a line to bring you up to date on everything.

As you know, I went home with Justine for a few days when our jobs were over. I had a fabulous time! I learned lots of things, like how to milk a cow, how to collect eggs, what you feed to a pig (anything at all, they're not fussy).

The last night I was there we had a bonfire on the beach. Cory came all the way from Louisbourg to be with Justine. It was Marc's idea for the four of us to have a beach party before I had to go back to Ontario. Was it ever romantic! There was a full moon that night. We toasted marshmallows. We sang Cape Breton songs. Marc told me he wanted me to come back next summer. I told him I hoped I could. Sometimes I wish I could live there.

When I got back to school in September, everybody wanted to know about my summer job and what it was like, etc., etc. Mrs. Greenberg (my history teacher) suggested I write an article about it and read it to the class. I described how the Fortress of Louisbourg got built the first time and then I explained how it came to be built the second time. I described my job and responsibilities. (I mentioned that I liked my boss!) Then I went on to tell about the film that was being made because I knew the kids would want to hear about that. At the end of the piece I said that the most wonderful thing happened to me in August when I learned that I wasn't an only child after all, and that I now had a sister.

Do you know what my teacher said when she heard that? She said, "Congratulations. I didn't know your mother had had a baby." Well, for a minute I couldn't stop laughing, and she gave me a strange look. It wasn't funny. It just sounded funny the way she said it. So finally I said that, yes, she did have a baby, but it was a long time ago. It was simply that I didn't meet her until last summer.

She still looked puzzled, so I told her the whole story. Well, not absolutely everything because that would take too long. She told me that this was a special experience, and she was glad I wanted to share it with others. And you know what? It turns out I'm not the only person who found out they had an unknown brother or sister. Two other kids came up and told me their stories of how their families were reunited. We are planning to form a club called the Secret Sibling Society. We're including you as a member. What do you think of that?

Love from your sister,

Andrea